ENTANGLED PAST

FAMILY TIES BOOK ONE

PALMER JONES

1

_____

"**E**verything is just _fine._"

Everly Clarke popped the bubble gum colored nail polish against her palm, taking out her frustration. Her house was her safe place, away from strangers and useless social conversations. This was her sanctuary after her husband left. But today changed that. It didn't matter how many times she told herself that she'd be fine, nothing was fine.

She'd been robbed. Wait. _Burglarized_ was the right term according to the middle-aged, overweight police officer who'd corrected her a half-dozen times. Too bad using the proper word choice didn't catch the idiots responsible for kicking in her door and tossing everything she owned onto the floor like an enraged toddler looking for candy.

There wasn't even a damn piece of candy in the house.

Everly rolled back in the computer chair until a wheel caught on the pile of pens and rubber bands littering the ground, stopping her movement.

"What the hell ever," she muttered to the mess around her. She didn't have the brainpower to deal with it today. Not after that same policeman had set his hand on her shoulder, turning her already stressful afternoon into a full-blown panic attack. After spending two years absolutely alone, anyone's hands on her body made everything inside lock up tight.

She hiked her foot on her desk and proceeded to paint each toe with excessive precision. This she could control.

Her bookcase stood bare, every book thrown onto the floor. Two dining room chairs lay on their sides. The curtains were piled in a heap on the floor. Shards of glass from a shattered vase covered the kitchen table and ground. Both desk drawers were dumped out entirely on the carpet around her. If there was a silver lining, she'd taken her laptop with her to the meeting.

Overall, the first floor was a damn mess thanks to whatever dipshit decided her house was a good location to find nothing of value.

She sat back and smiled. At least her toes were pretty.

Four loud beeps sounded from her cell phone. She jumped with the noise. There wasn't a single person she wanted to speak with today. Or any day, really, but especially not after the meeting-from-hell this morning and the break-in once she arrived home.

Tripp Wellington's name filled her screen.

Definitely wasn't talking to that jerk. She canceled the call, sending him to voice mail for a fourth time that afternoon. The man wouldn't give up. She hadn't heard a damn thing from Tripp since her husband's death six months ago.

Until today.

"I'm just *fine*," she repeated, wishing she believed it.

Everly painted on a second coat. The longer her nails took to dry, the better. The house wouldn't look so bad tomorrow. She fanned her toes with an old magazine, scanning the room.

Never mind.

Yes, it would.

A pounding on her door made the magazine fly from her hand as she screamed "shit!" and jumped up from the chair.

Her foot stepped on a pile of pens. The pile rolled out from under her, and she sat back down with enough momentum that both she and the computer chair tipped backward.

Everly waved her arms around, trying to gain balance, but flapping like a bird didn't help.

She fell, ending with both legs sticking up in the air. Her head landed on a pile of rubber bands and scattered printer paper. Not the softest pillow but better than the stapler her shoulder hit.

She closed her eyes, containing the moan of mixed embarrassment and pain. "This is so *not* fine."

"Mrs. Clarke?" A loud, male voice shouted through the door. "Are you okay? Open up." He thumped again.

Everly rolled to her side and stood. She moved to the door. "Go—" Her foot hit the upside-down glass bowl that she'd used to hold her keys. With the force of a soccer player, the bowl flew across the carpet, clanged on the hardwood floor, before breaking against the wall.

The front door sailed open. "Mrs. Clarke!"

A huge man loomed in the doorway. A shadow obscured his face as his body blocked out most of the late afternoon sunlight. He held a big, black gun with both hands.

Continuing her forward motion, she shoved one hand on the man's rock-hard chest, knocking him back, outside and slamming the door closed.

Her unsteady hands didn't cooperate with the doorknob. *Just lock, damn it.*

After a few fumbles, the doorknob locked. She grabbed her phone off the desk as the man shouted again, "Mrs. Clarke?" He knocked in rapid secession. "Please open the door."

"No." It'd come out with a whisper, her blood pounding too hard to yell.

"I'm here to help you."

Bullshit. And whoever broke into her house just wanted to redecorate. She hit '9' on her phone.

"He sent me to check on you. Are you alright?" The doorknob jiggled. "Call Tripp if you don't believe me."

Her finger paused after the first '1.' Tripp? Is that why he'd tried to call her all afternoon? She bit her lip and flipped over to her text messages. With wobbly fingers, she managed to type out a text to Tripp.

His reply was immediate.

That's my bodyguard. I sent him to make sure you are okay. Don't be difficult. Let him in to help.

Well, that concern was fundamentally unlike Tripp. Her edge of fear disappeared but suspicion took its place. Since when did Tripp have a bodyguard? And why did he even care about her at this point? He made it perfectly clear at the lawyer's office that he wanted nothing to do with her. He only wanted the stock certificate to the business.

She didn't have it.

Whoever owned the other fifty percent of ATLighting, Inc at this point could have it. Good luck dealing with a shady moron like Tripp.

Right then, she had a bigger problem: the gun-waving man standing outside her home. She crept across the floor and grabbed the umbrella leaning next to the door. After a quick second of weighing the cheap, plastic handle in her hand, she tossed it to the side. "Stupid," she muttered. It wasn't like she had some insane ninja skills and could do more than swing it at someone's head and hoped it hurt.

Tripp sent him. Everly brushed her hair back from her face, exhaustion sucking away the last of her energy. This day would never end. She balled her hands into tight fists and pulled in a deep breath through her nose. Face-to-face interactions turned her anxiety up to the max.

She relaxed her hands, pleased that the shaking had eased slightly. Talk. That's all she had to do. As long as he didn't touch her, she could keep her shit together.

With fake confidence, Everly opened the door, cool air brushing over her warm cheeks. The gun had disappeared, but the man's broad shoulders cast her in his shadow. He shifted to the side, crossing his arms and leaning against her doorjamb like a man who had all day and wasn't hiding a gun somewhere.

His shortish, dark hair looked purposefully messy. Intense but friendly brown eyes pinned her in place as a mesmerizing smile spread so slowly it twisted her stomach into a thousand more knots.

Oh, God.

The man was insanely gorgeous.

All the air in her lungs vanished.

She slammed the door in his face.

That was . . . crazy. She blinked, clearing the haze. For a moment, his smile seemed more lethal than the gun.

He said something unintelligible before knocking lightly. "Please open back up, Mrs. Clarke," he said, softer than before.

Breathe. Tripp sent him over to check on the situation. It was rude to leave him standing on her front porch. He didn't have anything to do with the tension between her and Tripp. Nor was he at fault for her stupid response to his good looks. Besides, polite manners should be afforded to gorgeous men as well as ugly ones.

She opened the door. That stomach-twisting smile had vanished, but he still propped himself against the side of her door frame.

"I texted Tripp." She cleared her throat. "He said he sent his bodyguard. I presume that's you?" Everly leaned to the side, scanning his waist for a holster. "What happened to the gun you waved in the air?"

He frowned. "I didn't wave a gun—"

Her focus shot back to his face. "Yes, you did." She demonstrated his actions. Maybe *slightly* exaggerated. "You barged into my house, brandishing a gun around. I think that's illegal. Do you have a permit?"

His eyes widened, and he straightened from his relaxed position. "Yes, I have a permit and you're wrong. I was not brandishing it—"

"Yes, you were," Everly snapped back, setting her hands on her hips to keep him from seeing her hands tremble. She could do this. Talking to another person wasn't so difficult. She was just out of practice. As long as he stayed on his side of the door, she was good.

He took a breath, the air escaping through his clenched teeth. "I'm sorry if I scared you, Mrs. Clarke. I heard a loud bang and thought you might be in danger after the break-in. Hazard of the job, I suppose."

God, she hated her married name. "Well," she said, crossing her arms, trying to ignore the way his English accent made her want to trust him for no other reason than it made him sound extraordinarily polite. "As you can see, I'm perfectly alright."

She was alright when he wasn't smiling. When her brain managed to think logically. The intense reaction to him confused her as much as Tripp sending over someone to check on her. If the bodyguard could keep his dimples under control, then she could reassure him of her safety and send him away.

"What was the bang?"

She flicked her hand over her shoulder. "I accidentally knocked a chair over." Not that anyone could tell with the mess.

His eyes searched the house behind her. She partway closed the door. He didn't need to know that she'd been in the chair when it fell over.

"And the glass breaking?"

"Tripped on a bowl."

He ran a hand over his hair, his bicep straining against his fitted blue short-sleeved shirt. She swallowed and snapped her focus to his feet. At one normal point in her life, a cute guy wouldn't rattle her this much.

"Cute" was such a damn understatement. A new word should be invented just to describe him. That smile and accent made a deadly combination. Regardless of the unexpected attraction, he needed to leave. If the world would leave her alone, aside from the occasional food delivery service, she'd be happy.

"Your house is a wreck."

"I'll be sure to send your compliments to the maid." Jerk.

He smiled again, flashing those stupidly adorable dimples. "Can I come in?"

~

INDECISION AND NERVOUSNESS flickered over Mrs. Clarke's face. Americans amused him. Back home, showing up unexpectedly at a house usually led to an afternoon visit and an invitation for supper. Instead, she'd slammed the door in his face. *Twice.*

Granted, he wouldn't have drawn his weapon while going on a friendly visit, but this was different. Someone had destroyed her house. When he'd heard the crash from behind the closed door, every ounce of his past training ignited in his gut. And for a damn good reason.

Finnian Hayes glanced at the mess in her home. It was a wreck.

She shifted her petite body, attempting to block the doorway again. Her action didn't hide anything since he could see clearly over her head and into the house, but he refocused on her.

"Why did Tripp send you here?" she asked, the question full of suspicion. He appreciated her caution. Now, he had to find a way past it to help her.

Finnian plastered an easy smile on his face. He didn't have anywhere to be. If she wanted to keep him outside, he wouldn't push. Working in undercover investigations for the drug squad taught him that patience is critical when entering a hostile environment. And he considered *her* to be a hostile environment.

"A friend of Tripp's on the police force let him know your house was broken into this morning while you were at the meeting. Tripp tried to call, but when you didn't answer all day, he sent me to check on you." Finnian rubbed the back of his neck, thinking of how to put her at ease. "I'm to look over your doors and windows for any security concerns. Make sure you're safe. Fix anything I can. I'm not sure how they entered your home, but I can install a new deadbolt, if necessary." He motioned to the bag beside him. "I brought tools."

Not exactly in his usual job description, but Tripp had requested it, and he cut the check. A check his family needed back home.

"Oh," she said, still looking at the ground. "I still don't see why Tripp cares, but regardless of why he sent you over here, I don't need your help." She didn't move to let him inside. The longer she stood, the smaller she appeared. Her head barely reached his shoulders.

A few golden strands intermixed with her light brown hair where it sat in a haphazard knot on top of her head. A car drove past the house, and she tracked the movement with concern. Based on her earlier reaction, the break-in had rattled her more than she let on.

Mrs. Clarke locked eyes with him for a brief second before looking down again. For the first time, he got a clear view of her blue eyes that made her look innocent of every sin ever committed.

How had a scumbag like Charles Clarke managed to marry such a sweet-looking woman? A busty blonde with heavy makeup and tight clothing fit Charles's style when he lived in Miami.

Finnian leaned down a little, trying to see her face. "It'll be a little difficult to help standing outside," he said with more patience than he genuinely felt.

Her head snapped up. Those crystal blue eyes flashed with determination. "I don't need your help."

He tried not to smile. Not such a little mouse anymore, was she? He liked that better, but she still needed his assistance. "I hate to contradict you, but yes, you do. Tripp said you lived alone and didn't have family nearby. Please, let me help." He held his arms out to the side. "I'm already here."

She stood straight, not moving an inch from the doorway. "I'm perfectly safe."

"Until today." When she didn't respond right away, he took it as an opening. "I'll be out of your way in ten minutes. Just let me double-check the locks and windows. I'll do a test on your alarm system."

She ran a hand over her messy hair, mumbling something he didn't catch.

"Mrs. Clarke—"

"Don't." Her body stiffened. She held up her hands as if to block him. "I'll let you in to poke around at my windows and doors, but don't call me *that*." She stepped back from guarding the doorway. "Everly. Please, call me Everly."

Everly needed more help than his security assessment. How had a lady like this survived being married to a domineering, womanizing man with a drug habit? It made sense why Finnian never saw Everly around Charles in the years he guarded him. She was better off in Atlanta, distanced from the world her husband had created for himself.

Finnian stepped cautiously inside the house. Keeping ample distance between them, he walked at her slow pace into the living room.

He paused, setting his hands on his hips and surveying the damage. He hadn't read the police report. Electronics and jewelry were the typical targets, and that's what he'd assumed the thieves wanted.

Not this time. That much was obvious. An expensive, flat-screen still sat above her fireplace. Her computer still sat on her desk. It was clear that the criminals searched her house for something in particular.

"Did they take any money? Jewelry?" he asked.

"No. They didn't take anything that I can tell." Everly wrung her hands together as she paced barefooted back and forth on the tan carpet. Pink toes. That explained the smell. Had she sat and painted her toenails instead of straightening up her house?

He caught himself before a laugh escaped. Women never ceased to amaze him.

She paused and studied him for a moment. "Did you know Charles? My husband? I know you're Tripp's bodyguard, but you had to be around Charles at some point? Or are you newer than that?"

Finnian's muscles froze. Tripp has specifically told him not to discuss Charles with Everly, but he wouldn't lie to her. "Yes. I knew your husband."

"Were you in Miami with him?"

He nodded, hesitant to answer her direct question. How much did she know of her husband's activities? A little? Nothing? Everything?

"Sorry. I know it must seem strange that I hate my last name. But you were in Miami. I don't think it's any secret that my husband and I weren't"—she held out her hands and shrugged, looking as though she needed to apologize to Finnian—"very close the last eighteen months of our marriage before he died."

Anger lit him from the inside out. She'd done nothing wrong and didn't need to act as though she had. No woman deserved their husband abandoning them the way Charles had. Not for that lifestyle. Not for that woman. He tightened his fists, remembering it was partly his fault.

She stared down at the floor, her fingers twisting the bottom edge of her white shirt.

"Everly?" She didn't seem to hear him. "Everly?" he

asked louder. Would she cry at her husband's memory? He may have died only six months ago, but the bastard wasn't worth it in Finnian's opinion.

Her lips twitched. "My name sounds nice when you say it." She met his eyes again, the fear or grief he'd seen moments earlier now gone. Her small smile became a little playful, and her eyes brightened the way he imagined they did before her husband ruined her life. "Are you from England?"

Focus. Concentrate on the job, not on her eyes. "Yes." He moved to the closest window. Nothing looked out of place. The lock secure. How had they come into the house? The front door looked intact.

Blowing out a harsh breath, like his presence forced her to clean, she bent down and shelved the books scattered around. "Don't be offended if I ask if you're from London. It's the only place I can think of right now."

Finnian shook his head and began rehanging her curtains. "I lived there for a time, but I grew up in the country, two hours outside of London." Working at his family's goat farm that needed even more money this month. As soon as Tripp paid him, he'd forward the funds home.

"I'm sure it's beautiful. I don't think you've told me your name."

Finnian turned at her lighter tone, catching a hint of female interest in her eyes.

She snapped her head down and pretended to look at the book in her hand.

The movement caused a strand of hair to brush across her soft cheek. For the first time in a while, that familiar trickle of temptation to flirt with a woman shot through his blood. Of all the women in Atlanta . . .

But he wanted to make her smile again.

"Finnian James Hayes." His English accent came through thicker than it had since he'd left home. When she looked up, he grinned. It was the way his sisters teased him made girls faint in his wake.

Everly didn't reward him with a smile or faint, but a light blush crawled up her neck to her cheeks. "Nice to meet you, Finnian James Hayes," she said, a little stiffer than he'd hoped, before shoving the last few books onto the shelf and turning to leave the living room. "Let me know when you're done."

He turned back to the window, pretending to inspect it again to ease off the quick thump of his heart. Everly wasn't so immune, after all. And it appeared neither was he.

2

An unexpected thrill fired through her. Finnian had confirmed it. His smile was a weapon. Judging by his confidence, he knew it. Too bad she couldn't stand her ground and flirt a little herself.

Flirt? Who the hell was she kidding? This was the first person she willingly let into her home since Charles left her for Miami two years ago.

Everly hurried to the kitchen, setting up the dining room chairs as she passed by them. She should tell him to leave. That she was fine alone. She didn't want the help or his company.

But that was a lie.

She peeked down the hallway, catching a glimpse of his broad shoulders. But for the moment she wasn't by herself. He was here to help.

She closed her eyes, willing herself to make conversation. "Why are you in America?"

"Work." He moved around the room to the other window, his head almost even with the top of it. How tall was he? He had to be well over six feet. Maybe six-three?

The simple blue shirt and faded jeans contrasted with his tanned complexion. He started to turn toward her.

Everly jumped back into the kitchen, careful not to step on the glass on the floor. This was stupid. Tripp sent him here for her safety. He wasn't there to give her a chance to dust off her rusty moves for the first time since she and Charles dated in college.

She pulled the broom from the closet and began to sweep up the broken glass. There wasn't much she cared for in the house, but she did like the vase. Her mom had sent it to her one year when she'd been sick.

"What in the bloody hell are you doing?"

"Jeez!" She spun around, her hand flying to her heart.

"You don't have any shoes on." He snatched the broom from her. "Are you out of your mind?"

"No." She stared at her empty hand. He just took the broom. Why would he take her broom?

Finnian shook his head. "I'll clean up this glass. You can start at your desk."

Something snapped with the demand in his voice.

She'd survived on her own after Charles left. If Tripp felt like sending someone to check her security, fine, but Finnian didn't have any authority to start barking orders. Charles had barked enough for one lifetime, and she might be scared of a lot of things in the world, but she hated people telling her what to do.

The desk could wait until tomorrow. Or the next day. Whenever *she* felt like doing it. Not when Finnian Hayes decided it needed cleaning. The same with her own damn kitchen.

She grabbed the broom back. "I'll clean wherever I want to. Are you done checking everything?"

He took the broom a second time. "Do you want me to

carry you out of the kitchen, or do you think you can make it without slicing your foot open on the glass?"

She snatched it back again.

Finnian mumbled something she didn't catch. He lifted her by the waist, taking three large steps, and then placing her in the dining room. He locked eyes with her, too close, before snatching the broom away a third time.

He walked back into the kitchen before she even had a chance to panic at his touch.

"Chill out and breathe," she murmured, ordering her body to perform a function that should be automatic. After inhaling slowly three times, she stepped back toward the kitchen, ready to kick him out, but he met her at the door.

Brushing past her, the heat of his body lingered. "That's done. I brought a bolt to mount on the inside of your door."

"Wait," she called as he continued into the living room. She had to gain control again. "No, thank you. The alarm company called the police. Obviously, it did its job." And she could order a bolt online and install it later.

"How did they get into your home?"

She opened her mouth and then shut it. Damn. He had a point.

He motioned around the room. "If they kicked the door in without even damaging the frame, your small lock isn't enough. Besides, look how much time they had before the cops showed up. I'm going to mount the bolt so that you're safer."

"I said"—she dropped her voice to make a point—"I'm fine."

The doorbell rang.

She squealed, staggering back a few steps until the wall stopped her.

Finnian raised his eyebrows, a smug look turning her anxiety into anger in a flash.

"Fine, huh?" He chuckled as he walked, no, he sauntered, to the door. His cocky attitude filled up her living room.

She'd admit that she was a little jumpy, but aren't most people after their house is trashed?

She wasn't going to budge on the bolt issue. Charles had pushed her around, even from Miami.

They'd had ten years of marriage. The first five were great.

The next two, things started to go downhill.

The final three ended with his death. She would not give in and let the first nice-looking man that paid her attention step all over her. This was her life. Her house.

FINNIAN ANGLED HIS HEAD, considering the short man wearing a gray uniform. "Can I help you?" He crossed his arms over his chest, taking up most of the door frame. His presence at Everly's house might deter someone from another break-in. The stranger didn't need to know he didn't live there.

"I'm here with the water department." The man glanced over his shoulder, apprehension vibrating off of him, cluing Finnian in that something wasn't right. Those instincts never disappeared.

The man cleared his throat. "I need to check the water quality inside the home."

Bullshit. "No."

His bushy eyebrows drew together. "No?" He shifted his

stance, planting his feet. "I don't think you understand. We need to make sure her water quality is correct."

Her. Why did he not believe Finnian lived there? It was almost too easy to spot the lie. A familiar rush of adrenaline warmed his limbs. Finnian wouldn't need his gun. An easy two-handed toss would send the man almost to the sidewalk on the other side of Everly's manicured lawn.

"You're not coming inside this residence." The guy wasn't with the city water department. No van in the driveway. No badge or identification. Finnian glanced over his shoulder at Everly, her back still pressed against the wall as if pinned there by some invisible force. If a random would-be-visitor scared her this much, he had no intention of letting her know that this man was casing her house.

Was he a party to the earlier break-in? Possibly. If they didn't find what they were looking for, maybe they sent him. Returning was risky. Unless the reward was worth it.

Dammit. And Everly was alone.

Finnian shoved his hands in his pockets. If he hadn't been here, would she have opened the door? He would install the bolt. Today.

"Well," the man mumbled and looked down the street. "I suppose I could come back—"

"Never." Finnian leaned down, eye-to-eye, putting as much warning in his voice as possible. "You will never come back here. If she has an issue with her water, she will call the city herself. Otherwise, if you come back, she will call the police." Finnian straightened to tower over him. "Or I'll handle you myself. Don't expect me to be too far away. Ever."

The man's eyes narrowed, but he snapped his mouth shut before retreating down the driveway. Finnian stepped onto the front porch, waiting while the man half-walked or half-jogged down the street until he disappeared around the corner.

Everly had no idea what she was up against if they were willing to risk witnesses passing by just to gain access to her house. Or to her? Either way, he didn't think a mere deadbolt would be a significant deterrent, but it was something until he could figure out his next move.

Finnian grabbed the toolbox he'd set on the porch when he first arrived. Taking one more look down the empty street, he closed the door. Nothing felt right about the situation. Rarely did he ignore his intuition. He picked up the bolt lock.

"Wait a second, what are you doing?" Everly rushed forward. "Who was that man?"

He measured the door, considering the best place to mount the bolt. "That man was not who he said he was, and I'm securing your door." Why was she against this? Someone was out there watching her. Didn't she understand that?

"Stop. Please."

At her soft plea, Finnian dropped his arms by his side and turned, ready to argue his point.

Everly stood a few feet away, her breath rushing in and out at an increased pace.

He swallowed down his next comment. Tripp had ordered him to secure her house, and now he needed to secure it for his own peace of mind. The entire time he protected Charles in Miami, he'd never considered Everly separate from the "Mrs. Clarke" that Charles and Tripp mentioned occasionally. Never imagined she'd be in danger. Was one of Charles's old business partners after her?

That was a gigantic leap beyond a simple thief stealing the silver.

"I need to put this bolt on your door, Everly," he said, gentler. "It's the best I can do for you right now." Short of sitting in her driveway all night, watching over her.

Her silent and unfocused stare bothered him.

"I'll be out of your way in a moment," he continued.

Everly blinked. "No." She yanked the deadbolt from his hand.

A harsh laugh left his mouth before he caught it. "What are you doing?" He stared at those innocent, blue eyes full of . . . what? Outrage? Frustration? Confusion?

He held out his hand, amused but still serious about her situation. She needed something more than a flimsy lock to protect her. "Please, give that back."

Everly hid it behind her back.

"Everly." It was like his little sister playing a game of keep-away. "Give me the bolt."

"No. I told you—"

"That you don't need my help," he shot back, loud enough that the fog cleared from her eyes. "I got the picture, dear."

This woman didn't have a single clue what she needed when it came to her safety. He rubbed his chin, knowing better than to insult her intelligence and say that outright.

"Give it back so I can install it and assure you of a little bit of safety. I'll leave right after."

"No." Tears formed in her eyes. "Go ahead and leave." With her back stiff straight, Finnian wouldn't be surprised if her strong will refused to let those tears fall. He appreciated the lack of emotions, as he didn't do well with crying women to begin with, but it hit him harder than usual.

Making her day worse was never his intention. He'd sit out in her driveway all night if that were his only choice and try again tomorrow. He stepped to his tool bag, ready to pack it up.

She jerked back, stumbling over the contents of her desk drawers and then over the computer chair. Was she trying to get away from him?

Her arms waved in the air as she tipped off-balance.

In one, long stride, Finnian was there. He swooped his arm around her, pulling upright tight against his chest. "Watch it."

She held onto his shoulders. A small, muffled squeal sounded more like a field mouse than anything understandable from a human.

His vision shifted. The light fragrance of apples clouded his head. A small pattern of freckles dotted across the bridge of her nose.

Her lips parted with an inhale, and fingertips dug into his shoulders, keeping their bodies impossibly close together.

"I, uh . . ." She closed her eyes, like someone waiting for a kiss.

Except, she began gasping for air.

That shattered the moment.

"Everly?"

She pushed hard against his chest, but he didn't let go. She'd pass out if she didn't get her breathing under control.

Her knees buckled.

He scooped her up into his arms. She weighed about as much as his nephew did the day he was born.

In three long strides, he carried her to the sofa and sat her down.

Everly scrambled to the far end of the couch, wrapping her arms around her legs, her knees tucked tightly under her chin. This was more than just the break-in.

The floral sofa sagged under his weight. "Do you need anything? Some water?"

She shook her head, the loose knot of hair on top of her head wiggling with the action and threatening to fall down.

Finnian moved a fraction closer, resting his arm on the sofa behind her, trying to comfort, not scare her further. Somehow, she'd curled her body into a tiny ball, those pink toenails poking out from under her black pants.

"Do you have anyone who could come stay with you? Or you could go stay with them? It might help your nerves to get out of the house. Anyone would be on edge after having it tossed this way."

"No."

"What about your mum?"

She pursed her lips a moment before answering. "She's in Indiana."

"Maybe you should go out there and visit for a time." His set his hand on her shoulder. She jerked, but he didn't move it. Didn't do anything. He waited on her like he'd wait on a skittish animal.

"I try to visit my family as little as possible. They have a lot more important things to deal with than a crazy daughter whose marriage failed." Her voice began to clear itself of the panic. "My mom would hover and worry."

Finnian reached forward and took her cell phone off the coffee table. "I don't think any mother would be too busy to hear from her daughter." He offered her the phone, but she didn't take it.

"She wouldn't, but she'd know something was wrong. It's not Sunday. We only talk on Sunday." She shook her head. "If I call her now, she'll be on the next plane out here. They run a store. She doesn't need to take the time away from it to be here for this."

He slid his thumb along her phone. When it blinked, wanting a face id, he held it up.

She frowned but didn't object.

It opened to the main screen. Four contacts. How did anyone have only four contacts? Not many people had eleven sisters and brothers, but still, friends? Relatives?

She gracefully uncoiled and crossed the room to look out the front windows. The blinds still stood open from when he'd checked the locks earlier. She crossed her arms and rubbed her hands up and down like she was cold.

"My mom likes to remind me that I shouldn't have let Charles leave for Miami. She thinks that's what led to my marriage failing." She sighed and massaged her temples. "They didn't know the half of it. I never told them about all the stuff he did. I never showed them the email he sent me."

Finnian held his breath. Of all the things he regretted about Miami, giving in to Tripp's blackmail and writing that email for Charles topped it. If Tripp had revoked Finnian's work visa, he'd be out of a job that his family depended on. So, without a viable choice, he'd been the scribe of a cruel email intended to keep Everly away from Miami.

But he'd hurt her. Not a distant "Mrs. Clarke." The woman standing right there suffered at his hands because he didn't stand up to Tripp and Charles. It wouldn't have made a difference in the end to anyone except his own soul.

"After my mom's lectures, and then the sympathy from everyone when Charles never came back to Atlanta, I decided I was better off on my own than answering everyone's questions." She looked back at him, the setting sun glowing behind her through the window. "I know my parents are there if I need them, but I haven't needed anyone for the past two years. I don't need anyone now. I don't need you here installing locks."

"You've been completely alone for two years?" No one? Not even her mother coming to visit since Charles abandoned her?

If Everly wouldn't take care of herself, then he'd do it for her.

He opened up the contacts in her phone.

"What are you doing with my phone?"

"Programming my phone number in here." He rose, his eyes intent on hers, daring her to say something. "I'm going to put on the new lock, and then leave you to your solitude. But promise me, if anything happens, you'll call. I only live about twenty minutes away."

"You really don't need to do that—"

He stepped closer, cutting her off with a hard demand. "Promise me."

She pouted, looking annoyed. He'd take it over scared.

"Do you know how bossy you are?"

"Only when I'm dealing with hardheaded women."

"I'm only hardheaded when people don't listen to me," she snapped back.

"Sorry, but I can't walk away when someone needs protecting." He'd done that once and still lived with the damn nightmares he deserved.

Her blue eyes didn't waver as he stepped toward her. That was progress, at least. He hated being the one to scare her.

She kicked her chin out, taking her phone. "I don't need protecting."

Silence settled around them with her lie. She might believe it, but Finnian didn't.

With a huff, she tugged down her hair. It fell far below her shoulders in long, soft waves. In another second, she'd whipped it back into a tighter knot. "Thanks for coming by and checking things out. You can tell Tripp I'll let him know if I find anything of Charles's that he might need."

"I'm serious, Everly. Promise me you'll call if anything happens."

She crossed her arms again.

Stubborn. The woman would test the Pope's patience.

"Everly . . ."

"Fine," she mumbled and turned to face the window again. "I promise."

Finnian relaxed at the forced promise. He looked past her shoulder. A van stopped in front of her house for a long five seconds before speeding away.

They'd come back. Now, the only question that remained was *when?*

3

The sunlight glinted off the gold statue of the Greek Goddess Athena with her shield raised as she protected the entrance to the ATLighting building. Finnian passed through its shadow on his way inside.

Everly hadn't called, which was a good thing since that must mean nothing happened after he left. He should get a damn medal for his willpower for not driving past her house, patrolling it throughout the night, hoping to catch sight of that van one more time.

But as much as he worried for her, the woman herself intrigued him. That one moment, holding her close, replayed again as he pushed through the doors of the skyrise. He didn't deserve to consider anything beyond a casual friendship.

Finnian nodded at the security guard positioned in the middle of the large rotunda. "Mornin', Bob."

Bob saluted Finnian with a coffee cup as he passed by. "Friday can't get here fast enough."

"I hear ya." Finnian shuffled along with the crowd. The morning traffic hadn't cooperated, causing him to be later than usual. Entering the building with the rest of the late crowd resembled the downtown connector with one fender-bender near Seventeenth Street and a stall in the center lane at I-20. The whole city almost came to a standstill.

"Hey, Kyle," Finnian said to another security guard standing between two bays of elevators.

"What's up, Hayes?"

"Traffic."

"Makes you want to call in sick, don't it? Just start the weekend on Thursday."

Finnian laughed and fell in line for the elevators that serviced the thirtieth through sixtieth floors. "Almost did."

Which was a lie. Finnian had never taken a day off sick in his life.

Stepping off the elevator on the top floor, the musky odor of incense religiously burned by Tripp's secretary, Shelley, overwhelmed the reception area. Her hair scarf resembled an overly ripe banana today.

"Good morning, Shelley."

Shelley smiled. "Well—"

"Hayes, come in here," Tripp called from his office.

"I hope it remains a good morning for you," Shelley said, rolling her eyes. "I'm about tired of that man's bellowing."

"Always a good morning when I see you." Finnian winked at Shelley as she laughed.

He entered Tripp's office, pulling the door closed.

Tripp sat down behind his oversized desk and motioned for Finnian to sit. The Atlanta city skyline provided the backdrop with the floor to ceiling wall of windows. Pretty. But between Miami, Atlanta, or the countryside back home, he'd take England every time.

"Tell me how Mrs. Clarke is doing," Tripp said. He wore

a suit in a deep, rich brown that nearly matched his skin tone perfectly. "Was she upset?"

Where did he start? Did he describe the doorbell scared her like the way his old dog ran and hid under the bed during a thunderstorm? Or that her pride made her stubborn enough to walk straight into danger? Or should he tell Tripp about her reaction when he held her?

His reaction when she'd pulled him closer for that one moment? How it made him want to fight any giant to protect her?

"She's a little shaken by the whole thing, but I'm sure she'll be alright." That wasn't a lie, but the rest of his response he'd keep to himself.

"Did you help?" Tripp asked with what seemed like passing interest.

"I installed a long deadbolt on her front door. The other lock just slipped when they kicked it open. Didn't even break the door frame. Only a battering ram would get through the bolt I installed."

Tripp leaned back, resting his hands behind his head. "I'm sure she appreciated your help."

He doubted that considering the verbal wrestling match that they'd engaged in over the bolt installation.

Finnian looked down at his hands. The attraction surprised both of them. Tripp didn't need to know that. Besides, he didn't seem so concerned with Everly when he encouraged Charles to leave her and live in Miami.

"I thought about riding out there to see about her again in a few days." Finnian leaned forward and rested his elbows on his knees, rubbing his palms together. "It's a little sad that she's so alone."

Tripp stood abruptly, his chair rolling back as he waved his hand in the air. "Nah, there's no need. Everly has always enjoyed being alone. When we first started the company, she sat for hours setting up the bookkeeping and audit trail in the computer system while Charles saw to the equipment and purchasing. I, of course, sold our services. She's just a loner. Always has been." He barred his teeth in an attempt at a smile. "From now on, you leave Everly to me. I'll check in with her later." He laid a hand over his chest. "She's my duty and responsibility. Shelley has next week's schedule if you want to take a look. This is your weekend off, I believe."

Tripp arched an eyebrow at Finnian's silence. It was a silent dismissal that Finnian had learned was bred into some of the wealthiest assholes he'd ever met since coming to America.

"Got it." He left Tripp to whatever it was he did all day. Probably causing more trouble for Finnian to clean up later.

When it came to Everly's safety, it didn't matter what Tripp said. His authority didn't extend to who Finnian chose to associate with outside of work. He did have this weekend off. Spending some of it arguing with Everly about her safety sounded like the best weekend since leaving home.

Shelley hung up the phone as he leaned on the counter to check the schedule. "Shelley, my dear—"

She held up a finger and called Tripp on the phone. "Mr. Wellington, the estate lawyer, just returned your call. The only additional information they found was that Mr. Randolf, Charles's personal lawyer, itemized out all his assets before making the will. Mr. Randolf asked him about the ownership of ATL, and he said that it was already taken care of." Shelley rolled her eyes. "No, sir. Mrs. Clarke wouldn't answer the phone for either lawyer today. Mr. Randolf left a message for you to call him if you needed anything else but that he was never involved in anything pertaining to ATL and the stock ownership."

Shelley hung up the phone and blew out a breath. "I swear that man is going absolutely crazy after they read Charles's will yesterday. I don't blame him. If Everly didn't inherit the stock, somewhere, someone has access to fifty percent of this business." She pursed her lips together. "I know I shouldn't speak ill of the dead, but I almost miss the jerk."

"Who?"

"Charles Clarke. At least when he was around, someone could keep Tripp in line."

Finnian straightened as Tripp's door opened behind him. Tripp headed straight to the elevator. "Finnian, I need to head to the bank and check the safety deposit box."

Finnian winked at Shelley, again, giving up on getting more information for now. "I'm on my way."

He followed Tripp onto the elevator and leaned against the wall. He didn't care about the fifty percent ownership in ATL. Right then, his only concern was how long he needed to wait before giving Everly a call.

EVERLY TRUDGED up the stairs at her home, gliding her hand along the smooth banister, each step causing the rock in her stomach to grow heavier and heavier. Finally, after ignoring seven phone calls, her upbringing reared its ugly head. She stopped being rude and called Mr. Randolf back.

It wasn't the lawyer's fault that Tripp was obsessed with this.

Had Charles ever mentioned the stock to her? Did she remember seeing anything when they delivered his personal items from Miami? What about his computer? The smooth, level-headed Mr. Randolf sounded completely flustered and frustrated by her lack of decent answers. She almost wanted to make up a few new facts to give the man some renewed hope in his life.

The door to the bedroom she'd shared with Charles stopped partway when she tried to open it. Big, brown boxes stacked taller than Everly blocked the entrance. The smell of old paper and cardboard enveloped her the further she pushed her way into the room. It'd been at least four months since she'd opened the door to the room. It could disappear and her life would be better.

She hesitated outside the room, looking at the maze of boxes around her. Instead of like a cute corn maze, old, painful memories surrounded her.

The first box she grabbed off the top of the first pile slid to the floor with an ungraceful thud. So what if anything broke? She'd tried to sweet-talk the movers to go straight to the landfill with all of Charles's shit from Miami, but they claimed it was against their policy. Her stupid neighborhood covenant wouldn't let her stack the boxes on the curb for the trash truck to haul away. That meant they ended up in a room she never used.

Now, to open it. A bead of sweat ran down her back. Opening a stupid box filled with useless junk should be easier than this.

"C'mon, don't be a baby," she mumbled. She sat down on a box and leaned forward. The tape ripped with the first tug. "Not very good packing."

She ran a hand over her face. Of all the blasted boxes in the room, she'd chosen the one she'd packed herself after she'd received the email from Charles, ending their marriage. Nothing in there pertained to ATLighting, but her hand betrayed her and opened the box anyway.

She picked up a picture album. It was nothing more

than pictures of birds. Charles's love of birds had gone from a cute personality trait when they dated to this full on obsession later. He knew every scientific name of the birds native to Georgia. He'd proposed to her by explaining the characteristics of the Agapornis: the love bird.

Their wedding album was next. She traced her finger over the cover photo of them, shoving cake into each other's face. Wow, they were young and right out of college and so happy.

A faint feeling of grief tried to well up from the memory. She pushed it away. No point in wishing for a different life. Charles ruined both their lives.

Flipping through the pages, their wedding day came flooding back. The bridesmaids she'd lost touch with. The groomsmen that Charles never called. Aside from Tripp. Tripp had always been around.

Tears threatened to fall, but she wouldn't let them. Charles hadn't cried a day over her; she wouldn't cry for him now.

No effing way.

Her phone rang a generic four beep ring tone.

She rolled her eyes and reached for her phone. Tripp and the lawyer wouldn't leave her alone.

But it wasn't them.

Finnian.

Her head fell forward. "Jeez." Not now. One issue at a time. He presented a whole new set of problems she didn't know how to handle.

As soon as the ringtone ended, it began again. She still didn't answer.

A text message lit up the screen:

Answer your phone or I'll come for a visit.

The phone rang again. Everly sat back against the boxes

stacked behind her. A phone call was the better option than trying to deal with him and his smile, face-to-face.

She slid her finger across the screen, answering it. Finally, she said, "Hi?"

"Good afternoon, Everly." His voice sounded far too cheery for her mood. "How are you doing?"

Everly shook her head, lying as she responded with a typical "Fine." No point in dragging him down into the emotional tombs of her former life.

"Has anyone been by? Any more guys asking about the water?"

"No. It's been quiet." She twirled the end of a piece of hair. "Did Tripp tell you to call and check on me?"

After a pause, he said, "No, I wanted to check on you. Make sure you were alright."

She sighed. In a different world, a phone call from such a good-looking guy would have made her day. But not with her current life and definitely not today, sitting surrounded by her late husband's things, with guilt, grief, and anger battling for top billing.

"Look, that's very considerate of you, but—"

"Don't mention it. I know what it's like not to have any friends or family around."

That made her pause. Was he alone too? But he had Tripp. He interacted with people.

Finnian James Hayes was a people person. He'd proved that yesterday.

Everly was not.

"I don't want anyone around." Could she make it any clearer?

His light laugh caught her off guard. "You're right. You don't want anyone around, but you definitely *need* someone, Everly."

There he went again, twisting her stomach into a knot when he said her name. "You don't know what I need, Finnian." The statement lacked the authority she wanted to portray. He got under her skin.

"I know you need to stay safe. And I also know you need a friend. You can't go through the rest of your life alone and isolated, hiding in your house."

She stood, wishing she had room to move. "I suppose you think you're the right person for the job, huh?"

"I think I am if the choice is between me and a house full of mangy cats."

"Cats?" That threw her off. What was he talking about?

"That's right. Cats. My Aunt Beatrice, on my dad's side, started off just like you. My uncle passed away, and she stopped visiting friends. Stopped coming to church. Stopped answering the phone. She slowly drifted away from the family and most human contact. One day, my mum loaded us all up, and we drove two hours to Aunt B's house over near Colwyn Bay. Cats. Everywhere. Twenty-three was my count. My dad was certain there were thirty or more. Couldn't even sit down in the house for fear you'd be meowing when you stood back up."

There he went, charming her when she needed to keep her distance. "I don't think I'm at risk for that." Looking around, she didn't have room for thirty cats.

"That's good to hear. I don't think my ego would have survived if you picked the cats over me as a friend."

She laughed. When was the last time a man, besides her brother, made her laugh? Sitting there, surrounded by everything she hated about her life, and Finnian Hayes made her laugh.

Definitely a dangerous man.

"Then I guess I shouldn't tell you that I'm allergic to cats, or else the competition might have had a different outcome."

He chuckled. "A win by default is still a win in my book."

"Finnian, why exactly do you feel the *need* to be my friend?" At one time, she considered herself a good friend to others. Now, she worried that not even a cat would want her.

"Because I have the *need* to make sure you'll be alright. I can't help it."

The way he said it poked at the sore spot in her heart. With her wedding album open, the easy way people can break their word shut down her brief moment of happiness.

"That's nice of you, but I don't—"

"Want to ruin this friendly moment by telling me, again, that you don't need me?" Finnian sighed and might have shifted the phone. "Remember, Everly," he said, drawing out her name with his accent. "I'm only a phone call away. Call me anytime, and I'll come to you. Have a good night."

Was he really that nice of a guy? "Bye," she said, pushing down the urge to stay on the phone.

Her cell phone screen showed five contacts. Five. She now had five contacts.

Mom.

Dad.

Her brother, Cade.

Tripp.

And now, Finnian. He made up twenty percent of her contacts after knowing him less than two days. How was that possible? She'd spoken with him more than her own mother this week. Thinking about it, it was more than anyone outside her family or her accounting clients since the funeral.

No wonder she had such a strong reaction to him. Human nature, right? A nice, albeit bossy person entered her life when she needed a little help. But friends? No way. Friends wanted to talk. And visit. And touch. Talking to her mom on Sundays and playing twenty questions was plenty.

Everly closed up the box. Finnian was a nice enough guy, but she needed to keep things the way they were. Safe.

She left the room. Maybe tomorrow she'd try again. Right now, every inch of her wanted to crawl in bed and sleep. That was the one thing she could always do. Even after the funeral. Even when Charles left her for Miami. She could sleep.

She passed through the kitchen, opting to skip dinner. After a long, hot shower, checking every window and door, and setting her house alarm, she crawled into bed.

And nothing happened.

What the hell?

Everly stared at the ceiling in her darkened room, her mind still circling around Finnian and his stupidly charming story. Thirty cats? That probably wasn't even true, but it brought another unexpected smile to her face.

Why had he really called? Why was she still thinking of him? She'd pushed him from her mind after his visit. Pushed away his dark eyes and broad shoulders . . .

"Ugh!" She rolled over on her pillow and squeezed her eyes shut. It was no use. The more she told herself not to think of him, there he was. Smiling in a way that made a blush start at her toes. She hadn't given men a thought since Charles left. Until now.

She stared at the black ceiling and bit her lip. Why fight it? It wouldn't hurt to think of him, for a moment. That moment when he'd kept her from falling, she'd held on. She'd pulled him close. Every pain in her heart peeled away as she inhaled the manly way he smelled.

She jerked awake, a little surprised she'd fallen asleep

that fast as the dream of Finnian standing on her front porch faded away. What woke her up?

She blinked, the dark shadows of her room coming into focus. She held her breath.

A footstep?

There it was again—a footstep in the flower bed outside her window.

She sat up, straining to listen, willing her ears to pick up another sound. Was it an animal?

A car door closed.

The hum of the heater died. Her bathroom nightlight disappeared, casting the room into thick darkness.

An eerie warm feeling flooded into her arms and legs as the thump of blood pounding in her ears drowned out the complete silence. The streetlights still shone through the blinds, as did the neighbor's security flood light.

Shit. Her power was out. *Only* her power.

Heart racing, she sat up on the side of the bed, reaching her shaking hand for her phone.

Should she run?

No. They were already on the side of the house, where the footsteps were, probably waiting for her. Even with the power out, the alarm company would be notified when a door or window opened.

But would that be too late? She dialed 911.

"Someone just cut the power to my house." She relayed her address as she stood up in the middle of her room, indecision heightening the anxiety. No. She would not freeze right now.

Think, Everly.

The 911 operator's voice remained calm. "Alright. Give me some more information. Where are they now?"

"I don't know. I have to go." Somewhere. She couldn't stay right there and wait for them.

"Ma'am, please don't hang up."

Everly hung up. She needed to think and save herself, not give someone a play-by-play of her murder at three in the morning.

The front doorknob rattled.

This was it.

If she couldn't run out of the house, what would she do? She was a sitting duck if she stayed in her bedroom. She turned in a circle. Maybe hide?

Her downstairs bedroom left her limited options. The closet was barely big enough to hold a few shirts and a vacuum. Her bed sat on the floor, but every bad guy knew to look under the bed. If she had a storage closet—

The window in the kitchen shattered.

Now!

Everly sprinted down the hallway and for the stairs.

Taking them two at a time, she darted into the old bedroom with Charles's things. Weaving around the columns of boxes, she worked herself back into the corner, partially inside the closet, also filled with boxes. Taking long, deep breaths, she refused to faint.

Her body shook. She squeezed her body into a tight ball. There was only one answer.

Fight. Everly would fight.

Loud banging began—like someone trying to kick in the front door. The entire house shook with their pounding.

Her mind flew to the deadbolt.

"Finnian," she muttered, pulling out her phone. With shaking fingers, she sent him a text.

HIDING UPSTAIRS. THEY CAME BACK. HELP.

4

The alert sound from a new text message pulled Finnian from his nightmare. The informant just blew his undercover mission. Sean had stalled their death sentence, giving Finnian and the two other team members time to escape. As usual, he woke up as the gunshot that killed Sean echoed through the warehouse.

Finnian reached for his phone. Tripp had a bad habit of using him as a personal taxi, but tonight he was thankful for the dream's interruption. His clock showed three in the morning.

And the text wasn't from Tripp.

Everly's name glowed brightly on the screen.

His body shot into action as he read the text, pulling on his jeans, sliding into a pair of flip-flops, and a T-shirt before grabbing his gun. He didn't bother with a holster. He intended to use it if they were in her house.

The twenty-minute drive took ten minutes, running near ninety miles per hour on the highway and ignoring most red lights. He called 911 on the way. The dispatcher on the phone gave him a shred of hope. She'd called before the alarm company had, but the homeowner had disconnected the call.

He slammed his hand on the steering wheel. Of course, she did, hardheaded woman.

Six police cars and an ambulance, lights flashing, sat parked at odd angles in the driveway and along the street.

Finnian braked hard, his tires screeching to a halt near a crowd of people gathered at the corner.

She'd better be safe. It'd been years since this much adrenaline and silent prayers coursed through his system.

Three cops ran toward him, all drawing their guns.

"Sir!" one shouted. "Drop your weapon!" Finnian set the gun on the ground before holding up his hands. He didn't have time for this shit.

"I'm her private security and former police." He turned around. "My wallet is in my back pocket with my identification. I have a license to carry in there as well."

Slowly, a hand extracted his wallet. Finnian's jaw almost snapped in half from the unnecessary delay. Where was she? Safe?

"He's clear," someone called out.

Finnian left them with his wallet and gun. He ran to the front door. The police officer standing there held up his hand. "Sir, I can't allow you to go in there."

Finnian gripped the doorframe as he tried to see around the officer. "Is she alright?"

His eyebrows furrowed together. "The homeowner isn't here. We think she might have run after they flipped the breaker to the house. That was an easy enough fix. I sent a few patrol cars to look for her. We apprehended one of the suspects. He's being questioned in the kitchen but not saying much. If there were others, they got away. Are you a friend of the homeowner?"

Finnian's patience reached its limit with the man's ramblings. "I'm her private security, and she didn't run. She's here." He ignored the officer's next question and pushed into the house, heading straight up the stairs with two police officers right behind him.

"Everly?" He shouted and checked the first room. A bed without sheets sat alone in the middle of the empty space. He pushed on the next door, but it stopped partway open. He squeezed into the room, filled with boxes. She could be in this mess and no one would ever find her.

"Everly?" He held his breath, listening.

"Finnian?"

"Thank God."

He looked back at the two police officers who'd followed him into the room. "Stay here." He wound his way through the stacks, somehow not hurling boxes left and right to make it to her.

There she sat, knees tucked tightly under her chin like before, her eyes glassy and wide with pure fright. He knelt down in front of her, careful their bodies didn't touch, remembering her aversion to it.

"Everly?" He called her name as softly as possible, a hard thing to do with his body wound tight. "Darling, are you okay?"

She lifted her frozen gaze to his.

Those beautiful eyes shifted from wide-open fear to recognition. "Finnian," she mumbled as she rocked forward onto her knees and wrapped her arms around his neck, almost knocking him off-balance and into more boxes.

His arms tightened around her petite body and his eyes closed.

Safe.

Nothing he'd experienced since coming to America

compared to this. He rested his cheek on the top of her head and breathed deeply. Her smell hit his memories, surrounding him with the vision of an early fall afternoon back home when the apple trees began to ripen. Perfect.

"How is she?" the officer called from the doorway, bringing Finnian back to reality.

Finnian ran a hand down her spine. "Are you alright?"

She sniffed and nodded. "I'm fine."

Fine? She was anything but fine. Finnian helped her stand, wrapping an arm around her back when her legs wobbled. "Steady," he murmured.

Her shoulder rose with a deep inhale. "I'm fine."

"I'm not sure you understand the meaning of that word." He looked to the officers in the doorway. "Make sure that scum is out of her house."

"He's already headed to the station," one officer answered.

Finnian took his time working his way back through the boxes, her hand firmly in his as he led the way. "What are all these boxes for?"

"Charles's things from Miami. I didn't want to deal with them." Her voice sounded as though she would shatter at any moment.

"I'll help you get rid of them." It was the least he could do for any assistance he'd provided for Charles Clarke to hurt someone like Everly. She didn't deserve the pain. She didn't deserve the torture she had to endure with these break-ins, either.

Because they weren't a coincidence.

He repositioned her beside him, his arm around her waist as they walked down the stairs, her legs unsteady. He'd pick her up and carry her if she'd let him.

The police officers quieted as they entered the room.

She squeezed a little closer.

She needed him. A quick snap of pride shot through his body. He'd not felt that since well before Sean's death.

"Ma'am?" A police officer began, waiting for Everly to lift her head. "Are you up to talking about what happened?"

"My house!" Everly's mouth dropped open as she took in the living room, everything tossed about in a hurried job. "Again. The S.O.B. trashed it all again."

"I understand if you'd rather come down to the station to discuss this."

She shook her head and sat down on the sofa. "I don't want to go anywhere."

Finnian sat beside her, his arm moving to her shoulders.

"I'm fine, Finnian." She leaned away.

"There's that word again. Remind me to give you the proper definition later."

She frowned but didn't reply.

He removed his arm but remained hip-to-hip with her. Each moment she retold the story, the footsteps and the power outage, increased his outrage at whoever did this. The police seemed to dismiss it as nothing more than a return job, the burglars trying to get what they left behind.

That didn't make sense. Anyone who cased the house knew she didn't leave. They'd expected her to be home. Only one idea remained: Everly was their target.

Everly retold the story three more times, and the police collected fingerprints. The man they caught didn't say anything meaningful. Still, the police assured Everly they would call in a few days to discuss prosecution. Finally, they left, taking with them the noise and chaos.

Finnian closed the door behind the last one, bolting the lock that had held throughout the ordeal. He sighed and rested his head against the door. For the first time, since leaving England three years ago, he had a connection to someone. The one woman who needed space and distance to function.

But tonight, it was different. No one had ever held onto him like that—like he was her only lifeline. It was stress from the situation. He knew how that affected emotions.

Finnian shut his eyes tight against the quiet whisper that it was more.

A ticking sound came from the living room. Everly hunched over her desk, her fingers flying over the keyboard of her computer. She'd taken down her hair, the scent of apples faint in the air.

Finnian shook his head. Now wasn't the time for that train of thought. She'd be upset. He opened his mouth, but nothing came out. How did he tell someone it was alright when it wasn't?

What would his mum do?

"Can I fix you something to eat?"

She jumped when he spoke. "No, thank you." She repositioned her hair on top of her head. "I'm so confused. What would anyone be looking for in my house?"

You. The answer resurfaced. The robbers hadn't searched through anything like before. Yeah, they trashed the place, but it was fake. The police thought the alarm scared them away, but the scum they caught looked more like part of the crowd Charles and Tripp associated with down in Miami. Like the drug mobsters that Finnian had interacted with long ago.

"I'm glad they didn't take my laptop." She typed for a moment. "Charles's lawyer, Mr. Randolf called me yesterday and asked that I look through Charles's things for anything referencing ATL and a random trust fund he located in my name. He sent me an email with limited information on the trust. Basically just the name." She huffed. "And I tried to look for the ATL information upstairs in those boxes." She cradled her chin in her hand and sighed. "I didn't make it past one box last night. Now, I am attempting to hack into Charles's email account. I'm just grasping for answers at this point."

"Like a trust fund from your parents?" He propped a hand on the desk and leaned down to see the screen.

She half-laughed. "Uh, no. We aren't the type of people to have trust funds. I don't know who set it up. I assume Charles. Knowing him it's illegal." She typed in five more attempts into Charles's email account before it locked her out for twenty minutes. "Charles obviously changed his password after he left for Miami."

She angled her head toward Finnian, now only inches away. Her eyes didn't rise to his but lingered on his mouth. It almost hurt to resist the pull. She was tired, exhausted, and one problem still existed.

He placed a hand on her shoulder.

She jerked in response. The computer chair rolled over his foot as she scrambled away.

"I'm sorry!" She covered her mouth with her hands. That small indication of interest a moment earlier switched to embarrassment. "I didn't mean to squash your foot."

"Give me a chance to look for information." He grinned, trying to put her at ease. "My toes may be a tad safer sitting in the chair than standing behind it."

~

HE SAT at her computer desk barefooted and wearing a simple white undershirt untucked with his hair messy. His jaw tightened when he concentrated on another Internet search. A hint of cologne hung in the air around him, not helping with her unexplainable attraction. She wiped her palms on her pajama pants.

Without hesitation, Finnian had shown up in the middle of night. Instead of leaving when the rest of the police did, he stayed with her to figure this out. She squinted her eyes over his shoulder at the computer.

Almost five in the morning. No matter how much she appreciated his help, the truth remained that she still craved her solitude. She wanted to figure this out on her own. She'd come a long way since Charles left her. It would be stupid to hand over her life to another man. *Fool me once, shame on you . . .*

Finnian slammed his hand on the table.

Everly gasped when her heart attempted to escape from her chest. "What?"

He muttered something in . . . what was that? French? Or maybe English, and she just didn't understand him through his accent?

He ran a hand through his hair, causing it to stick up in short, dark spikes pointing all different directions. "I'm not surprised she'd be involved."

"Who?" Everly leaned over his shoulder, moving as close as she allowed herself. The screen showed a Miami address. "What are you looking at? Do you know what this is?"

Finnian stood without warning, causing Everly to stumble out of the way.

He began to pace. The muscles across his shoulders bunched under his shirt.

She sat down in his vacated seat. The computer screen showed the legal documentation for a condominium in Florida registered to the "Everly Clarke Family Trust."

Well . . . that laid it out pretty clearly that there was a

trust in her name. What the hell was Charles thinking? And family? What family?

"The lawyer, Everly. Where is his number?" Finnian leaned over her, his long arms reaching around like an embrace. He clicked on her email. The heat from his body made her want to run away and crawl closer.

Did he care that her blood pressure would kill her if he didn't move soon? The air in her lungs felt thick when she tried to take her next breath.

"There it is." His cheek brushed her temple as he jotted down the number on the notepad beside her hand.

He stepped away, pulling out his phone. She didn't need a crazy lunatic after her. Death would come quicker if Finnian didn't keep his distance.

She ran a hand over her hair. How did it always get so messy? She yanked out the ponytail holder and threw it back up.

He paused in dialing, watching her as she finished fixing her hair. Shaking his head, he pressed the last two numbers.

"It's barely five in the morning, Finnian. You can't possibly call Mr. Randolf now?"

Finnian locked eyes with her and held the phone up to his ear.

Everly ground her teeth together. He would call the lawyer despite her opinion, as usual. Maybe she should start telling him to do the opposite of what she wanted to be done. He was *amazing* at doing that.

Finnian began to pace, swearing when he redialed the number. He had to redial two more times before someone answered.

"I need to speak with Randolf!"

Everly crossed the room, holding her hands up. "Finnian. Chill out." He'd scare the poor lawyer.

"Randolf! What do you know about that trust?" He
flexed his hand by his side. "That trust. Everly's trust," he
shouted.

Everly leaned near the phone, trying to listen.

"I said, what is the meaning of your email to Everly?
Email!" He snapped his mouth shut and shoved the phone
to her. "He can't understand me," Finnian grumbled with
what could be described as a combination of a pout and
scowl, both corners of his bottom lip turned down, but he
looked ready to throttle someone.

She took the phone, pressing her lips together. It
shouldn't be funny. The entire situation should feel
harrowing and have her crying in the corner. Finnian
changed that.

Hell, Finnian had changed everything in only a few
short days. She bit her lip. That shouldn't make her happy.

"Don't you dare laugh," he snapped.

Oh, she didn't dare. Shifting her tone of voice to extra
sweet, she said, "Mr. Randolf, I want to apologize for my
friend calling so early."

Finnian threw his hands in the air and faced away
from her.

A small laugh did escape.

"No, not a problem. Who was that? I couldn't
understand a thing he said." Mr. Randolf's voice sounded
rough from sleep.

"A frustrated, bossy Englishman."

Finnian cut his eyes at her over his shoulder. Even with
the apparent annoyance at her, his intense, direct look sent
tingles down the back of her neck.

She cleared her throat, needing a glass of water. "Mr.
Randolf, can you tell me more about why you were asking
about a trust fund? What worried me is that I've had people

break into my house twice now. I'm wondering it has something to do with it. Or maybe it pertains to ATL? What do you think? It started the day the will was read. We found a Miami address registered—"

"Everly, you might want to let the man answer." Finnian rested a hand over hers that had twisted the bottom of her shirt into a knot. He plucked the phone from her hand and put it on speaker.

"I hope I can answer a few of those questions, Mrs. Clarke."

"Everly." Once this ordeal was over, she would change her last name. No point in keeping it. She'd happily rejoin the world as Everly Fischer.

"Yes," said Mr. Randolf. "I forgot. Everly, I found out, just yesterday, about this trust." It sounded like he shuffled papers on his end of the phone. "Where are my glasses? Oh, here they are. It all started yesterday when I discovered that a trust fund is holding the ownership of a condo in Miami. You, Everly, are named a trustee of that trust."

Finnian shoved his hands in his pockets, his scowl darkening as he stared at the phone as if Mr. Randolf would be intimidated into speeding things along.

Everly couldn't hide her amusement. It had to be a lack of sleep that made the large, disgruntled man like Finnian "cute" right then. Nothing about Finnian should be cute. Puppies were cute. Not a gun-toting security guy that looked like he could rip apart a phone book with his hands.

"What does this mean?" Finnian said, his voice a deep growl, his muscles tense. He might be cute like a puppy, but there was no doubt he could protect her.

"I, apparently, own this mysterious condo through a mysterious trust." Charles was shady, but he didn't play games when it came to business. "I don't understand why he would put this in a trust."

"I don't either," Mr. Randolf replied. "Or why he didn't tell me about owning the condo."

Finnian's tan face drained of color before flushing. He ran a hand through his hair. "Bloody hell. You own the damn condo." He began to mutter, looking up at the ceiling as though he was having a conversation with her ceiling fan.

Mr. Randolf continued. "I'm not sure who lives there now, if anyone. I never knew any of this existed until yesterday when I researched the trust." The sound of shuffling papers echoed through the phone. "If you give me a few weeks—"

"A few weeks?" Everly stepped closer to Finnian and the phone. "Someone broke into my house. Twice. If these break-ins have anything to do with ATL or this trust or a damn condo," to use Finnian's words, "I don't think I have a few weeks. We need to figure it out, and we still don't know who Charles left ATL to, do we?"

The volume of Finnian's imagined conversation with the ceiling fan increased. Definitely speaking a different language. It had to be French.

"Finnian?"

He snorted like a bull and looked at the front door, away from her. He shook his head, as if in disbelief of something.

"What is it? Do you know something about this condo?"

His shoulders sagged as he faced her. Instead of the frustration seen earlier, when he reminded her of an adorable grizzly bear, his look softened into an apology.

That wasn't good.

A ball of nerves tightened in her stomach.

"That's Claudia's address," he said in a low voice.

"Who is Claudia?"

He grimaced. "Everly." He shook his head. "I'm so sorry."

Miami.

A condo in Miami.

That must mean Claudia . . .

Finnian laid a hand on her shoulder and cupped her cheek with his other. She had always assumed that Charles had another woman down there. Now she had a name and another reason to hate Miami.

But Finnian confirmed it. "Claudia was Charles's mistress."

5

Claudia's name tasted sour. Everything about his time in Miami with Charles sent a rush of cold anger and burning shame through his blood. From the parties to the drugs, Charles had lived his own life to the max while ruining Everly's.

And Finnian had stood by and watched it happen.

Mr. Randolf still shuffled papers on the other end of the phone call.

A tear escaped, rolling down Everly's smooth cheek. He wiped it away with his thumb. Crystal blue eyes searched his for answers he didn't have. Her mouth parted as she sucked in a ragged breath before stepping away.

She was strong. She'd taken one blow after another to her emotions and was still determined to stand on her own.

"Just one more moment," Mr. Randolf said.

Finnian scrubbed his hand over his head. How much would Everly want to know about Claudia? Most people underestimated Claudia based solely on her looks and past. She'd recognized a weak, wealthy man in Charles Clarke and pounced on him. Was she worried that Everly might kick her out of her condo? Hell, it wouldn't take much more than a flick of her hand to hire men to harass Everly like this. How far would she go to keep up the lifestyle she loved?

Everly stared past his shoulder, the gentle sound of her breath the only noise in the room.

Her innate softness was a stark contrast to Claudia's sharp edges. She stood six feet tall with her white-blond hair adding a few inches on top, and more plastic surgery than his own annual salary could pay for. The last night Finnian saw Charles alive, Claudia had worn a barely-there dress in the oddest shade of yellow. It was lodged in his memory for some reason.

Everly wrapped her arms around her stomach. "Charles's mistress lives in a condo that belongs to me." She closed her eyes, her lips pressing into a thin line a moment before she spoke. "Alright. Are you sure? Are you sure she's still living there?"

Finnian rubbed the back of his neck. It'd be easier to lie, but she'd been lied to too much already.

"Last time Tripp mentioned her, she was still there."

Her brow creased, but her eyes stayed closed. "Tripp? What does he have to do with her?"

Finnian's mouth opened. Jumbled thoughts raced through his mind, none of them coherent. He'd hardly understood the relationship himself.

Her eyes opened, filled with hurt and punching straight to his soul. "Tell me, Finnian."

He'd try. "Charles made Tripp promise to take care of Claudia." He reached for her hand, hoping to offer her comfort. "We all assumed Charles would leave the condo to her."

That knocked her out of her daze. "Mr. Randolf?" She

snatched the phone off the desk and moved to the other side of the living room. "How do I find out more about this trust? I mean, for all we know, Charles put other things in there besides housing assistance for his mistress. He was a piece of shit in about a dozen different ways, but Charles didn't do anything without a purpose in mind. He did this for a reason. He created a secret trust for a reason."

She was right. Something was off about the situation.

"Well," Mr. Randolf started. "That will be a little tricky. I have a few legal aides researching it, but, honestly, contacting the person who registered the trust is your best option. They may have had a conversation with Charles and could explain more. I'm afraid since I have nothing to do with it, no one will speak with me. But don't worry, the attorney-client confidentiality keeps everything between the two of us. That means I won't be telling anyone about this trust. I won't discuss anything you do with Tripp. You can guarantee it."

"Thank you. Who set up the trust?" she asked. "Do you know that?"

"John Harriman."

Finnian sat back down at the computer. John Harriman? It sounded familiar. Why? He typed in the name, bringing up a picture and his history of arrests. Again, another character who looked like he belonged to the mafia crew in Miami. More than likely, he'd run across Mr. Harriman at some point or another.

Finnian turned around as Everly ended her call. She looked dead on her feet. Her eyes opened a little slower with each blink as she started picking up books scattered around from the last break-in.

He shut down the computer and stood. Stretching his arms, every inch of his body reminded him he hadn't slept in almost two days. Tripp's social engagements kept him out most of the night before.

"It's been a long night. Let's get some sleep."

She stopped straightening the room as her eyebrows raised high.

"Oh." He smiled, a half-laugh escaping, "I meant I'll sleep on the sofa." Not that curling his body around Everly, knowing she was one hundred percent safe, wouldn't make for some incredible sleep.

He crossed the room to rehang the curtains. Again. Tripp didn't want him to associate with Everly. Finnian smiled to himself. He really didn't give a shit what Tripp wanted at this point. Meeting this woman had changed the game.

"You don't need to stay. I'll be fine. You can go home." She stacked the books tossed about the room on the coffee table. "I'll finish cleaning this and then take a nap."

"I'm not leaving here after you had to hide for your life not three hours ago." She needed the protection, even if she didn't want it.

Her spine stiffened, the haze of sleep disappearing for a moment.

He held up his hands and softened his voice before she could kick him out. "Please, Everly. Let me stay. We can figure out our next move in the morning. Or afternoon. Whatever time it is when we wake up."

Everly sucked in a big gulp of air, gearing up for another argument, but none came. Her shoulders drooped with exhaustion. "Fine." She picked up a few more books, letting the last one fall onto the top of the pile. "But just today. I'll finish cleaning when I wake up. I doubt I'll even sleep for an hour." She stalked past him and out of the room, down the hallway past the kitchen.

A door closed a moment later.

He looked down at his bed for the next couple of hours. It wouldn't be the first time he slept on a sofa too short for his height. The glorious thought of falling asleep would have to wait.

Finnian headed into the kitchen. He needed to patch up those shattered windows and clean up the glass.

DID her clock really say four? Everly's eyes, swollen and scratchy from crying and lack of sleep, squinted at the glowing numbers. Ten hours of sleep. She yawned. Another ten would probably do the trick. Her muscles ached as she stretched her arms, and a dull pulsing pain began at the back of the head. This morning had left her emotionally drained. First, the break-in last night, and then the conversation with Mr. Randolf.

Claudia.

That's right. She finally knew the name of her husband's mistress. She squeezed her eyes shut. Finnian had been so sweet and almost apologetic about the entire situation. It wasn't his fault Charles was a piece of crap.

The old concept of not speaking ill of the dead didn't apply to her ex-husband. Not after everything he'd put her through. His life still put her through hell with the break-ins, and now a surprise trust fund to furnish his mistress a house. What the hell was the point of that?

Everly would sell it. No way would she support a woman like that.

She sat up, looking at her reflection in the mirror mounted above her dresser. She grimaced. It was bad. Sadly, she couldn't blame the way she let herself go on Claudia.

When had she become so pale? And thin? Why hadn't she noticed before? She used to worry about fitting into a pair of size eight jeans. Her yoga pants were barely tight on her.

She plopped back on her bed and stared at the ceiling. Why would she have noticed? No one cared what she looked like going to Walmart at six in the morning to avoid the crowds.

Her phone chimed. She reached for it on her nightstand.

IT'S SUNDAY AND I HAVEN'T HEARD FROM YOU. IF YOU'RE NOT TOO BUSY, I'D LOVE TO TALK.

Typically, her Sunday conversations with her mother gave her something to look forward to each week. Just enough contact with her family to make her feel not alone on the planet. But lying to her mom was uncomfortable, so she'd skip it for today.

SORRY. I WAS UP LATE LAST NIGHT AND SLEPT IN. LET'S TALK TOMORROW.

She definitely couldn't write to her mom that a gorgeous Englishman slept on her couch all day or that she'd had men break into her house earlier.

DATE?

Everly rolled her eyes but felt the beginnings of a smile. Subtle hints were not her mother's forte.

NOT REALLY

Her phone rang. Predictable Elenore.

"Hey, Nora."

Her mom's high-pitched laughter echoed through the phone. "You did have a date, didn't you?"

"No."

"You said 'not really' the first time. Who is he? How did you meet? Is he a client?" Her mom's excitement suffocated her for a moment. "I had no idea you were back out there, playing the field. I'm so proud of you."

Not sure a pushy man invading her life was "back out there" in the sense of dating, but she wouldn't correct her mom. "He's . . ." What did she say? "He works for the ATL. Tripp sent him to, uh, to fix the door. The lock broke."

Silence. Her mom was thinking. Never a good sign.

"Were you up late with him? It's nearly four in the afternoon. Are you just waking up? You sound like you do when you wake up."

Nora, as she and her brother usually referred to her mom, wanted to know every little detail of every possible moment. The more gossip and juice she could squeeze out of Everly, the more she demanded. Sometimes, it was easier to give in since her mom was like a freaking detective. That's why Everly had distanced herself. She always asked too many questions of her about Charles.

"I've been up," she lied. "We ended up talking for a little bit last night."

"Oh! Is he cute? Is he tall?"

"Yes."

"To which question?"

"Both, but it doesn't mean anything."

Her mom sighed. "You've hardly interacted with anyone in years, and you're saying that talking with a cute handyman half the night isn't important? I know you and Charles had some difficulties at the end of your marriage, but he passed away six months ago. Remember, you're only thirty-three. You have a long life ahead of you."

"Mom—"

"I know. It's your life, and you don't want to talk about it."

Everly smiled at Nora's imitation of her voice. "I gotta go, Mom. Love you."

"I expect a longer conversation with you tomorrow."

Everly grimaced. "I'll try."

Discussing her true feelings with her mom, either about Finnian or Charles, was pointless. Once she set her opinions, her mom went about trying to mold the situation to fit them. If she talked about Finnian with that overwhelming excitement gushing through the phone, Everly had no choice but to become just as excited. That was dangerous.

For the first time, her mom wasn't too far off the mark. Nothing would work out long-term with Finnian. After Charles, she had zero interest in marrying. She'd never let anyone in close enough to hurt her again.

Everly looked back at her reflection. Still, it didn't mean she had to look like a complete slob in front of Finnian.

After a quick shower and finding some makeup that wasn't too dry or too old to use, she dried her long hair. She marveled at the mass hanging in a limp, dull stream down her back. No wonder it kept falling out of her ponytail. Had it really been more than two years since her last hair cut?

Grabbing a pair of scissors, she held them up to her collarbone. A small thrill shot through her as the scissors sliced through the first section of hair.

She trimmed one side and then the other, trying to even it out until she gave up. It was a start. Maybe someday she could find the nerve to go to a beauty salon for a real haircut. With a little eye makeup and some lip gloss, the old Everly reappeared in the mirror.

Baggy jeans and a beige sweater finished her first attempt to re-enter the human race. Not necessarily the fashionable side of society, but a step-up from yoga pants. At least these pants had a button. That made them "real."

She paused at the door, ready to face Finnian. Her worry over her looks was a petty thing, really. Over the past few days, the turmoil should have caused her to crawl into her shell and hide until it passed. This attempt at normalcy was Finnian's fault. Why couldn't he be wimpy and short with bad skin?

A half-laugh bubbled out. Who was she kidding? It was more than some superficial attraction to a man.

He was nice. Big and growly and plain, ole' nice. After her history, that was as sexy of a personality trait as a man could have.

Finnian's muffled laugh floated down the hallway.

Following the sound, she tiptoed into the living room. He'd cleaned her house. Aside from the plywood screwed over the kitchen windows, it looked exactly how it did before the break-ins. She paused at the entrance to the living room.

"Now, Megan, love, you can't just run off and leave us. Who's going to cook me that magnificent apple amber pie I love so much?" He laughed again. "I don't care if I'm in America. Australia is even farther. First, Germany, then America, and now Australia. I thought you were liking California. I was hoping for a visit soon."

Her heart sank. Who was she kidding? Megan was probably some gorgeous model that traveled extensively. She looked down at her misshapen sweater and old jeans. No competition here.

"No. I don't care if you want to see the world." He shook his head. "Not today, no. I'll try to make it to church service next week. I know, but I told you something came up. Well, yes, it does have to do with work. Ah"—he rubbed the back of his neck—"just a little extra assignment the boss is making me handle. Nothing important."

Everly's dejection snapped into indignation. "Extra assignment?" she said.

That was a lovely way for him to describe her. Here, she thought he was nice because he might like her, a little. Nope. Just another damn assignment from Tripp.

His head whipped around. "I need to go, Megan." Finnian's eyes stayed intent on Everly. "Goodbye, love."

"Oh, don't let me interrupt your conversation with Megan. I am just an obligation, after all. A little extra work on Sunday. I didn't ask you to stay, you know."

His eyes stayed trained on her. "You cut your hair. It's cute."

She stormed to the kitchen, away from his compliment.

"Wait."

How did she even entertain the idea that he was different from Tripp and Charles? The entire race of men must have gotten together to learn how to act as though they cared. His casual flirting with Megan bothered her way more than he needed to know.

Let a guy in, and they'll find a way to screw you over.

She spun around, unleashing the hurt tainting her blood, deserved or not. "I've told you before I don't need your help. I appreciate you coming to see about me this morning and straightening my house today, but you're welcome to leave anytime."

She yanked open the refrigerator, glass condiment bottles rattling together on the door. A pitiful sight. The shelves consisted only of butter, jelly, and ketchup. Settling on water, she pulled the pitcher out.

Finnian's hand slammed the door closed. "I can very well see that you're not a morning person. Or afternoon at this point. And I don't know what bug crawled in your bed, but I don't appreciate it being taken out on me."

Pushing past him, she grabbed a cup out of the drying rack and poured the water. "Go away, Finnian. I know Tripp has more important things for you to do than to babysit me." It was better this way. He'd leave eventually, like Charles did.

"It's my off weekend. I've nothing to do but stand in your kitchen and have you yell at me for reasons I don't understand."

"Go visit Megan. I'm sure she misses you. I am sorry the boss is making you 'handle' me. I've handled myself for the past few years just fine. I've my work, and you have yours." She drank the cold water, ignoring him standing there, watching her like she'd grown two heads.

She'd been wrong. The attraction was so obviously one-sided that it brought back the dull headache from before. Alone. That's how her future would look. She was committed to that before Finnian ran to her rescue in the middle of the night. Nothing had changed.

As soon as she finished her water and set the glass down, his hands clamped down on her shoulders.

He spun her around. The panic of someone touching her had disappeared.

No. Not just someone . . . Finnian.

"Megan does miss me. As does Rebecca, Aislinn, Katherine, and Bridget. Not to mention John, Brady, William, Oliver, Leo, and Elliot. And don't even get me started on my mum. What did you expect me to tell my family? I can't tell them I'm watching after the widow of my late boss, making sure some psychopath doesn't kill her!" His voice ended near a shout. He adjusted his hands, his eyes trailing down to her feet and back up in one, quick sweep. "Or she doesn't end up starving herself to death, first. God, Everly, do you ever eat?"

Shoving his hands off her shoulders, she jerked away. "I'm not starving to death."

What were they even arguing about now? Everly stormed back to the living room, sitting in the computer chair he'd just left. The computer screen showed Finnian's last search for John Harriman and a different address in Miami.

All of the anger drained out of her. "Shit," she mumbled as she laid her head down on the desk, guilt pressing in all around. He'd cleaned her living room, fixed her windows, rushed to her house in the middle of the night . . . and she yells at him.

For what? Because he doesn't think of her how she thinks of him? She shouldn't even want him around. She bumped her head against the desk. Why was this so freaking confusing?

Her chair pulled away from the desk and swiveled around. She came nose to nose with Finnian as he planted his hands on each arm of the chair.

His irritated, brown eyes locked with hers. "Don't get comfortable. We are going somewhere to get food." He interlaced her fingers with his and tugged her out of the chair. "Get your purse or whatever it is you carry."

Everly snatched her hands back, that same defense against someone bossing her around rolling through her system.

He crossed his arms, complete confusion in his expression. "What is your problem?"

All thought of apologizing flew from her mind. "You, Finnian. I refuse to let another person see me as nothing more than an obligation and dictate my life. I need to stay here and work."

He leaned close. "You can work later. I need to eat, and so, do you. We're leaving to find food."

She kicked her chin out. "You can leave. You installed the deadbolt, Finnian. I assume you know how to operate it and can let yourself out."

"Cute one, Everly, but I'm not leaving without you. It's not safe, and you need to eat. Give me one good reason for us not grabbing dinner."

Everly ran a hand through her hair, the shortened length catching her off guard. "I'm not hungry."

"What did you eat for dinner last night?"

The challenge in his question made her more and more peeved when she couldn't answer. What had she eaten for dinner? A banana? No, she ate that for lunch. Last night seems so long ago.

"Exactly," he said with a smug look on his face that poked at her temper. "We *both* need to get some food. It'll help your temper and mine. Grab your shoes. I'll meet you in the car."

"Ugh!" She squeezed her hands into fists. "Do you even know how to interact with someone without dictating their every move?"

She expected him to push back or fight. Instead, his eyes softened a touch. He placed his hands on her upper arms before gliding them down to her fists. Her hands fit inside his wide, warm palms.

Gently, he urged her hands to relax until their fingers interlaced.

His strength was undeniable, but here he was, being sweet and simply holding her hands. "I'm trying to learn how to interact with you, Everly." He stroked the inside of her wrist with his thumb, rough and calloused. "I'm beginning to realize that you don't like being bossed around."

Her lips twitched. "You're *beginning* to realize it? You catch on quickly, don't you?"

"You've given me a few clues." He brought the back of her hand to his lips, the gesture making her forget why she was mad to begin with.

With his brown eyes holding hers, he turned her hand over, kissing the inside of her wrist. "Can I please persuade you to go eat dinner with me?"

Persuade . . . seduce . . . they had different vocabulary for how it made her feel. She sucked in a deep breath, his lingering cologne pushing her over the edge.

Hell, it worked.

"Fine."

~

FINNIAN CHECKED HIS WATCH. What was she doing in there? Didn't she realize that at any moment his body would stop functioning from lack of food? He'd missed breakfast and lunch. But as much as he needed the food, she needed it more. He'd never seen a cupboard as bare as hers.

The door opened. Everly stepped out in an old pair of sneakers with a purse strapped across her body. She looked so . . . normal.

No, normal would never describe her. She was such a conflict of emotion. One minute she looked as though she would fall apart, then she was ready to fight the men that chased after her. And she always seemed ready to bite his head off for telling her what to do.

But there were moments, like the one a few minutes

earlier, that he let down his guard and she stopped trying to control the world, and they connected. And it was dangerous.

She wasn't a woman to take to bed and walk away. But she wasn't a woman to settle in for a relationship with, either.

Once she found out about his role with Charles, that he'd written the email ending their marriage, that he'd helped with Claudia, those encouraging looks would disappear. It would be all-out anger and venom, and he'd be out of her life.

Everly managed to sit down in his small car and avoid touching him. The sweet smell of apples surrounded her. It replaced his hunger for food with a craving for something else he couldn't have.

"Before you say anything and ruin the moment." She pressed her lips together, a tiny dimple forming at the corner of her mouth. "I want to say thank you."

The reply 'no problem' stalled on the tip of his tongue. Thanking someone for help wasn't easy and shrugging off the effort didn't feel right.

"You're welcome." He nodded once and concentrated on backing out of the driveway. "If it is alright with you, I was thinking of Chinese food."

Her nose wrinkled. "I don't like Chinese food."

"How is that possible?" He pulled onto the main highway heading toward downtown Atlanta, the city skyline visible. "Outside of my mum's and sister's cooking, it's the best food I've ever tasted. I'd only had it a handful of times before leaving home. I eat it three times a week, at least."

Her mouth dropped open. "Three times a week? How can you look so good and survive on Chinese take-out?" A crimson blush crawled up her neck, and she suddenly became very interested in picking at her fingernails. "I didn't mean that you looked good."

"So, you think I look bad?" He faked a look of hurt. "That's a disappointing development."

Her head snapped up. "I didn't say that."

Teasing her was fun. "Then, you do think I look good?"

"I just meant—" She ran a hand through her hair. "Oh, shut up, Finnian," she said with a small laugh.

"Well, I think you look very pretty." He flicked a finger through the end of her short hair. "I liked your long hair, but this suits you too. You didn't need to dress up for our date."

"Date? Do you drag all of your dates to dinner against their will?"

He enjoyed this side of her. The funny, sarcastic personality that wasn't damaged by her husband. "I didn't drag you. You walked out all on your own." He wiggled his eyebrows. "But if that's something you're into . . ."

She tried to contain a laugh but failed. "You're impossible. Besides, baggy worn-out jeans and an old sweater do not constitute dressing up for a date." She tugged on her sleeve. The sweater looked nice, but the jeans were too big. How much weight had she lost?

The light conversation made him press on instead of circling back around to Charles and ruining the moment. "Then let's go to the mall. You can find some new clothes, and we can both find something to eat."

She crossed her arms and slunk down in the seat an inch. "I don't like to shop."

Impossible. A woman who hated to shop? He'd never met one.

"What are you laughing at?"

He stared at her until his traffic light turned green. "That was a joke, right?"

"No. I really don't like to shop."

He rubbed a hand over his mouth. "Never have I heard a female utter those words before. I think your entire sex just kicked you out of the club."

Everly rolled her eyes. "And you're an expert on females?"

He pulled into the parking deck attached to the mall. "I grew up surrounded by six of them, including my mum, and shared only one bathroom. Now, I have five nieces, one on the way, and two sisters-in-law." They stepped out of the car in front of the entrance to a large department store. "But they all have this one thing in common." He motioned to the store as he held open the door. "Shopping."

The thumping bass of techno music blasting through the speakers pounded through his chest. Bright colors, ripped clothing, and teenagers surrounded them. Everly twisted the bottom of her sweater into a knot as her eyes darted around the crowd.

He placed a hand on the small of her back to urge her forward.

"It's so"—she stepped down the aisle—"loud." She cut her eyes up at him. "Why do I feel old all of a sudden?" She picked up a hanger with something that once resembled a shirt, slashes through the sleeves and down the back. "Am I really out of touch with what's fashionable?"

"You're not old." He took the shirt from her and set it back on the rack. "You expect to pay for the entire shirt when you buy one. That's normal."

Finnian let her set the pace as they moved from this department. Right before entering the main mall area, they passed through the women's department.

She slowed, her forehead wrinkling as she scanned the

racks of clothing. "Maybe I should look for something new to wear."

"Oh?" Finnian tried to sound casual. "I didn't think you'd actually listen to me since I'm so bossy and everything."

The corner of her mouth twitched. "When a guy is an expert on women, you listen."

"Where would you like to start?" He rubbed his hands together and surveyed the clothes around them. Nothing struck him as something his sisters might wear, but this was America. "What about this?"

She wrinkled her nose and shook her head. "You might be an expert on women, but you have zero taste in women's clothing."

The mint green jacket looked nice. It had silver buttons, which seemed fashionable, and tiny silver threads running through it.

She patted his arm. "My grandma would wear that."

"Oh." He looked back down at the jacket. Why did that sound like an insult?

"And she's dead."

Finnian hung the jacket back up, trying his best to keep a straight face. The pants hanging with the jacket had an elastic waist and tiny roses embroidered on the cuff. Maybe she was right.

Everly grabbed his arm, tugging him toward the mall entrance. It was the first time she'd touched him on purpose aside from when he found her in the closet. Progress. How far they progressed was up to her, because each moment spent with her confirmed his attraction. The woman was remarkable, and that wasn't simply his protective side.

"I think I can manage on my own." She pointed to a

bench inside the main mall area. "I'll meet you over there. Give me about ten minutes."

Finnian thought back to the time he drove his sisters shopping. They never took ten minutes to do anything. Hours, more than likely.

Finnian scanned the department store. Whoever broke into her house this morning had likely done so expecting to find her sleeping. He couldn't shake the feeling someone, maybe someone sent by Claudia, tried to get to Everly. Leaving her alone like this wasn't part of the plan.

She touched his elbow. "I'll be fine." Her cool fingers skimmed up his arm and curled around his bicep before dropping by her side. She blinked, staring straight ahead at his chest. "You can go."

Wait. What was that about? A touch from her sent a thousand sparks through his body. "Everly?" After a beat of silence, she looked up. Hell, those eyes killed him. He grazed his thumb along her chin, tempted to kiss her right there. "I'll be right outside if you need me."

No matter how many reasons he came up with, staying away from her on a one hundred percent personal level proved impossible. He wanted more. But he'd have to let her set the pace. He'd die before he hurt her.

Finnian left Everly to her shopping, keeping an eye out for anything suspicious. Someone was still out there.

A lady with black hair and bright red lipstick smiled at him from behind the makeup counter as he exited to the mall. He gave her a grin and a wink.

"Oh, you are dangerous, sugar," she called before laughing loudly.

Dangerous. Yes. To anyone that contemplated hurting Everly. He was very dangerous.

6

E verly smoothed her hand down the ice blue cashmere sweater as she stepped out from the changing room, tossing her old clothes into a trashcan on the way past. The splurge on a pair of tall, brown boots worn over her new dark jeans, two sizes smaller than her old ones, was worth it. Instead of remaining mad at having thrown away the past two years of her life, maybe it was time to look at her future.

"Honey?"

Everly stopped when a short, round woman standing at the makeup counter waved her hand in the air.

"Come over here, sweetie." She snapped her fingers. "My, my, you look five hundred percent better than when you first walked into the store."

Everly forced a smile through her embarrassment. "Thank you?" She started to turn, but the lady reached out and touched her arm.

Her immediate reaction was to jerk away, but she managed to barely flinch as she put distance between them.

"Whoa, there. My, you're skittish. I think you need a few

things to finish the look. I'm Judith." She tapped her name badge. "You need a free makeover today."

"No, I have someone waiting for me."

Judith whistled low. "I saw that fine specimen of a man you walked in with." She quirked her eyebrow. "Is that your brother?"

"Brother?" They didn't resemble each other. "No."

"Uncle?"

Everly shook her head.

"Cousin?"

Everly crossed her arms. "He's not related to me."

Judith slapped the stool next to the makeup counter. "Bless your heart, Sweet Child, but you are in need for some Miss Judith magic."

Everly's muscles twitched. Running away was an option, but the unforgiving fitting room mirrors agreed with Miss Judith's assessment if she were honest with herself.

"Maybe just a little blush."

Judith's face split into a wide smile. Her full cheeks covered the bottom part of her eyes. She patted the small stool. "Sit down, my candy cane. I was down on my luck, once. A woman can spot that in other women. I'll get you looking like you belong back in the world. Whatever got you down won't be a second thought after you see what I can do with you."

The makeover took an additional twenty minutes. Now, headed out of the store, her insides twisted with nerves with each click of her boot heel on the marble floor. She caught her reflection in a darkened store window to her left. Charles would have hated her outfit. Good.

Finnian leaned against a pillar in the middle of the mall, his back to her as she approached. Almost every female that walked by took a second look at him. Even a little girl craned her neck to look up at him.

He still wore a fitted white undershirt and jeans with flip-flops. That's all he threw on when he'd run to her in the middle of the night. His profile revealed the shadow of dark stubble along his jaw. He was there for her. She'd try her best to remember that the next time he bossed her around.

Not that she'd let him, but she might try to ask him nicer to stop.

She tugged down on the sleeves of her new sweater. Would he like her in this?

Taking a breath and standing up straight, Everly tapped him on the shoulder.

He turned. His eyes paused briefly on her face before they ran down to her new boots and up.

"You look great." He glanced down at her empty hands. "What happened to the clothes you wore here?"

"I didn't think they were worth keeping. Sorry, it took so long. Let's get something to eat. I know you must be starving." She couldn't read his face, but he motioned for her to lead the way.

She fell in line with the crowd of other shoppers, her hand clenched on the strap of her purse. A new outfit didn't make the anxiety of being around others disappear altogether. But being with Finnian made it a little easier to handle. A person rushing by bumped into her. He turned around and held his hand up, as if to say "excuse me," and kept walking. See, she could do this.

Her phone chimed—a text from Mr. Randolf.

"What is it?" Finnian's arm brushed her shoulder as he read the text with her.

I found a bank account in the trust's name. I emailed you the details for you to contact them.

Everly flipped to her email, refreshing it twice before the email showed up. A bank account. What else had Charles done?

Maybe the bank could email her the bank statements. Selecting the number he listed, she called. A recording came on, giving business hours. She dropped the phone to her side. "Mr. Randolf found a bank account for the trust. It's Sunday. Of course, the bank isn't open right now."

"We're going to get run over if we stop right here." Finnian rested his hand on her shoulder and moved them out of the walkway, near the wall.

Everly looked back down at her phone. "I've never heard of this bank before. I wonder why he didn't use his usual banker." Even more secrets. Was there a reason?

Finnian didn't appear to listen. He rubbed his thumb back and forth across the top of her arm before sliding his hand down at an unnervingly slow rate.

The music and voices in the mall faded. It turned into a hum in her ears as his serious expression concentrated on touching her. Combining his touch with the soft cashmere against her skin caused a shiver to rush down her spine.

His dark eyes met hers as he encircled her wrist within his grip.

One small tug and he brought their bodies close.

She inhaled, the scent of him filling her head.

He angled his head down. His thumb brushed back and forth over the pulse in her wrist. "Your sweater is nearly as soft as your skin."

The rumble of his accent tightened her stomach. His intentions were clear, but she couldn't do this. Not here.

She needed space.

Everly thrust her cell phone between them, breaking the contact. "Alright. Well, did you know that Charles had a bank account at this bank?" She returned to searching for the bank rather than acknowledge the trembling in her legs. "Did you ever go there with him?"

"No," he said, his voice huskier than before.

Her fingers flew over her phone, distracting her from the hulking man beside her. That moment had proved she wasn't dead to the world after all.

Finnian stayed close but didn't touch her again as she flipped between the email and searching the Internet, trying to find one more thing. Anything that would explain the bank account. Anything to keep from having to face Finnian after that . . . moment.

Finnian's hand covered her screen. "Everly, darling, we can call them tomorrow. But I won't make it to tomorrow if I don't eat something."

"Oh, sorry." Sliding her phone back into her purse, she kept pace beside him to the food court, completely ignoring whatever was happening between them. That's all she could do. If he didn't mention it, she wouldn't either.

The fantastic smell of cheesy pizza hit her first, inciting an unfamiliar feeling of hunger and eliminating the question of what she should eat for dinner. She would concentrate on the mouth-watering pizza. Not the mouth-watering Finnian.

FINNIAN EYED the third slice of pizza Everly intended to eat. He'd seen his own sisters put away their share of food, but they all outweighed Everly by at least a stone. Maybe two.

The blue sweater matched her eyes to perfection, and the feel of her body under the softness of the fabric generated ideas he should ignore. Probably just a lack of food and sleep. A wretched excuse. His core training revolved around discipline in the police force. In a measly ten seconds, Everly Clarke almost destroyed his restraint by simply wearing a damn sweater.

One decision had been made: he had every intention of stepping forward with the relationship if the opportunity presented itself.

But he'd pick a better location than in the bloody mall.

"I think we've established you don't eat."

She took a large bite of pizza and raised her eyebrows.

"If you never leave your house, how do you buy normal things?"

"Normal things?"

"You know. Like toilet paper?"

She chewed slowly as her eyebrows pulled down in deep thought.

Toilet paper? His involvement with Everly needed to remain on friendly terms but asking her how she buys her toilet paper ranked at the top of the least romantic things to say. His brothers would rag on him until next year if they knew.

"I order most everything online, or I go somewhere early in the morning." Everly concentrated on her pizza, trying to avoid eye contact with him. Did she feel the attraction? Was she interested?

No need to rush anything. Tripp might have some strange aversion to him seeing Everly, but that wasn't Finnian's problem.

"You know, I'm glad my Aunt B doesn't have the capability or knowledge of how to order things online," he said.

She canted her head to the side. "Who?"

"My aunt. The one I told you about. With the cats."

That same small dimple formed along the corner of her mouth. Good. He wanted to make her smile more.

"Oh, I forgot about her. What did she do if she didn't leave her house and didn't order things?"

"My Uncle William catered to her every need. That's my Da's younger brother. He'd take her anything she wanted. Like the time he brought her a cat pool."

Everly set the slice down and reached for her water. "A cat pool?"

Finnian leaned forward, glad he held her attention. "She claimed that her cats wanted to go swimming. It was truly the craziest thing you'd ever hear when Aunt B started on the subject."

"She really thought her cats wanted to swim?" Everly smiled. Any person passing by would think they were two ordinary people having dinner together. No crazy past. No criminals chasing after her. No mysterious trust fund or mistresses. Just Finnian and Everly.

"Well," he said, rubbing his chin, feeling the result of missing a shave. "I was more worried that the cats actually spoke to her. Uncle William, being the loving and adoring brother he is, did as she asked. He found one of those little swimming pools for children and set it up in the backyard. Guess what?" He paused, sipping his drink.

She shifted closer. The pizza was forgotten. "What?"

"Those mangy animals jumped right in and swam around."

Her mouth popped open. "Are you serious?"

He shrugged a shoulder. "Partly. A few of them sniffed around the edge, but the rest took after Aunt B and wouldn't even leave the house."

She threw a balled-up napkin in his direction. "You're

horrible," she said between laughs. "I bet you don't even have an Uncle William."

"I do. My parents named my brother after him. Turned out just the same. He does anything my sisters ask of him, and they exploit that knowledge every chance they get. He's driven them shopping twice as many times as I have."

Her smile dimmed. "You miss them."

"The cats?"

"No, your family, silly."

"Of course." He'd missed his family every day since he left England. At least, until he sat across from Everly. The need to fill his time with work to ignore the loneliness had disappeared with her. He'd rather fill his time with her than anything else.

She broke eye contact first. "You said you came to America for work. Why not stay in England?"

"Opportunities." It was a part-truth. The rest of the story wasn't a happy one, and he didn't need to bring it down on Everly when she was enjoying herself. "Nothing I found in England paid enough." Her hesitation stopped him from explaining his family's farm. "What?"

She laid down the half-eaten pizza. "Is having money that important to you?"

He caught her tone, annoyance mixed with something else? Regret? "I suppose it's important for everyone, isn't it?"

Her chair scraped against the tiles as she stood. "No, it's not. I need to use the restroom. Excuse me."

Everly left without waiting for an answer. What had he said? That he needed to work for the money? Why else did people work if not for money? For the joy of it, he supposed.

Finnian wouldn't apologize for working and sacrificing himself to make sure his mum and siblings didn't worry.

Shifting in the metal chair, he attempted to relax as Everly disappeared down the hallway to the bathrooms.

Did she compare his need to save his family farm with how Charles Clarke worked to sustain his cocaine habit? If so, he had a few words to say that would definitely be less romantic than asking about her toilet paper habits.

He scanned the food court as he ate in the last bits of rice from his Chinese food. The mall was the first place he'd visited when he'd arrived in America. The constant noise of people talking around him helped with the homesickness.

A tall, thin man walked along the wall of the food court's outer edge.

Finnian set his fork down slowly, the recognition immediate. The name wouldn't come to him, but he knew that man from his time protecting Charles. It couldn't be a coincidence. He sat back, his mind flipping through every lowlife person he knew from his past, trying to place the guy.

Someone that worked with Lorenzo or Ray. It was a weird name. Snake? Frog? Something stupid.

The man in question turned the corner toward the bathrooms.

The chair flew to the ground as Finnian ran.

There shouldn't be anything wrong. Paranoia. An overwhelming need to protect Everly as the memory of Sean pressed in when he got this familiar rush of adrenaline mixed with fear. Personal fear. Sean was personal.

Everly was personal.

Finnian wove around people, making his way across the busy food court. He turned the corner and rushed into the hallway for the restrooms.

Empty.

He listened as he took quiet steps on the concrete floor,

his shoulder brushing the cold, cream-colored tiles on the wall.

The exit door at the end of the hallway jerked opened, the metal squeaking in protest, but no one entered.

Finnian slowed. Pressing his back against the wall, he reached for his pistol. His hand met empty space. Shit. In the car.

He flexed his fingers. That was alright. He'd handle the situation without a gun.

To the left, the women's bathroom door flew open.

Everly's new boots emerged first, kicking and flaying around in midair, the man he'd recognized attempting to gain control of them.

The back door opened wider. Oh, hell. The guy from the water department reached out to take ahold of her.

Finnian tensed, studying the situation. It was all connected.

Everly's boot kicked at the side of the man's head as Finnian sprinted forward. A third man held up Everly's shoulders as he carted her out of the bathroom. Duct tape covered her mouth and wrapped around her hands. She bucked her body, twisting and wiggling, trying to escape.

This wasn't happening.

Finnian full-body tackled the man carrying her legs. The two of them fell into the concrete wall hard.

He ducked a punch, coming up and slamming the guy's head back into the wall.

The guy crumpled to the ground.

The second man dropped Everly's shoulders, letting her fall like a rock as he brought his fists up for a fight.

Everly moaned when she hit the floor.

The sound turned Finnian's blood to ice. He slammed

his fist into the guy's face, knocking him to the ground to slump beside his friend.

The exit door banged closed as the last man ran.

Finnian squatted down next to Everly, now curled up in a ball on her side. They were after *her*. He'd been right. He knew that man. They called him Lizard. He worked for Lorenzo.

Lorenzo hated Charles, but why in the hell were they after her?

She jerked with his first touch on her shoulder.

"Everly, love, it's me." He brushed her hair away from her face. "You're safe." Not for long, but for now.

A mixture of rage and panic radiated from her wide eyes. Finnian helped her up to sit. A long rip at the shoulder seam in her new sweater fired him up again. She'd struggled against the bastards.

He wanted to chase down the last scumbag, but he wouldn't leave her again.

He felt for the edge of the tape along her cheek. Leaning forward, he pressed a kiss to her forehead. "This will hurt."

She squeezed her eyes tight. Finnian ripped the tape from her mouth. A small moan of pain escaped, but nothing else. The redness of irritated skin appeared around her lips. He brushed a finger over the mark. "I'm sorry."

"Sir!" A security guard's hand clamped on Finnian's shoulder.

"Let go and get me a knife." He held up Everly's wrists taped together.

The bumbling guard fished out a pocketknife, but his hands shook too much. Finnian snatched it away. "Give it here before you cut her."

The tape fell away. Everly rubbed her wrists. Her eyes

remained downcast, but a tear dripped from her cheek and formed a little damp circle on her jeans.

"The police are on their way," the security guard said. "I'll need you both to stay."

Finnian helped Everly to stand, but her knees nearly gave out. "Let me hold you," he murmured next to her ear as he slipped his arms around her waist to support her.

And to comfort himself.

She tucked into his chest, hiding her face. How many more times would he have to do this before she was safe? Small, uncontrollable shivers ran through her body. And even then, the scent of apples from her soothed a small edge of his emotions.

Lizard sported a long red gash dripping blood down his cheek. Had Everly done that?

The hallway filled with police and spectators. The police evaluated the two unconscious men. One officer radioed for an ambulance.

Finnian tightened his arm around Everly and waited for the questioning to begin. Telling the police that he wasn't a little disappointed that he hadn't killed the piece of shit when he slammed his head into a wall didn't seem like the best thing to say at the moment.

"Thank you, Finnian." She looked up at him. "Again."

Unable to stop himself, he kissed her forehead again and closed his eyes. It'd been close this time. Too close. Whatever they were after was big.

Whoever was behind the attacks wouldn't stop until they got it.

Or got Everly.

"Miss, can you recount what happened?" A police officer, barely old enough to be out of high school, flipped open a notebook. Everly's ringtone sounded from the bathroom.

She glanced that direction, her body tense.

"Stay here with the police. I'll get it."

Her hands fisted in the sides of his shirt.

That response killed him. He cupped the side of her face. "You're safe now."

Everly nodded and released him. Making sure she could stand, Finnian left them to retrieve her purse.

It laid on the ground in the last stall, her wallet and keys beside her phone, the strap broken. He'd buy her a new one.

"Hello?"

"Yes. This is Home Security Protection. We have an alarm going off at your residence. The front door triggered it."

He stopped at the exit of the bathroom. This was bigger than he'd imagined. What in the hell did these people want? "Tell the police the homeowner won't be back to the residence tonight, and they'll need to secure the front door. We'll be by in the morning. Board it up if necessary." He ended the call, his eyes meeting Everly's from across the hallway. She looked abused but strong. Good. She needed to keep that strength until they figured out their next step.

"They broke into my house again, didn't they?" Everly asked, interrupting the police officer's question.

"Afraid so." His own phone rang in his pocket. Tripp would be the only person calling him at this time of night. He cut off the ringtone and leaned against the wall next to her, his chest pressed against her shoulder.

Finnian's phone rang again.

"I'm fine, Finnian. Answer your phone." Everly continued to explain what happened as well as the history of the break-ins.

Finnian didn't listen. He couldn't if the police didn't want him to chase down the one that got away. He didn't need any more incentive by hearing her relive the story of the past few days.

"Hayes," Finnian answered when he didn't recognize the number.

"Mr. Hayes, I'm calling to report an intruder alarm at your residence. Both front and back doors were opened."

He grumbled a few colorful phrases in French to keep from offending Everly. He didn't need any more of a reason to catch the S.O.B.s after the hell they'd put her through, but now he had it.

"Ask the police to secure the residence. I'll be there sometime tomorrow."

He ended the call, shoving the phone into his pocket. They both needed a different place to stay tonight.

Everly's strength to get through the questions amazed him. Every so often, she snapped at the police officer until she'd finally had enough.

"I'm done answering the same questions I've answered before." The redness around her mouth had faded, but her sweet blue eyes held a new fire. "I don't know the men who tried to take me, but my house has been broken into three times. If any of your detectives want to figure that riddle out, they can give me a call. Everyone in the Atlanta P.D. has my cell phone number."

She pushed off the wall and stormed back to the mall without even a glance at Finnian. He caught up to her in a few steps and wrapped his arm around her shoulders, pleased she didn't pull away.

"I'm sorry you got involved with this. That idiot cop didn't think the break-ins and this were connected." She leaned into him. "Did I hear you say something about your house?"

"Yup. They hit my place as well, and this is absolutely connected." And it was connected to her. It wasn't random. There wasn't a chance in hell that Lizard was involved by accident. Not after his boss's ties to Charles and Tripp. But why did they want Everly? She had nothing to do with the business.

Finnian guided her back through the mall, through the department store, and into the parking garage before she spoke.

"Wait." She stopped him with a hand on his forearm. "Where are we going if you just told both of the alarm companies that we wouldn't be home?"

Good question. Tossing her over his shoulder and hauling her to England was his first thought. Pass her off into the protective hands of his mum and siblings while he took on whoever did this.

But based on her reaction to leaving the house for dinner, it was unlikely that he'd get her on an international flight. "I thought I'd take you to a hotel for the night." A place nearby that he knew the security for the building well after Tripp stayed there. Everly was his number one priority, no matter the cost.

She twisted her lips to the side, a sexy smirk making his anger fade a little. "You move pretty fast. Is that an English thing?"

Despite her intended joke, the possibilities ran through Finnian's mind before he could stop them. He dropped his arm and stepped away, pretending to reach for his keys in his pocket.

"No, I think I picked that one up in America."

"Don't blame your bad habits on us."

He returned her smile. "Who said anything about it being a *bad* habit? You might miss something good if you move too slow."

They both stopped at his car, staring at the slashed tires and shattered windshield.

"Finnian? Is that French?"

He caught himself muttering in French again. He'd picked it up from his brothers as a way to keep things from their mum. It wasn't until he was in high school that his mum let him and the rest of the family know that she could speak fluent French and knew every bad, dirty, foul-mouthed thing they'd said to each other.

"Yes. Sorry."

Her laugh caught him by surprise.

"What's so funny?"

She laughed again, but it sounded forced. She threw her hands in the air. "This entire situation! I've done nothing but keep myself away from everyone. First, it was to protect me from Charles."

Finnian's fists balled in response. "Protect? Did he ever—"

"No. He didn't hit me or anything. How he made me feel wasn't much better. I never dressed or acted the way he wanted me to. He didn't give me subtle hints. His discussions about my appearance typically ended with him storming out of the house." She shifted closer to Finnian. "You've met this 'Claudia,' right?" Her teeth caught her bottom lip. "I'm not asking for details, but do she and I, I mean, are we similar?"

"No." He shook his head. "You're far too beautiful to be compared to the likes of her." He hadn't meant to say it exactly like that, but Everly's cheeks blushed a pretty shade of pink, and a small dimple formed beside her pursed lips.

He fisted his hands tight and let them relax. Ignoring his urge to reach for her was hard. "Let's head back inside and purchase a few things before I find somewhere for us to stay."

"Should we split up? You go to the men's department, and I'll head back to the women's?"

He straightened to his full height, challenging her to argue with him. "You'll be lucky if I let you out of my sight to even use the restroom again."

7

"We should've had the cab drive us to a cheap motel, Finnian. We could've gotten two rooms for the price of one . . ." Everly's suggestion died on her lips. She pushed through the revolving glass door and entered the sparkling hotel lobby. The beautiful hotel sat at the corner of two of the busiest streets in Buckhead near Lennox Mall. A place about four levels outside her comfort zone.

"Wow." Everly craned her neck up. Thousands of lights twinkled in a massive chandelier covered in crystals.

"I didn't know light fixtures were so intriguing to you," Finnian said as he fell in step beside her.

She swung one of her shopping bags at him but missed, leaving them both laughing.

She'd replaced her torn blue sweater with a pink one with the same soft fabric. Finnian hadn't exactly commented on it, but he'd taken care not to touch her in the cab ride over.

And she'd missed the connection.

Her boots produced a rhythmic tapping sound on the wooden floors as they crossed the lobby. Her shoulder brushed his arm and she shifted away. The hyperawareness of him had melted from nervousness into excitement. They still needed separate hotel rooms.

Two grand staircases swept up to the second-floor balcony on either side of the entrance, with two more large crystal chandeliers suspended in the air over the reception area's center. The faint scent of roses made her smile. Even the air smelled fancy.

She risked a look at Finnian's profile. He'd purchased a few clothes himself, including the white button-up dress shirt he wore now with the top button unbuttoned. He still looked as deadly as he had when he'd charged at the men trying to kidnap her at the mall. No matter what he put on top of it, she would forever have that raw image ingrained in her memory.

Followed by the tender way he'd held and kissed her. It solidified that they were beyond the "friend" category. Defining what they were seemed impossible, though. They'd just met. Did people really have these instant connections?

"Good evening," Finnian said to the receptionist as he leaned on the counter, giving her that charming smile he could summon at a whim.

The petite blonde flashed her dimples.

Everly hated her.

"Hi, I'm Sandy."

Everly rolled her eyes at the high-pitched, baby-like voice. Did men really like that?

"Nice to meet you, Sandy." Finnian deepened his accent.

Everly crossed her arms. Obviously, Finnian did. The man could give James Bond a lesson on flirting. Fine. If he wanted to flirt with a girl barely old enough to buy a beer, that was his problem. It made their "instant connection" easier to ignore.

"We need a room for the night."

"Two rooms," Everly added, her tone a little surlier than she expected. Jealousy wasn't an emotion she enjoyed.

"Damn it," he muttered, barely audible. "*One* room, please, Sandy."

Everly and Finnian locked eyes. His typical irritated look replaced the smoldering one he'd given Sandy. Safety was less of a concern than the teetering self-control that raced through her each time he touched her.

Everly had heard in strange parts of the world that men and women sometimes slept in the same bed and didn't have sex. She glanced at Sandy, whose attention stayed one hundred percent focused on Finnian. Sandy understood. A thousand bucks said those odd women weren't sharing a bed with a man like Finnian Hayes.

"Sandy?" Finnian kept his gaze focused on Everly a second longer before turning back. "Do you have any rooms on your restricted floors? You know, where you use a key card to get to obtain access."

"Yes, sir. Right now, we have one suite available for the night."

"You don't have any other rooms on the restricted floor?" Everly crossed her fingers under the bags she held down by her side.

"No, I'm sorry. We still have a few guests remaining from a wedding this weekend. Just that one suite left on the restricted floor."

Everly crossed her arms. "How many beds?"

"One, ma'am." Sandy cleared her throat, and it sounded like she stifled a laugh. Her attention shifted to Finnian. "King-sized."

Everly shook her head at Sandy. Those disgustingly cute dimples deepened.

Finnian shrugged. "That's plenty big enough."

This time, Sandy didn't bother to hide her smile. She nodded her head. "Oh, I can imagine it is."

Leaning closer to Sandy, Everly dropped her voice and tried to plead with her. "Then, you can imagine why I need two beds."

"No," she began, slowly taking in every inch of Finnian's height. "I can't."

"You're not helping."

"I think I am," Sandy shot back.

"Leave Sandy alone. She can't make another room appear." Finnian leaned down, putting his lips near Everly's ear. He rested a hand on her waist and whispered, "Remember what happened not two hours ago. You are not staying in a separate room. I'll sleep on the floor if I make you that nervous." His warm breath across her cheek caused a shiver down her spine despite the sweater she wore.

He pulled back. His mouth hovered close to hers a beat before he straightened.

Her mind drew a blank as she looked to Sandy, whose cheeks turned a brighter shade of pink the longer she stared at Finnian.

"Does the room have a sofa bed?" Everly's voice sounded far away as she asked the question. Control. She needed to get in control.

Sandy sighed and shook her head as she mumbled "some people," as she clicked through the computer screen. "Yes, ma'am."

Did Sandy just emphasize the word 'ma'am'?

"We'll take it." Finnian reached to his back pocket. Everly followed the movement. She snapped her head up to the chandelier when she realized where she was looking. He must have gotten new jeans as well. They fit. Nicely.

"That will be nine hundred and fifty-two dollars."

"What!" No way were they paying that much for a hotel room. "For one room?" Finnian started to hand over a credit card, but Everly pushed his hand away. "We are not spending that kind of money on a hotel room."

"We will."

She knew it was to keep her safe, but still, she would not let someone spend that kind of money on her. Finnian already said he needed this job because of the money. And to throw it away for her? Not going to happen.

"I'll pay." Everly dug her wallet out of her purse. "Here." She passed over a credit card.

Finnian growled her name.

Sandy didn't move as she looked between the two of them, both of their cards reaching toward her.

"Ugh! I don't need—"

"You've given me a laundry list of the things you don't need, Everly." Finnian's brown eyes narrowed at her in a challenge. "Sandy, darling," he said louder, pushing his card farther in her direction. "Run it."

Sandy gave her a delicate shrug and took Finnian's card. "One king size suite coming up."

"Traitor," Everly said to Sandy and put her wallet away as she stomped to the elevators to wait for him. She tuned out the rest of their conversation as she let the irrational irritation overcome her. Better to stay angry than risk sharing that king-sized bed. If she stopped and focused on everything that he'd done for her, she was toast.

The nice guy routine, mixed with a healthy dose of superhero complex, made Finnian hard to resist. But she would. She needed to survive on her own. He'd dominate everything if she let him.

A few rowdy shouts preceded a group of guys stumbling into the lobby. One of them blew a kiss at Sandy before heading to the elevators. Seven of them, all in their early twenties, laughed and slapped each other on their backs like they'd won some award. Everly huffed. Probably the award for being the drunkest idiot in Atlanta. Definitely not the type of people she wanted to deal with at the moment.

She gripped her shopping bags tight against her chest. After being bumped into at the mall a half-dozen times and nearly abducted, a simple elevator ride with these yahoos shouldn't cause a panic attack. Look how far she'd gotten with Finnian touching her.

"Hey, there," one with hair the color of burnt copper said as he leaned in her direction. "You lookin' good tonight, sweetheart."

Everly managed a polite smile before staring back at the elevator numbers. The illuminated number ticked from nineteen to eighteen. It was on its way down. Maybe Finnian will take a little longer with Sandy, and they'd catch the next elevator.

"Oh, oh, oh," another guy called. "Boom! Struck out, Chad."

"She has a more sophisticated taste than a lowlife like Chad." A man moved forward, his tie a little crooked, and he definitely had a heavy dusting of glitter on the side of his face from whatever woman he'd encountered earlier. He hooked his arm around her shoulders. "You just forget about Chad. He's getting married next weekend. But I'm free."

"Lucky me," she replied, every muscle from her neck to her toes seized in response to his touch. Nothing prepared her for a complete stranger pulling her close into his sweaty body, ripe with overused cologne and stale beer.

She jerked to the side, but he held her. This wasn't a guy trying to kidnap her. He was obviously drunk and an idiot. It would be alright. Finnian was right over there.

"I'm sure you have better things to do. Let go of me." She twisted to the side, forcing the guy to drop his arm.

"C'mon, babe."

So cliché. "I'm not your babe."

He laughed and hooked his arm across her shoulders again. "Don't be like that. Honey, what you need is a real man."

She filled her lungs to scream.

"You're right," Finnian's deep voice, thick with his accent, sounded from behind them. "She does want a real man."

The leech swung around. Everly tripped over her bags, nearly falling as he pulled her around with him.

Finnian looked pointedly at each of the seven guys. "Since none of you fit the description of a real man, you're all welcome to leave." He shifted his stance. That threatening glimmer in his eyes turned deadly when they locked on with the idiot whose arm still pinned her to his side. "Stop. Touching. Her."

"Hey man, we're just having some fun."

"And I'll have fun breaking both of your arms."

Finnian's matter-of-fact statement finally got through. The guy held up his hands and moved away. "Chill. Damn."

After taking a deep breath of clean air, she stepped to Finnian's side. Someday, maybe, it would be her turn to rescue him.

The elevator door opened, and the guys piled inside. Everly wished he'd wait for the next one, but he guided her in and pulled her to the corner with him. Setting her in front of his chest, his hand snaked possessively around her waist.

When Finnian held her, the panic never came. More like hot thoughts that made her want to press into his body for more connection.

His fingers began to barely rub along the side of her stomach, the sweater's soft material like silk against her skin. He probably thought the motion would calm her down. Not a chance.

She closed her eyes, pushing away her sexual desire churning to life after being dormant for so long. Hell, this would make the rest of the night miserable knowing they were in the same room together.

The guy who'd grabbed her risked a glance at Finnian before snapping his focus back to the front. The scowl on Finnian's face must be extra fierce.

They all rushed out as the elevator opened on the eleventh floor, one man falling to his knees in the rush and his friends leaving him to fend for himself as he crawled the rest of the way off.

Finnian reached around her, slid the card into the reader, and pressed the button to their floor. His fingers continued to caress her skin through the fabric, weakening her knees with each stroke.

Everly let her head fall back on Finnian's shoulder, closing her eyes. The past two days had been hard, but in some strange sense of the universe, worth it to have found Finnian. If only life were normal.

If only she were normal.

The doors opened on their floor. She broke the physical connection and marched ahead. She wouldn't need much more convincing to keep that sofa bed folded up and unused if he kept touching her that way.

"This is us." He motioned to a room and opened it. She walked in ahead of him, twisting her shoulder to prevent brushing up against his chest.

The room was as impressive as the lobby. The champagne-colored walls complemented the mixture of off-white carpeting and dark wooden floors. Teal and blue pillows covered the sofas and coordinated with the same pillows on the large bed off to the side. A long set of windows, flanked by deep burgundy ceiling-to-floor drapes, revealed the Atlanta skyline at night. She immediately spotted ATLighting Inc's building with the double towers and green-tinted lights shining at the top.

Finnian moved behind her, his reflection clear in the window. The fairy-tale setting and quietness soothed her anxiety from the day. The tranquil colors in the room drew her closer to the peacefulness she needed. Despite her argument to go somewhere cheaper, she was safe here.

Safe with him.

She turned. His face didn't hold the look of desire she'd expected from their brief encounter on the elevator.

Everly sighed. "I know you must be upset about the guy putting his arm around me. I was too busy preventing myself from hyperventilating to push him away effectively. I knew he didn't mean anything by it. It wasn't like the guys trying to drag me from the bathroom." She set her bags on the sofa. "I fought the ones at the mall."

"I know you did, and I'm very proud of you. I'm not mad about a couple of drunk college guys that hit on you." He shook his head. "Can you—" he halted his words, his fingers skimming along the edge of her jaw with a featherlight touch. "You know that I have feelings for you, right? I'm not doing this for Tripp or Charles or anyone else. I'm here for you. I'm here because I *can't* be anywhere else but with you.

It doesn't make sense, I know, but I'm involved and right where I want to be."

Her mind clamored to understand the words. He liked her. Too bad he'd confessed it with a glower.

"You didn't just embarrass me downstairs. You insulted me."

The thrill from his declaration disappeared as quickly as it had formed. "Insulted?" How? When?

"Yes, insulted." His voice grew tense while his brown eyes took on a sharp edge. "I witnessed criminals attempt to drag you out of the back door less than two hours ago. Before that, I found you huddled in your closet, hiding for your life, shaking, barely able to stand." His hands flexed and unflexed. "I need to do more than I have to keep you safe. I know the security guards at this hotel, and I knew the cost of staying here. You argued, in front of a stranger nonetheless, and insulted my instincts to take care of you. I can't keep you safe if you second-guess everything I do."

Here she stood, in a beautiful hotel room, instead of trying to claw her way out of the trunk of a car or worse. All because of Finnian and those instincts. Her heart stuttered and ached. Why hadn't she met Finnian before Charles? When she wasn't damaged goods? When she could accept his help without the fear of giving up her independence or becoming helpless again?

But she couldn't change the past.

She slipped her arms around his waist, resting her cheek on his chest, soaking in his strength. Hurting him was the last thing she wanted to do.

He pulled her tight to his body.

"I'm sorry." She wouldn't give up trying to survive on her own. It meant too much to her, but she understood pride.

She swallowed past the lump in her throat. "Thank you. For everything."

He kissed the top of her head. "I'll do everything I can to get you through this. Trust me."

"That's hard."

His body relaxed. "I know." He held her for a long time, his fingers trailing up and down her spine, gliding softly over her sweater.

If only she could curl into him for the night, let him hold her this way, and know it wouldn't lead to more complications.

But it would. She didn't have the resistance to turn away from him. Not tonight. Not after everything that'd happened.

Everly rose on her toes and kissed his cheek, the stubble from not shaving rough on her lips. "Goodnight, Finnian."

He stepped away. "I'll take the sofa." He began emptying his pockets onto the desk as she crossed the room.

She turned at the door, risking everything by admitting to her feelings. "You should know that I like you too. I'm not sure what that means for me or for you. I don't know how to process it after everything that's happened. But I'm trying to."

He froze, his expression unreadable, but the impact of his words hit straight to her heart. "I understand. Just know you've only to say the words, Everly. I'm here, ready to cross the line."

But what would happen once he did?

THE KING-SIZED BED looked twice as large with Everly's body curled up into a tight ball in the middle of it. The pajamas she'd purchased lay folded on a bench with her other new clothes, untouched. Finnian pulled the blanket over her, the back of his hand brushing across the pink sweater at the top of her shoulder.

Her stubbornness frustrated him, but it didn't change his determination. Right this moment, for tonight, she was one hundred percent safe, and that meant more than anything in the world. The apology helped ease the insult but watching the emotions swirl through her eyes when she'd admitted that she returned his feelings sent a rush of need through him.

A need to protect her. A need to treat her the way she deserved. A definite need to kiss her.

Leaving her to sleep, Finnian closed the pocket doors to the bedroom. He pulled the gun out of from the back of his waistband, setting it on the coffee table next to the sleeper bed, now taking up most of the living room.

A song played in Everly's purse. Finnian pulled it out, hoping to silence it before it woke her up, but he laughed at the unexpected rap song as her ringtone. The screen showed a blond man in dark sunglasses framed by a bright blue sky. He looked like a movie star.

Who the hell was Cade?

"Hello?" Finnian didn't know what prompted him to answer other than complete curiosity about a man calling her.

"Who is this?" A younger male voice asked.

Finnian stood and stared out the window over the Atlanta skyline. "Who is this?"

"You're not in a position to ask me that. You're answering my sister's phone. Who are you?"

Sister. Finnian relaxed his shoulders. "I'm Finnian Hayes."

"Who? Wait a second. Are you the guy that Tripp sent to check up on her?"

Finnian rubbed a hand over the back of his neck, not sure how her brother knew. Was he friends with Tripp? That could cause some serious issues. "Yes."

"Nora didn't mention you were English. I emailed Everly a few times tonight. She usually emails me right back. I wanted to razz on her about the 'tall, cute handyman' that kept her up all night talking. At least, that's how Nora described it."

So, she thought he was cute? Finnian sat down in the closest chair. "I wouldn't exactly call me a handyman, but I suppose I'm pretty handy. Who's Nora?"

"Our mom."

Had she told her mum about him? He settled back in the chair, glad of the phone call. After her declaration that she liked him too, this secondary encouragement started to clear his mind to move forward . . . tomorrow.

"Where's Everly?"

"Sleeping."

"Whoa!" Cade mumbled something. "Sleeping? I called her house. No one answered."

"We're at a hotel." Finnian squeezed his eyes shut. Why had he admitted that? He's supposed to keep her hidden, not declare to the world where she was staying for the evening.

"A what?"

Too late now. "Hotel."

"Man, I don't know what to say. It's not like my big sister to go to a hotel with a man. I feel like I should protect her. Read you the riot act or something. I've never had to be the protective brother before. Might be kinda cool."

"I have been the protective brother before, and it's

incredibly frustrating because the sister never wants the help and doesn't listen to reason." His Meg was as hardheaded as they came. Always seeing whomever she wanted, regardless of what her brothers thought of the louse.

"Yeah. I bet Everly would hate it." He laughed. "Might have to try it just play with her someday."

"Sweetiekins," a woman said.

"Not now," Cade answered.

"Sweetiekins, come back to bed." The feminine purr and kissing sound made Finnian smile.

Clearing his throat, he leaned back into the chair. "It's okay, Sweetiekins. You're obviously busy." He managed not to laugh too loud. "I'll tell your sister you called."

Cade gave up on the tough brother routine and laughed with him. "Alright. I hope she gets a chance to at least email me back tomorrow. Bye."

Finnian ended the call before he was privy to anymore of Cade's life. Some things were better left in the bedroom, and that included Sweetiekins and his lady friend.

He put her phone on vibrate so the ring tone wouldn't wake her up. Leaning his head back, he closed his eyes. All the 'what-ifs' about the trust fund, the condo, and Miami prevented sleep earlier that morning after showing up at Everly's house. Exhaustion began to creep over him like a blanket.

The phone vibrated on his leg. Without opening his eyes, he answered it. "Yes, Sweetiekins?"

"Well, now," Mr. Randolf began, his chuckle rumbling through the phone. "That's a much nicer greeting than the wake-up call you granted me this morning."

Finnian's eyes flew open. "Oh, Mr. Randolf. I thought you were Everly's brother."

"Is that what he goes by now? I always thought he preferred Cade."

Finnian smiled. "Judging by Sweetiekins' current company, I'm guessing he has a variety of nicknames. What can I help you with?"

"First, I'm afraid I had terribly rude manners this morning and didn't ask you for your name."

"Finnian Hayes." He moved to his bed for the night, stretching his legs out. "Do you have any news?"

"Yes, a little, at least. I'm afraid the solution may cause Mrs. Clarke, I mean Everly, some distress. It's actually rather fortuitous that you answered the phone. Maybe you can help break the news to her. Is she around?"

"She's sleeping."

"Well, this has to do with that condo. It is being foreclosed on this week."

Claudia would be tossed out of the house along with all her dresses covered in sequins and dozens of pairs of shoes. She'd have to find another man's piggy bank because Charles Clarke's well just ran dry. It shouldn't cause Finnian this much pleasure.

"Should we let it go into foreclosure? Would that be the best thing for it?" Why would Everly want the condo, anyway? It would only have bad memories. Plus, how could she have enough money to pull it out of foreclosure. It was a million-dollar condo. Not the kind of money she had hiding in her sofa cushions, and based on what she'd said about Charles's will, he didn't leave her much.

"Not in this case. Because her name is associated with the trust owning the stock, it could do damage to her personal credit. No one could come after her legally for the debt, but the trust's name is Everly Clarke Family Trust. I worry that it may come back to haunt her one day. Although she only works as a bookkeeper right now, she still maintains her professional CPA license. Since she's the trustee, I'd hate for the accounting board to get wind of it. I don't think Charles ever set up a trustee to administer the trust. If he did, I haven't located him. John Harriman is the only name I've found registered to the trust, thus far."

After a pause, he continued. "The bank holding the mortgage hasn't received a payment in six months. Charles was a very wealthy man. Based on the contents of the will, or the lack of contents, really, I believe that there may be a good sum of money in the bank in Miami that would cover the costs of pulling it out of debt."

"So, what happens now?" Finnian held his breath for the worst possible answer.

"There's no time left. She's going to have to handle this in person since we don't have a trustee to act on her behalf." Mr. Randolf sighed loudly into the phone. "She's going to have to go to Miami. Tomorrow."

8

Everly stood in the doorway, watching Finnian sleep on the sofa bed across the room. For the first time in a while, her growling stomach had acted as a well-timed alarm clock. The pizza reminded her body that good food, beyond peanut butter and crackers, actually still existed in the world. The quick call to room service ensured the new trend of eating real meals would continue, starting with some pancakes and eggs.

Her cell phone sat on the desk near Finnian, plugged into a charger. It was sweet he'd think to do that for her. She tiptoed across the room. She picked up the notepad beside her phone, cocking her head to the side, trying to decipher what was scribbled on it. Did he write in French? No, she recognized 'flight' and 'arrive.' His handwriting looked like her little brother's did in first grade.

"Good morning." Finnian's deep voice, raspy from sleep, sent a warm tremble through her. She turned as he pulled back the sheet and stood up, shirtless in just his jeans.

She snapped her mouth shut, afraid she might make a fool of herself gawking at him. Or drooling. Apparently, under his shirt he looked like the superhero he'd played. Well defined muscle and a sexy layer of dark hair covered his chest and down the midline of his body.

"Morning." She couldn't formulate much more of a greeting. He must work out all the time. No wonder he could throw that guy against the wall.

He cleared his throat.

Her eyes snapped up to his. How long had she stood there staring at his six-, no, eight-pack abs?

Finnian's amused smile made her want to crawl into his bed.

No, her bed. Back into her own bed. Alone. To hide.

Everly glanced at the rumpled sheets on the sofa bed. She licked her lips as her throat ran dry from her rarely used imagination.

His amusement had vanished when she looked back. His eyebrows raised in a silent question as he hooked his thumbs into the front belt loops of his low-slung jeans. "Did you sleep well?"

She followed the movement until her face flushed hot. Holding up the notepad like a shield between them, she blocked him out before she could embarrass herself further. Did he hypnotize all women with his shirt off, or was it a personal affliction?

She pointed to the front of the notepad. "What is this?"

"What?"

Everly swallowed, trying not to stare at his body, his face, or the bed as she held out the notepad. "All this writing. I found this on the chest, I mean desk." Her eyes diverted to a spot over his shoulder. "The desk over there."

Finnian chuckled and grabbed his shirt, ending her unnatural obsession with his body. Glad he found her discomfort so amusing.

"Travel information. We have to go to Miami."

Her eyes searched his for answers, all those delicious, sexy thoughts vanishing. "Oh, no. No, I'm not going to Miami." She couldn't. The thought of Miami used to make her physically sick. All because of Charles. He destroyed her life when he left to move down there.

"Yes, you are. The lawyer called after you went to sleep." His teasing look disappeared altogether. "I already bought the plane tickets. We fly out in a few hours."

"Ugh! Why do you think you can take charge of everything? It's not your decision if I go to Miami or not." She slammed the pad of paper on the desk. "I told you before. I refuse to let someone dictate my decisions again. I don't know why you, Charles, or anyone else thinks they know what's best for me."

His face hardened. He crossed the room in three large steps. "Don't you ever compare me to Charles Clarke, again."

She stood up straight and refused to let him intimidate her, but he ended the fight before she had a chance to join in.

"I'm taking a shower." He stalked to the bathroom. "By the way, Cade called for you late last night. I wouldn't call him back, just now. He sounded like he had company. He wanted you to respond to his email." Without any more of an explanation, he stalked out of the room. His exit was followed by the hum of water through the pipes.

Everly sat down in the chair at the desk. Cade had called? He never called her. She squeezed her eyes shut. And Finnian had talked to him. This should be interesting.

Grabbing her phone, she pulled up her email. Three emails from him yesterday. All asked about the "tall, cute handyman." Everly dropped her head in her hands.

Seriously, Nora? Her mom couldn't leave well enough alone. She had to dish to her baby brother.

Everly ran a hand through her hair, thinking of Finnian. She appreciated everything he'd done for her, but did he have to be so controlling? Why did they need to go to Miami today? He obviously didn't feel the need to give her the reason.

It was her life at stake. Her sanity. Didn't she get a vote? She picked up the pad of paper, the writing still illegible and not helpful. She let it fall back on the desk and rested her chin in her hands, giving in and pouting for the moment.

"Bossy Englishman."

The knock at the door made her jump from her seat. Even stupid room service made her jumpy after last night. She crossed the room as the sound of water from the shower shut off in the bathroom. Perfect timing. Maybe if she plied him with food, she could get Finnian to finally understand that she needed to be included in these decisions.

She opened the door. The smell of pancakes, sausage, and coffee blended into a heavenly bouquet. When was the last time she had syrup and butter together? The server cleared his throat.

"Sorry." She smiled and motioned him into the room. "It smells delicious. You can set it over there, please."

"I hope everything is how you ordered it, ma'am."

The bedroom door panel slid open and slammed into the wall. Finnian stepped out in jeans, barely zipped, with a gun in his hand.

The server stumbled backward.

Everly braced him from falling, her hand reaching under the tray and saving it from ending up on the floor.

She took in Finnian's body and that same affliction began again. God, he was magnificent.

"What the hell are you doing?" Finnian took a menacing step into the room.

After ensuring her food was safe, she rushed over to Finnian, shoving him back into the bedroom with two hands on his damp chest. "Me? What the hell are you doing? I ordered room service. You know. Food. Like bacon, eggs, and pancakes. I don't think"—her hand wrapped around the hand that held his gun, pushing it down against his leg—"we need your firearm. The bacon is already dead."

He kept his intense focus trained over her head at the server. The china rattled from rushed movements as he set out the dishes. Finnian's chest heaved under her hand. It didn't matter anymore if the server threw the food on the ground. The fresh smell of soap mixed with Finnian's own scent captured her attention.

A muscle in his cheek ticked. He seemed oblivious that she even touched him, and yet every inch of her responded. The pulse in his neck jumped in rhythm with her own. What would happen if she kissed him right there?

She trailed her hand down his chest and over his damp skin, admiring the dips and curves of his muscles. The door closed as the server left.

Risking everything, she pressed her lips to the center of his chest, where his heart steadily beat. The superhero routine messed with her determination to yell at him for the plane tickets.

He gripped her butt with his free hand, pulling her hard against his body, her sweater soaking in the rest of the water on his skin. She gasped, her body instantly on board with the idea of more.

"Everly," he growled, dipping his head and kissing a spot

behind her ear. "What is this?" He pressed his lips to her throat.

But it wouldn't be something simple with her. With everything so chaotic, she didn't have the mental space to keep herself distant and not go falling in love. She did like him, but she would never let herself love him. That hurt too much. It gave him too much control.

Ignoring the heat building low in her stomach, she patted his chest and pulled away. "This is breakfast. If you don't like pancakes, I can order you some waffles."

"What?" His eyes narrowed. "Waffles?"

"I know some people prefer waffles to pancakes."

His English accent deepened as he grumbled, "I have no idea what you're talking about."

She crossed her arms, a little pleased that she'd managed to distract him. "I would have pegged you for a waffle kinda guy, anyway. Perfect little squares. You can neatly fill each one up with syrup before cutting them into equal-sized bites."

He rolled his eyes, placing his gun on the bed and buttoning his jeans before turning back around. He opened his mouth to speak, but she continued.

"I'm a pancake girl. Haphazardly cut with the side of my fork, each bite sopping up the syrup that didn't manage to soak in."

"I don't care about pancakes or waffles." His chin dipped as his dark eyes locked with hers. "I'd rather discuss this." He motioned between the two of them. "Us."

She beamed a smile at him. "Nope. I don't have any answers for your questions, so for right now, we're going to eat." She turned to walk to breakfast, hoping they'd moved past his anger and her desire. Her heart sank when his hand clamped down on her shoulder, and he stepped between her and the room service set up on the table.

"Everly." He paused and closed his eyes as he blew out a long breath. It reminded her of those self-help books where they tell you to count to ten before losing your temper. He might need to keep on counting because he didn't look hungry for her or breakfast when he opened them again. More like a touch of murder aimed her way.

"You shouldn't have ordered room service, especially without letting me know. Someone attempted to kidnap you last night. You need to be more careful with who you let into the room."

"So, I can't even open the door now?" She moved past him, away from the food. She chewed on her bottom lip, hating to consider he was right. Maybe she should have told him about the room service, but she wasn't used to answering to anyone. That's the way she liked it.

Long, thick beige curtains framed five large windows revealing the Atlanta skyline drenched in the early sunlight. Everyone else on the streets below went about their Monday morning commute without worrying about men chasing them for some unknown reason. Once, a long time ago, that'd been her.

It was a thousand years ago.

Could the men chasing her see them right now? She let out a nervous laugh. Was she safe anywhere?

Finnian's arms wrapped around her shoulders, pulling her until she leaned against him. "I know you're upset about going to Miami, but we need to go. I'm starting to think that Claudia might be behind this. The only way to find out is to confront her."

She relaxed back into his embrace. "I wondered about Claudia when you first mentioned her living in the condo."

"It's just a theory. With all the drugs and illegal gambling Charles was into, it could be anyone that had a score to settle. They probably assume you inherited ATL and all the money that went with it."

She closed her eyes. "Drugs?"

A moan rumbled through his chest. "You didn't know about the drugs, did you?"

Everly shook her head. "I don't want to go to Miami and confront drug dealers."

"You won't have to. I'll handle them if necessary." He leaned down. His lips close to her ear. "I'm not going to leave you until I know you're safe. We'll get through this. I promise."

Leave. Of course he'd leave. That's why keeping her distance was for the best.

Finnian's lips pressed against her hair above her temple. "Try to learn to trust me." He kissed that spot behind her ear again. "Don't always jump to the worst conclusion about everything I do." He moved lower, kissing the side of her neck. "I'm doing this all for you. Please believe that."

His hand spread wide across her stomach. His other hand planted low on her hip, locking her in place.

"I'm trying," she whispered as he kissed the top of her shoulder, wishing life were simpler.

"Why do you smell like apples? It's driven me crazy since the first time I held you." He nuzzled his lips back on her neck. "God, Everly, say the word. Please."

He'd placed her in charge of them moving past this point. She'd done nothing but complain about wanting control in the decisions, and now, she wished he'd take back the power and kiss her and not let her overanalyze it.

"Alright." Finnian squeezed her hip. "I need to get dressed."

She nodded, her head bobbing back and forth like her neck was made of rubber. The heat from his body lingered on her back as the door to the bedroom closed behind her. What would it take for her to dive into a relationship with Finnian without fear?

~

THE LINE LEADING up to security wound its way five rows deep. Flying out midmorning on a Monday always meant longer lines, but Finnian didn't care. As long as nothing disastrous happened, they should make their flight on time and be in Miami in a few hours.

"Is that your phone?" Everly asked, reaching for her phone in her purse. "Or mine?"

"Mine." He set his duffel bag on the ground, regretfully answering it. "Good morning, Tripp."

"Hayes. I got your message that you were going to have to take off this week."

He winked at Everly, enjoying the cute smile she gave him in return. They'd apparently moved past the drama from this morning. But not sexual tension. That still hovered over them with each touch and look. And there'd been plenty. Once they made it to Miami and sorted this mess out, he'd take her out for a real date. And hopefully end that date with the kiss that was inevitable.

"Yes, sir. I already rescheduled the week so that the other guys have my shift covered. Sorry for the short notice. Something came up. I'm about to go through security at the airport right now, so I need to—"

"What? Where are you going?" Tripp's anxious tone was unusual. "The police came by earlier. They were concerned that Everly didn't go home last night. Since I'm listed as a contact with the security company, they came here to do a wellness check." He paused for a moment. "Is Everly with you?"

Finnian hesitated. Tripp wouldn't be happy. "Yes, she's here."

Her eyebrows shot up.

"I told you not to associate with her anymore!" Tripp shouted loud enough that Everly heard every word. She mouthed, "Why?" Tripp continued. "I said I'd handle her. This is direct insubordination, Hayes."

"She called me." Finnian waited for a reaction. "Because we're friends now. She needed help, so I'm helping. I'm taking that vacation time you promised when I was first hired."

Everly huffed out a breath and rose on her tip-toes, trying to listen to the conversation. Finnian smiled as he leaned down and shared the phone. Anything to have her close again.

"You think I'm going to believe that the two of you are just friends? Where were you both last night? I had my driver drive past your house at five in the morning on my way to work today. Your car was gone, and crime scene tape crossed over the door. And now you're flying somewhere together." Tripp laughed harshly. "Amazing. After four days, you've managed to crawl into her bed."

Muscles across Finnian's back bunched tight. "Hey—"

"I'm not jealous of you, though. Charles always complained about how dull she was. Lifeless. That's why he finally stopped suffering through sex after finding Claudia."

Finnian straightened so Everly couldn't hear anymore. What had gotten into Tripp? He turned away and lowered his voice. "I don't have any desire to hear what Charles had to say on the subject. Or you, for that matter. I work for you. You don't dictate my personal business."

"Everly is *my* business. I'll take care of any issues she's having."

"She's a grown woman who can make her own decisions. She called me. Not you. I'll see you next Monday." Finnian ended the call. What on Earth was he going to say to her?

Her hair covered part of her face while she stared at the ground. That must have been devastating for her to hear. Tripp blamed Everly for Charles leaving. No matter the money, come next Monday morning, Finnian would put in his two-weeks' notice. He'd had enough of Tripp. Like it or not, he'd have to call his brother to help cover some of the farm costs until he found another job. Brady would have to get over whatever issue he had with the family and help out. Their mum needed the help and their dad told them all before he died to watch over her.

"Everly, darling, please look at me." He laid his hand on her back. "Men say stupid things to other guys to justify their actions. Whatever Charles said to—"

"He was right." Everly looked at Finnian, an unexpected storm brewing in those innocent eyes. "I was dull. Boring. Lifeless. It's hard to have feelings for a man that treats you like a pet he bought and regrets it once he got it home." She began to pace in the small area as the line for security moved forward a few steps. "I'll tell you when I started being dull in bed. He came home from work one night." Her voice rose as she gestured her hand in the air, narrowly missing a woman next to her. "He told me to be dressed in something sexy and ready in ten minutes. That we were going to a strip club." She stomped her foot. "A strip club, Finnian!" Her shout caused a few people to look up from their phones.

Finnian nodded and politely smiled at the onlookers.

Everyone needed to go back to their own little world and ignore her outburst. But Everly seemed to gain her footing on the subject along with the attention of most of the people around them.

"I told him that if that's the kind of woman you like, then no wonder you can't last more than two minutes before you give up!"

Two women behind them in line looked Finnian up and down. Wait. Did they think . . .

"No," he scrambled, "she's talking about her ex—"

"I went." She poked him in the chest with a finger. "Just to prove that I wasn't some prude. But then, two strippers showed up on my doorstep at three in the morning because *someone* had invited them back to the house."

"Dude," a young man said down the line as he shook his head at Finnian. "Not cool."

"She's not talking about me," he shot back.

Everly didn't acknowledge his statement. "So, yeah, after that, I became lifeless. Husband or not, the minute you chose strippers over your wife, you don't deserve to share my bed."

The woman next to him mumbled, "Well, I never," under her breath.

Great. The entire damn line thinks he's the scumbag she's ranting about.

Everly ran a hand through her hair. "Since you told me about the drugs and gambling, some of those things have started to make sense."

A TSA agent down the line rose on his toes at the mention of drugs. Enough was enough.

Finnian pointed to Everly and addressed everyone around them, raising his voice over the rumblings of his inadequacies. "She's talking about her ex-husband. Not. Me."

Everly faced Finnian, her hands planted on her hips and her face more alive than he'd ever seen it. His words caught in his throat. Who cared if everyone around them thought he was the pathetic loser she'd just described? Everly was magnificent, fired up this way.

"I just want someone to want to be with me because they like me." She squeezed her eyes tight. "I'm not Charles's wife anymore. I'm not weak." Her blue eyes shot open. "And I know what I want." She wrapped her hands around Finnian's neck, pulling him down into a kiss.

She parted her lips under his in their next breath, her moan of relief sending him over the edge. Nothing resembled the sweet, innocent kiss he'd thought to give her a dozen times before now.

Her body buzzed with energy underneath his hands. The sugary taste of syrup from her morning pancakes lingered on her lips and tongue.

The crowd's cheering grew when his hands slid into the sides of her hair, cradling her face, and taking over control of the situation. She purred as her hands ran over his shoulders, down his chest, and over his abs.

Too much.

He broke it off. Any longer and his brain would forget to keep things rated for family television.

"Oh?" Everly stepped away as she brought her fingers to her lips. She looked around at everyone watching her with a blush spreading across the bridge of her nose. "I'm sorry, Finnian."

The line moved forward, but Finnian stopped to lean down in front of her. "I'll endure all the yelling you can dish out if it ends with a kiss like that." He winked. "Let's make it a little more private next time."

The young guy from earlier moved past them as the security line snaked around. He held up his hand. "Dude!" Finnian high-fived him and then shrugged at Everly's confusion. He'd have to explain it to her later.

A new security area opened up, the line moving quicker than before. They made it through without any problems, but they still needed to rush to make the plane. He took her carry-on bag from her and shouldered it with his own.

"Thanks." Her embarrassment lessened as they stopped at the line to board their flight. "I don't want to do this, but," she paused, the dimples in her cheeks deepening. "While we're stuck together, we need to set some rules."

"Rules?" Yeah. He had a rule. Like not to kiss him like that in public where he couldn't properly kiss her back. Or run those soft hands over his body and not let him reciprocate.

"From now on, I want to be included in all the decisions." She waved the tickets in front of him. "If you'd explained why we needed to go to Miami, I might not have been so mad about it."

He rubbed a hand over his chin, glad the hotel had provided a razor and a little embarrassed that his mind had lingered on the kiss since hers obviously hadn't. "I have a rule of my own. You remember that I can keep you safe, and sometimes things aren't up for discussion if I know what needs to be done. Your safety trumps everything else. Including your pride."

Her eyes narrowed. She didn't have to like it. This situation turned personal the moment Finnian laid eyes on Everly. The fact he'd caused any part of her pain when he protected Charles killed him inside. Now, someone wasn't just after Everly. They were after something that Charles hid away from even his own lawyer. They were willing to kidnap Everly to get it.

If he could protect Everly, maybe it would absolve him of some of the sins he'd committed on behalf of Charles. Maybe he could prevent another tragedy like Sean's death.

"Fine." She turned away as it was her turn to hand her ticket to the flight attendant. "But I will never be happy about it."

Finnian pulled out his phone as they boarded the plane. "I'll arrange a car to pick us up at the airport." She made a noise, like a grunt or a growl, as they sat in their seats. "Sorry." He handed her his phone. "Would you like to do that?"

9

"Which door is it?" Everly paused as she stepped off the elevator, holding her purse strap close against her body like a shield. Time to confront the mistress. It was a moment no wife ever wanted to do. The one shred of silver lining was that Charles was gone. She didn't have to listen to whatever bullshit answer he'd come up with to justify his actions.

"The second one on the left," Finnian said, his voice close behind her. "The one that's open."

She ran a hand over her hair, hoping the flight hadn't damaged the effort she'd made straightening it before they left the hotel that morning. She was a different person now than she was a week ago. The clothes gave her a small boost of confidence. She could face Claudia without looking like the second place, defeated wife.

It was time to finally find out what made Claudia so much better. What did Charles see in this other woman?

"Stop fidgeting. You look beautiful." Finnian's soft accent soothed her.

She shook her head, readjusting her grip on her purse. "I hate getting so nervous."

"Hey," he said, tipping her head up with a light finger under her chin. "You've come so far in the past few days. You're doing great." He searched her eyes before lowering his head, lightly touching her lips with his. It was their first kiss since the spectacle at the airport.

And it was perfect.

Because it was Finnian.

"You call that azure?" A woman screeched in an uncommonly high-pitched voice.

Finnian grimaced as he pulled away. "There's a voice I wish I never heard again. Let's get this over with." He patted her hip. "I'll be right behind you."

Claudia's voice echoed through the hallway. "I told you to paint the wall azure! That's kerulean. If I wanted kerulean, I would have told you kerulean."

Everly glanced back at Finnian, but his expression remained grim.

"You mean, cerulean?" A man replied in a soft, diminished voice.

"I know what I mean." Her voice rose higher. "I said it, didn't I? It says it right here on the can. Ker-U-Lean."

"Yes, I see that, but the shades are practically the same in this sunlight. I thought . . ."

"Oh, you thought, eh? I'm not paying you to think!" Claudia yelled.

Everly jumped with the shout, pausing only a step away from the door.

Finnian squeezed her hand. "She's in a mood. Do you want me to go first?"

"I have to do this on my own." Did those words just leave

her mouth? Everly swallowed. "Give me a second to introduce myself. Then you can come inside."

He winked. "You're the boss."

She could do this. She could take back her life. After taking a fortifying breath, she stepped into the open doorway.

A tall, garish woman peered down her nose at a man in a bright pink Hawaiian shirt. Her bleached blond hair stood almost five inches on top of her six-foot frame.

"Oh good, the cleaning lady is here."

Wait, what? Everly glanced down at her new jeans and cute boots that she'd purchased last night. Did she look like a cleaning lady? Maybe in her old clothes but not these.

Snapping the gum in her mouth in loud, annoying pops, Claudia motioned Everly into the condo. "Well? Nothing's getting cleaned with you standing there. You can start in my bathroom." She wagged her jeweled finger in Everly's face. "Mind you, don't touch my things. Clive said he was sending a new girl out and that I needed to keep an eye on her."

No. No way in hell this was Claudia. The teased hair and caked-on makeup that looked as though she'd not washed her face from the party the month before didn't resemble the woman Everly had pictured. Where did Charles find her? A Trashy Woman of the Month Club?

She snapped her fingers in Everly's face, and her eyes widened, but the penciled-on eyebrows didn't move. Face injections? "Hell-loooo?" If possible, her volume rose higher. "Did you hear me?"

"Yes, but I'm not—"

"Good. Get to work. Now, Mr. Mizolini, let's start at the beginning." She flounced across the floor to twelve-foot windows as her red, sheer robe flowed behind her, revealing her dangerously skimpy micro-bikini. She motioned toward the view of the Atlantic Ocean. "That is azure." Pointing to the small streak of blue on the wall, she said, "That is kerulean."

"Cerulean," he corrected her again.

Everly kicked her chin out, trying again in a louder voice. "Excuse me." She held up a finger. "But are you Claudia?"

Claudia adjusted the red bikini top. As hard as she tried, that ample chest would never fit into those small triangles. Silver high heels clicked across the travertine tiles as she approached Everly.

"Ms. Richardson to you. Don't make me call Clive. I'm not paying for a social visit. The bathroom is that way. The commode isn't going to clean itself." She fluttered her hand at an open bedroom door. "Get to work. Chop-chop."

Something snapped deep inside. Charles had dismissed her as nothing more than an annoying obligation. It wouldn't happen again. "I'm not here to clean your bathroom, Claudia." Hell if she'd call the woman "Ms. Richardson."

Claudia rested her hands on her waist. "Oh, really?"

Just tell her. "I'm here—"

Finnian stepped into the doorway.

Claudia's face almost split in two with her sudden smile. "Well, hot damn!" Claudia waltzed across the floor with her hands set on her perpetually swaying hips. "If it ain't the sexiest Englishman to visit America." Her voice smoothed out from the harsh tone she'd used moments before.

To his credit, Finnian didn't seem aware of the flimsy bikini. His expression remained cold and distant. "Claudia." He smiled, but not in that "special" way he could. His voice sounded strained. "We have a few things to discuss."

Why couldn't she command a room like that? Walk-in

and say what needed to be said. Easy, Finnian had never been scared of anything a day in his life.

"You know," Claudia said as she eased herself closer to him. "I was thinking just the other day that I require a bodyguard with your credentials." She squeezed Finnian's bicep, her smile widening. "*Exactly*, your credentials."

"I already have a body to guard." He moved past Claudia, winking at Everly. "I need to introduce you to someone."

"The cleaning lady?" Claudia's eyes narrowed, watching his every move like he was her dinner. Or dessert. "We've already become acquainted. Although at the pace she's moving, I doubt it will work out. Clive will fire her like he did the last one."

Finnian's hand rested at the nape of Everly's neck, a move that instantly conveyed possessiveness. And although she wanted to be independent, it thrilled her because it went both ways. He was hers for the moment.

Judging by the way Claudia straightened, she'd gotten the message.

"You're mistaken. This is not the cleaning lady." His accent deepened. It was the only giveaway that Claudia bothered him.

Claudia crossed her arms, her massive chest resting on her forearms and threatening to spill even further. She looked between Everly, Finnian, and the decorator, who stood a few feet away, openly listening to their conversation.

"Don't tell me *this* is your girlfriend? I'd hoped that with Charles gone and Tripp staying in Atlanta, we'd have a little time to explore our own options." Her eyes narrowed at Everly. "I'm not sure if I want to go exploring anymore if this is your type. Homespun and sweet as apple pie. It's unlikely you'd be up to handling me."

Homespun? She didn't feel like Laura Ingles Wilder, but if that remark meant she was the complete opposite of Claudia, she'd take it.

Finnian rested his hands on Everly's shoulders, drawing her back to his chest. "I happen to love apple pie." Her heart hitched. "But we're here for a reason. This is Everly."

Claudia shrugged. "Great. I'm Claudia, you're Finnian, and now we're all acquainted. What's your point?"

Everly's worry shifted into disbelief. It's not like Claudia accidentally bumped into someone's car in a parking lot and left before exchanging insurance information. Claudia had lived with Charles, a married man, for at least a year and didn't even recognize his wife.

Claudia's mouth dropped open as her arms fell to her side.

Everly patted Finnian's hand still on her shoulder. Never mind, the recognition part just kicked in.

"Everly"—Claudia's breath hitched—"Clarke?"

She forced her lips up into a smile. "Nice to meet you."

Claudia stared at Everly as though she'd grown three heads. Maybe she had for even venturing to Miami.

But now that she was here, standing across from the "other woman," she was glad Finnian pushed her into coming. She needed the closure. So much had happened since the reading of the will. This was one more step in the process to moving on.

The painter poured a different blue shade of paint into the small container. The movement seemed to wake her up.

Reality snapped back into Claudia's eyes. "Is this some sort of sick joke?" She swiveled her head left and right. "Will cameras pop out at some point?"

With a firm voice, Finnian said, "No. It's no joke. Everly has business to discuss with you. In fact," he said, looking at

Mr. Mizolini. "You can leave. Claudia won't be painting the wall azure, cerulean, or any other blue."

"Okay, I don't know what you think you're doing right now, but it's not cute Finnian." She took two long steps to a small gold cigarette case, flicking it open and puckering one between her lips. The lighter's flame licked the end of the cigarette. She took a long drag before pointing at Everly and causing her half-dozen bracelets to jingle together. "Why is she here?"

Everly angled her body in front of Finnian. Control. Maintain control. This was her condo. "Why don't you ask me yourself?"

"My guess is that you came down here out of curiosity?" She pushed her sheer robe back, setting her hand on her hip and giving everyone in the room a clear view of her body. Trashy or not, her perfectly curvy body made Everly's look like a schoolboy.

"Partly," Everly began. "But it goes a little deeper than that now."

"The condo—" Finnian cut off his sentence with one quick glare from her. This was her problem. He might keep her safe, but her history with Claudia made this personal.

"What about the condo?"

Everly stood a little straighter. This was it. She'd rehearsed this part in her head for most of the airplane ride. "Are you aware of who owns this condo?"

"Tripp told me it was the company's, and I could stay here. Those were Charlie's wishes. He always wanted to take care of me." She took another deep puff on the cigarette, the smoke mixing with the fake vanilla scent and paint and making Everly's stomach turn.

"The condo isn't owned by ATL." Everly tilted her head up. "I own it."

FINNIAN DIDN'T WANT to touch Claudia, but he couldn't leave her lying on the tile floor, unconscious. After carrying Everly, Claudia's weight resembled a male linebacker. Or one of his large-ass brothers.

He held her away from him. Hopefully, her sickeningly sweet perfume that reminded him of the dumpster in the alley behind a bakery shop would stay with her and not soak into his shirt.

He set her down on the curved couch. Everly tossed a blanket over her. Good. He didn't need to see if her bathing suit shifted during the ordeal.

Claudia's head rolled to the side, and she moaned.

Finnian caught Everly's confused look. "She's prone to drama." He ran a hand over his hair as Everly's teeth tugged at her bottom lip. "Are you about to laugh or cry? Hard to tell with you lately."

She laughed once, although a tear escaped before she wiped it away as quickly as it appeared. "I don't know anymore. Charles left me for"—she motioned to Claudia —"her. I know that sounds horrible. I'm probably judgmental, and Claudia is a nice person."

"No, she's not."

Everly met his eyes and half-laughed. "Thanks. I needed that."

Finnian's heart eased. The worry that had plagued him for the past few hours, since he'd told her about going to Miami, began to dissipate. Everly could handle this. He knew she was strong enough, but she finally realized.

Claudia shifted with a theatrical moan, her movement causing the blanket to fall from her body.

Everly huffed and covered her again. "I don't need to see

all the reasons Charles left me for her. What isn't on display I can fully imagine."

"I don't understand it either." Finnian pressed his lips together to keep from explaining his thoughts. He still had a lot to figure out when it came to his feelings about Everly.

Claudia put a hand to her head. "Wha-what happened?" She tried to sit up, and Everly leaned over the back of the couch to help. As much as she had every right to hate Claudia, she was still nice. She couldn't help it. It wasn't right that someone like Everly ended up in a situation like this.

"You fainted after I told you the condo belonged to me."

Claudia reared back, like Everly's hands were on fire. "Oh!" She patted her hair. "I can't believe this. Why would Tripp lie to me?"

Tripp's lies were starting to mount. Everly might want to handle her affairs with Claudia and the trust, but Tripp was his. "I have no idea," Finnian said. The ownership of the condo was public knowledge. Tripp had to know that Everly owned it.

Finnian held out his hand to help Claudia stand. Luckily, she adjusted her top and wrapped the robe around her body.

"What will happen now? Are you kicking me out?" She looked to Finnian for an answer. He opened his mouth but motioned to Everly. He'd never live that one down.

"Yes." Everly's mouth curved into a sweet smile. "You have two weeks to find a new place to live."

Finnian coughed to cover his amusement at the flick of pleasure in Everly's eyes as she said those words.

Claudia pressed her lips together for a moment, her gaze shifted between them. "I see. And, uh, where are you two staying?"

"Here," Everly said.

Finnian and Claudia both snapped their heads around to Everly. She knocked her chin up a fraction. "I own the condo. I'm staying here. I'm sure as hell not paying for somewhere to stay. That wouldn't be very economical."

"I see. Well, if Miss Apple Pie isn't inclined to share her bed, remember, Finnian, my door is always open." Claudia leaned her back against the kitchen counter in an invitation.

"That's very hospitable of you." Everly's voice remained flat and proper. "But that won't be necessary. There's plenty of room for us to stay." She cocked her head to the side. "Or else that two-week notice I gave you can be cut down to two hours."

Finnian bit his lip and silenced his immediate agreement to both Claudia leaving and the sleeping arrangement. As much as he wished it wouldn't matter, he didn't want her to be caught off guard. He cleared his throat and lowered his voice. "There's only one spare bedroom, Everly."

She didn't flinch, but one delicate shoulder shrugged. "One's enough." Finnian tried to swallow. His throat wouldn't work. The prospect of being with Everly had officially topped anything else since coming to this country.

Would she let him hold her tonight? Touch her? A strange heat grew along Finnian's jawline and up to his cheeks. Had the air conditioner stopped working?

Claudia barked a laugh and slapped her hand on the granite. "My word, Miss Apple Pie can make a blind man blush with those sweet and innocent insinuations." She sauntered closer to Everly, leaning down like she was whispering a secret. "I read once that blushing is the color of virtue." Claudia narrowed her eyes at Finnian. "If that's the case, I'd sure like to be the one to rid Finnian of his." She nudged Everly like an old man telling a dirty joke before cackling again.

Everly's eyes widened. She looked at Finnian and then snapped her gaze to the floor. He opened his mouth to dispute it and maintain some dignity, but what could he say?

Nothing. He tried to push the conversation past his apparent virtuous blushing. "We need to get to the bank before it closes."

Everly strode from the room. He moved to follow her, but Claudia reached out and stopped him.

"Seriously? Apple pie?" She arched a thin eyebrow. "I would've never have guessed."

"Two weeks." He pushed past her. His mind had more important things to concentrate on. Their sleeping arrangements that night was one of them.

The elevator doors closed, leaving him to wait for the next one. Was she mad? Upset? He was so damn proud of how well she'd handled herself.

Everly waited on the sidewalk. The blue long sleeved shirt and jeans were out of place in the warm Miami heat. Even though it was early October, it was still beach weather for many people.

Did Everly enjoy the beach? Would she wear a bathing suit and swim in the ocean? If the anticipation of sleeping in the same bed didn't distract him, images of her in a bikini would drive him crazy.

He laid his arm across her shoulders. "I'm proud of how well you handled Claudia." He kissed the top of her head. "You impressed me."

"We're not sleeping together tonight. I can sleep on the sofa."

That's a blunt way to approach the subject. He pulled

her closer to counteract the disappointment. "No, it's okay. I can sleep on the sofa." The curved sofa that barely contained Claudia's height. He'd take it over leaving her alone.

She relaxed against him. "Thanks. I just couldn't stand the thought of her inviting you to her bed. She's already taken one man away from me. I can't compete with that."

"There's zero competition, Everly. Believe me. Let's get going."

He interlaced his fingers with hers and strolled the four blocks to the bank. As the doors opened, the cold air conditioning rushed out in a loud *swoosh.*

Behind a receptionist desk stood a woman, a few inches shorter than Everly, with a fake smile plastered across her bright red lips. "Can I help you?"

Everly rested her hands on the counter. "I need to speak with someone about getting copies of bank statements."

Finnian remained a step behind her, giving her full control. It was something he had to think about. Protecting people was in his nature.

Protecting Everly took that basic need to a whole new level. But he'd let her take control as much as he could. She needed it.

"Okay, I can help you with that. We charge five dollars to print each month." She typed into the computer, pausing to push her glasses up. "What is the account number?"

"I don't know." Everly pulled out her wallet, handing over her license. "I'm the trustee of a trust. I need the bank account statements. Can you look it up by my name?"

"I can try." The receptionist sighed, a little put out to make an effort. She typed into the computer. Her eyes, already enlarged by her thick lenses, widened. "Oh, my.

Why, yes, I can print these statements for you. You're listed as an owner on the account."

Everly smiled as the lady typed a few more times. Finnian laid his hand on her shoulder, pleased when she shifted slightly in his direction.

"One moment." The receptionist, a new light gleaming her eyes, hurried away. She went to a small room, then gestured and pointed at them.

"What's that all about?" Everly leaned back, allowing her body to rest against his.

"I have no idea. About tonight . . ." Another woman rose from behind a desk in the small room. He squeezed her shoulder. "Never mind."

The woman straightened her skirt as she walked across the lobby. "Hi, I'm Missy Gable, the branch manager. You're Mrs. Clarke?"

"Yes," Everly said, her voice tight, probably with the use of her married name. "Is there a problem?"

"No, no. Not at all. I'm happy to finally meet you. Laura is retrieving the prints. They're rather long, so it may take a few minutes. I'm hoping you continue banking with us. I understand Mr. Clarke passed away recently. I'm sorry for your loss."

Everly tilted her head. "Thank you." It sounded more like she was surprised by the statement than appreciation for the sentiment.

Laura rushed back toward them, a stack of paper in her hands. "Here we go, Mrs. Clarke."

Everly opened her wallet. "How much for the copies?"

Ms. Gable waved her hand at her like she was swatting a fly. "No, no. No charge. Not for one of our *best* customers."

"Thank you?" Everly took the prints and her license back from Laura. "I may need to withdraw funds to cover a mortgage of my husband's that's become past due. Other than that, I'll be in touch if I need anything else."

Ms. Gable stepped forward, grabbing Everly's arm.

Everly jerked her shoulders back, and Ms. Gable dropped her hand. "We have several other investment opportunities with the bank. The money sitting in the checking account isn't earning anything. Savings, money market, or CD would be a better option."

Everly pressed harder against Finnian's chest and nodded. "I understand. I don't plan on moving the money from the bank, so additional interest-earning opportunities would be nice."

Ms. Gable's smile widened. "Great! I look forward to hearing from you." She handed her a card. "Call me anytime."

Everly took the business card and the envelope of bank statements and walked out ahead of Finnian. She slid the paper from the envelope, missed the first step to the sidewalk and stumbled.

Finnian caught her around the waist. "Better not try reading and walking down stairs, darling."

"This would throw anyone off." Everly held up the first page of the bank account between them, blocking her face.

"Is that a four?" It was his turn to be off-balance. "He has four *million* dollars sitting in your account?" He knew the man was rich, but that was a little ridiculous for a side savings account.

"The big question is why." She frowned and flipped through a few more pages of the bank statements. "He wanted this money kept secret. But from whom? Tripp? Claudia? Me?"

"Someone, that's for sure." Or maybe another player in Charles's circle. Finnian knew a few of them, and there were probably even more shady characters that Everly's late husband had kept to himself.

Shaking her head, she pulled out her phone. "I'm tired of guessing. We need to pay off the condo before it goes into foreclosure so I can get back and confront Tripp. He has to know something. Why else would he care that you're with me in Miami?"

"Pay it off tomorrow." He covered her phone with his hand. "We're here three more days. The foreclosure isn't scheduled until Wednesday. First thing in the morning, we'll come back to the bank and handle it." His fingers threaded through her hair, cupping her cheek. "Let's grab some new clothes, a bite to eat, and then walk on the beach."

Something normal for once in their unexpected relationship.

"I'm up for the clothes and food, but not for the beach." She shook her head and looked away. "Not yet. I've hated any thoughts of the beach since the first time he made the trip down here."

There he was again, Charles's ghost wedging between them. Finnian wouldn't push. She needed to reconcile herself with the past. Then, maybe, she'd be ready to move forward.

EVERLY GRIPPED the plastic handles of shopping bags full of Miami-esque clothes as she followed Finnian into Charles's condo. No. Into *her* condo. She owned it, and it was about time for her to start remembering it. But the bravery she'd harnessed to confront Claudia earlier vanished as exhaustion from the day set in.

"Claudia," Finnian mumbled a greeting and nodded his head in Claudia's direction, sitting on the sofa. It had to be an effort for him to *not* be charming. For some reason, Everly had turned into the third wheel instead of . . . whatever she was. How well did Claudia know Finnian? Asking the question meant dealing with the fallout from his answer. He didn't seem to like her, but that didn't mean they'd never had a past relationship.

"Hey there," Claudia said and leaned to the side to look at Everly. "And here's Miss Apple Pie. Glad you returned."

"That's not my name."

"Fine. I suspect you think I should call you, *Mrs.* Clarke? Although that title doesn't suit you since there wasn't much of a marriage between you two based on what Charlie told me."

Finnian shifted his body, just a little, putting himself between her and Claudia. His broad back blocked her view.

Claudia's barb was meant to insult her, but it was the truth. Everly raised her hand, hesitating before setting it on Finnian's lower back and stepping beside him. It would be easy to let him handle it.

She'd hidden from life and conflict long enough.

"You can call me Everly." Her voice sounded calmer than expected. "I'm not a fan of using my married name."

Claudia waved her hand in the air. "Whatever." Now dressed in a pair of black exercise pants and a tank top in the loudest neon green Everly had ever seen, she flipped through a gossip magazine. "I see you went shopping. Not sure we have clothes down here that will suit you."

"I managed alright." She let the shopping bag hang by her side. She touched Finnian's arm, wanting to see him a little longer but knowing she didn't have the energy to handle Claudia. "I'll see you in the morning."

Sleep would help. She shut the door to her bedroom, letting the weight of the entire world fall off of her shoulders. Hot shower. Soft pajamas. Cozy bed. In that order—no compromises.

The bathroom was white. Only white. White tile with white fixtures and white bathmats. It was oddly calming and unsettling. Afraid to show how dirty even her hands were, she touched the shower faucet with the tips of her fingers as she blasted the water straight to hot.

As she climbed out of the shower, a knock on the bedroom door made her pause. She let her head drop forward. "Oh well for my plans to sleep."

Quickly, she dressed in the new pajamas she'd purchased, one hundred percent bamboo fabric in a pretty mint green color, and crossed the room.

"Everly?" Finnian's soft accent drifted through the door.

"Just a minute." She ran the towel over her hair, taking with it most of the water. This had to have been the longest day. Was it really only this morning they'd shared a kiss? They hadn't so much as shared a kiss as she had attacked him with her mouth in the middle of a crowded airport.

She cracked open the door. He held up a glass of wine.

"I don't drink much."

His smile grew, inch-by-inch, and her heart sighed. Being charming and sexy must be bred into his DNA.

"Then, don't make me drink alone." He pushed the door open and held out his hand. "C'mon. She's gone to her room. No reason to hide out in yours."

"I was getting ready for bed, not hiding." But she relaxed as she realized they were truly alone with Claudia's door closed.

He set her glass of white wine on the coffee table next to

a second glass. Her heart stumbled a little at the trouble he'd gone through. Maybe just a sip.

"I spoke with the police back home. Tripp went to your house."

Everly sniffed the wine. It reminded her of peaches and apples. "Of course, he did. He's apparently inserted himself into my life."

"Did you interact with him a lot when Charles was alive?"

"No." She curled up on the couch, tucking her feet under her. Finnian turned off the kitchen light. The last rays of sunlight glinted off the ocean just beyond the windows.

"Tripp's around because he's looking for the ATLighting stock. Must be strange knowing that some mysterious person owns fifty percent of your company." Finnian sat down beside her. Heat from his thigh soaked though her thin shorts. She snuggled a little closer. "I don't have any illusions that he gives a crap about me. Hey, do you think he left Claudia the company?"

"I don't think she'd keep it a secret if she did. Claudia is a lot of things but she is who she is. I don't see her waiting for some perfect timing to declare herself half-owner to a company as profitable as ATL."

Picking up the glass, she focused on the liquid swirling around. She closed the gap and laid her head on his shoulder. "This is so simple right now. No Tripp. No random thugs chasing us." She leaned back and looked up at his profile as he sipped the wine. The next thought, "just us," was on the tip of her tongue, but she couldn't go there, so she changed directions. "Do you still think Claudia was the one behind all the attacks?"

"No. First, she's not acting unusual at all. This is her usual level of strangeness. Second, she left her phone out, and I went through it." He took another sip. "There were no calls to anyone that would be involved."

"Just like that," Everly snapped. "You snooped through her phone."

He arched an eyebrow. "Remember I was in the police, Everly. If I think anyone of interest was involved, I'm going to check into it."

"What about going to our police? Should we give them a chance to solve this before we get in too far, and it gets even more dangerous?" That made the most sense. Let the authorities handle the men chasing her before either she or Finnian ended up hurt. Or dead.

"I've thought about trying again." His body tensed, the muscles along his shoulders bunching for a moment before he relaxed. "My greatest worry is that we'll never know the truth if we go to the police. We'll have to get them involved, but not yet. I have too many questions that will go unanswered. Depending on who is behind this, they may have the police in their back pocket."

"This sounds like a bad thriller movie." But she'd have to believe in him. He'd asked that of her before, and she'd keep pushing herself to trust him fully. It was hard.

"If it's not Claudia, then who is it? You have to have some clue, right?"

The question hung between them. Finnian stared at the wine in his glass before finishing it in one long drink. Was he holding something back, or did she imagine it? She sipped her wine, a little proud when she didn't grimace at the unusual taste. Whoever said that it tasted like grape juice was dead wrong.

He took her glass and set them both down. "Didn't your mum ever tell you if you make a face, it'll freeze that way?"

Maybe she hadn't kept her reaction to the wine a secret. "No, but she did tell me that my nose would grow if I lied."

He chuckled and bumped his shoulder with hers. "Don't lie too often." He brushed his finger across the tip of her nose. "You hav'a very cute nose."

"But I'm afraid yours may grow soon."

The small hesitation before he answered gave him away. "I haven't lied."

"You've withheld the truth."

"I've withheld a theory. I'm not obligated to give you all my theories on this. I run scenarios over and over in my mind." He leaned toward her, pressing his lips against her forehead. "Let me do my job."

"I'm trying."

He kissed her temple. "I think it may be time for bed." She cocked her eyebrow, but he shook his head and patted the back of the sofa. "You're currently sitting on my bed, remember."

"Right."

"I almost forgot. Let me show you what Claudia gave you."

"An apology," she muttered. "Farewell letter. A vacant guest room to rent."

"Not likely. She left you this." Finnian motioned to a laptop that sat closed on the glass coffee table. "It might be the closest you'll get to an apology from Claudia."

A note on hot pink stationary had *Everly* scribbled on top of the computer.

"Did you snoop?"

"Of course. I wouldn't let Claudia upset you again if I could avoid it."

God, he was sweet. She unfolded the note.

Miss Apple Pie,

I'm not sure why I didn't hand this over when Charlie died, but some small voice told me to keep it as a souvenir. If you can manage to break into it, maybe it will give you some of the answers you're looking for. For what it's worth, he never stopped loving you.

Charles's guilt and love for her were two vastly different ideas. She ran her hand over the top of the computer. Answers. But how much could she find and how much had died with him?

"Do you think you'll try to look?"

"I don't think I have a choice. If I can even get into it. Maybe we can find out the answers to a few of our questions." She covered a yawn. "But I won't start tonight. It's been a long few days."

She started to stand up, but Finnian grasped her knee, keeping her seated. "Everly, dear, would it be brutish of me to ask for a goodnight kiss?"

A warm glow spread in her body. Walk away or dive in? Who the hell was she kidding? She'd take what she wanted for once.

Everly stood, amused when the hope in his eyes started to fade. She straddled his lap, both knees sinking into the soft sofa cushion.

"I never did get to finish making my point at the airport." She smirked, running both hands up his wide chest. "You told me not to kiss you in public next time." She liked this better. Unlimited amount of touching, feeling his strength.

He gripped her thighs and then tugged her hips higher on his lap. "I'm glad you've taken my suggestion."

The door to Claudia's room opened. The dang woman came walking out like she was entering a ballroom, arms out to the side, her robe trailing out behind her.

Everly tried to scramble off of him, but he had other

plans. In an unexpectedly graceful move, Finnian stood, both hands under her hips as her legs automatically wrapped around his waist and carried her to the bedroom.

"Finnian!" she whispered, averting her eyes from Claudia, who laughed loudly from the kitchen. "Shit! That was so embarrassing." She slapped at his shoulder. "Put me down."

Finnian kicked the door closed behind him. "No. Not if you only want down because of her." He turned, sat on the bed, putting them back in the same position as they'd been on the sofa.

He kissed her neck, a delicious hum of expectation building with each press of his lips. "Now," he murmured, his teeth grazing her earlobe. "You were saying something about making a point." He pulled back and raised both eyebrows. "Well? I'm waiting."

Everly kissed him. Any shred of insecurity remaining from a few minutes before vanished as her lips parted over his. She didn't just want to make a point that she could feel like a real woman. It went beyond that.

She pressed her chest against him, hyperaware of her lack of bra as the smooth fabric rubbed against her skin. The intimate way their bodies fit together brought delicious ideas to her mind.

Everything clicked as the rest of her fear vanished. She wanted more.

She wanted Finnian.

Badly.

Her soft moan echoed in the quiet room. It was too much too soon. Too much uncertainty of life surrounded them both.

But their kiss grew wilder. No man had ever kissed her with such a juxtaposition of dominating strength and tenderness. She hugged him tighter, craving it even though it was scary.

He broke the kiss and squeezed her thighs. "Let me touch you, Everly."

"I . . . I can't have sex with you." It sounded like the half-hearted refusal it was.

Finnian's lips explored the curve of her throat. "I have a fierce need to touch you. Nothing more." He slid both hands up the curve of her hips, under her shorts and panties, to grip her rear. "You need this, baby."

Need what? Sex or an epic make-out session that made her second-guess every single thought or idea she had on the subject? It was cliché to think it'd never been this good before, but it wasn't a lie. It had *never* been this good.

He rolled her hips forward, causing a surprise shot of pleasure from the friction of her body against his.

Oh. *That's* what he meant. She opened her mouth to tell him she didn't need his help for that either, but his dark gaze intensified, cutting off her argument as he moved her body again.

And again.

Each slide of her body against his doubled the pleasure and made her regret her "no sex" decision.

Finnian tilted his head back. "Kiss me again."

Everly wrapped her arms around his shoulders, kissing him over and over. Her world clicked into place. It was easy to be with him. His taste. His smell. She loved everything about Finnian.

He cradled the back of her head with one hand as his other slid between their bodies.

The anticipated orgasm slammed through her with his light touch. She buried her face against his neck, muffling the uncontained moan of his name.

Finnian shifted her on his lap, still teasing her with his fingers, the pleasure never fully releasing its grip.

She moved against his hand, wanting more.

His shoulders tensed, and he growled deep in his chest. He reached under her shirt and covered her breast with his hot hand.

"Again," he ordered, slipping his fingers underneath her panties.

Her body arched back as it complied with his demand, sweet pleasure hitting hard.

It stole her breath and most of her brain. She clung to his body, letting every single irrational thought run free. She wanted to stay with him, hide from reality, and run away to England to start a new life.

He silently stroked a hand up and down her back as she floated back down to earth.

But hiding wasn't an option. Not anymore. Not from Finnian. Not from the rest of the world.

10

F innian picked her up and laid her on the mattress. Everly needed a solid night's sleep.

And he needed space to make sense of every hard-core emotion he'd been hit with since coming to Miami. Tonight, she'd come apart under his hands, giving him control the way he'd asked her a dozen times before. But it worried him that he couldn't live up to his promises.

He straightened, but she reached out, stopping him. "Stay."

It was what he wanted, but he wouldn't take advantage of what just happened. "That's not necessary, dear. I can sleep on the sofa."

"Please. Sleep beside me tonight." She hit him with her beautiful eyes. "I want you here."

A sweetness like Everly's deserved someone worthy of it. He wasn't, but he'd gladly be the recipient of it. She'd find out about the email, about everything he'd done in his life, and walk away soon enough.

He turned off the bathroom light before taking off his

jeans and shirt, setting his gun on the nightstand beside him.

As he laid down in the bed beside her, she rolled his direction, curling tight against his chest. "Thank you for staying."

He kissed her temple. "Never thank me for this."

"I wish everything could freeze. No one chasing me. No Claudia. No Tripp." She half-laughed. "No millions in a bank account." She pressed her lips to the center of his chest. "Just this."

The concern that he wasn't enough vanished. There wasn't a choice in the matter. He'd find a way to be enough and keep her safe.

"Someday, it will be." He'd make damn sure of it.

EVERLY SAT along the edge of the bed staring at Charles's laptop. She'd spent most of the morning attempting to login, trying dozens of passwords, hoping to access whatever secrets might be hidden. This piece of equipment might contain the answers to all of their questions. Who was after them? Who really had the stock? Why in the hell did he stick this condo in a trust fund for her?

But only half her brain was even focused on the task. The other half still mused over waking up next to Finnian.

He'd held her all night, his hand wide and warm across her bare stomach. She'd slept hard until he'd murmured "good morning," and mentioned starting coffee and left. Too bad, he hadn't lingered a little longer. Those dreams might have turned into a reality.

Now, diving headfirst into the emotional abyss of Charles's personal computer, her day had begun. The risk of finding even more of her ex-husband's transgressions eliminated her need for coffee. Who knew what was on this computer.

One bright spot was that she and Finnian would visit the registered agent today. It was the man who set up the trust fund, and as far as Everly could tell since the damn laptop wouldn't unlock, he was the only other person in the world who might have an answer as to *why*.

Her phone rang the familiar rap song. Cade's face with his blond hair and sunglasses flashed on the screen before she answered it.

"You're up early." It would have to be close to five in California. "Or going to bed late, which is my guess."

"I wish. Up early. I flew to Indiana last night to help Dad at the store. Mom called and dropped a not-so-subtle hint that they were changing out all the displays and that our sixty-five-year-old father didn't need to move everything himself." His voice dropped to a whisper. "She threatened to start following me on every social media site possible."

"Ouch. Nothing like Nora 'liking' those pictures of you at that wet T-shirt contest you judged last year."

"I took those down after she blackmailed me into accepting her as a 'friend' on Facebook. I still block her from seeing half the pictures I get tagged in."

Everly laughed. "Yes! Nora is ruthless."

"Glad she passed that along to both of us," Cade said.

Once, a long time ago, Everly used to feel invincible. Like she could stand up to anyone. She studied accounting expecting to command a boardroom or be CEO of a major company. Her mom had taught her by example never to be someone's doormat. That piece of advice worked until Everly ended up in love with the person walking all over her.

"Hey, what's wrong?"

Everly glanced back at the laptop. "Everything."

"Your hunky handyman giving you trouble already?"

"No, not exactly." Everly studied her pink toenails. "How much did you know about my marriage?" Maybe it was time to let her family into her life. Cade might be the best place to start.

He sighed. "I know Charles made you sad, and I hated him for it. Took a lot of self-control to stay in California instead of flying to Atlanta to beat him up."

Her lips trembled into a smile. "My big, bad, baby brother always saving the day."

"Nobody makes my big sis cry. And I'm not so little anymore. Just hit thirty. I've been watching some YouTube videos on self-defense. I think I could handle myself. But what did you want to tell me?"

Here it went. "Charles left me for another woman." At his silence, she continued. "He moved to Miami a couple of years before he died to live with her. He owned a condo that she lives in along South Beach. Got into drugs and other things I'm not sure I even want to know about. He had another life down here."

"Wait," he snapped. "You're in Miami now? Alone?"

"I'm in the condo"—she sighed—"with his mistress."

"Shit, Ev. Do you want me to come down there? I never liked Charles, but damn, now I wish I had beat his ass."

She sniffled. Since he'd learned to walk, Cade had protected her. "Well, he's dead, so it's a little late for that."

Cade let out a harsh laugh. "He should be thankful for it. How long are you in Miami? Do you need me to come down there once I finish here?"

"No. You have all those interviews set up in California next week. After two different degrees, you need to find a job to help pay for your debt. I know you have to have a ton."

"You're more important. I'm here for you, Everly. I don't want you to go through this alone."

Here was the moment. Did she continue to lie to her family? "I'm not alone."

His playful tone of voice returned. "Ah, yes, the hot, English handyman. Did he follow you to Miami? Let me know the moment that one steps out of line. I'll come and handle it. I don't want to miss my opportunity again."

"Finnian is great, Cade. Besides, I need to learn to handle things myself." She'd hidden from the world and herself long enough.

"Just be like Nora and never back down. Hey, we should put that on a shirt or something." Her mom's voice yelled in the background, and Cade groaned. "There's the warden. I gotta go. Give me a call when you get back home. Let me know how it goes."

"I will."

"Oh, what happens to the condo now?"

That part was still hard to comprehend. "I own it."

"Sweet! Just mail me my set of keys. Oh, kick the mistress out first, though. Love ya. Bye." He hung up before she started laughing. Oh, Miami wouldn't know what hit them if she let Cade loose in this city.

FINNIAN LISTENED to Everly's laughter. He leaned against the kitchen counter, sipping his coffee and watching the small white crests of waves roll into the shore. Cade had called her based on the ringtone he'd heard a few minutes ago from the bedroom.

He squeezed his eyes shut against the light from the sunrise that distorted his vision. He welcomed the burn from not sleeping. Unrelenting reminders of his past pounded into him. Mainly, their upcoming visit to John Harriman and exposing Everly to Charles's history.

Finnian made the connection between Harriman and Charles yesterday. Harriman's relationship to a Miami-based mafia helped him miss jail time twice, thanks to a crooked judge who dismissed several racketeering charges. He might not work directly for the family any more, but it was too close.

Finnian was delivering Everly right to him.

Talking her out of the meeting seemed pointless. She wanted and deserved answers. It didn't negate the fact that someone was out there, after them, and he didn't know who. That made protecting her challenging when she wouldn't stay hidden.

Going to the police was the logical option, but what could they do? They didn't even believe them the last time.

Finnian heard the murmur of her voice through the door, followed by her laughter. He had to find a way to secure her happiness. But he needed more time to figure out who was behind it. Involving the police might escalate the problem before he found a solution. He couldn't screw up if John Harriman's family was involved. How far would Lorenzo and Ray go?

Sean. Every decision he made circled back around to that one person. He sipped at his coffee again, not tasting the hot, bitter liquid. A similar organization of men took Sean's life away at sixteen once they found out the police were involved.

The kid wanted a better life, and Finnian let him down.

He frowned at the coffee in his cup.

And, again, he was taking Everly to meet a member of organized crime.

Idiot. He rubbed his hands over his face.

The door to the bedroom opened. Everly stepped out, purse in hand, looking beautiful as usual as she walked to the kitchen. Her light blue tank top flowed around her and matched her eyes.

"Are you okay?" She set her purse down and reached for a coffee cup. "You looked ready to fight just now. Are you mad at the coffee or the world?"

He took her cup and poured the coffee for her. The underlying danger of meeting Harriman forced Finnian to make his mind up about one thing.

Her teeth tugged at her bottom lip as her forehead wrinkled in concern. "What's wrong, Finnian? I want the truth."

Everything. A future without Everly was impossible. Only one option remained. Without a doubt, he'd protect her with his life.

EVERLY REACHED for the coffee he'd poured, but Finnian set it out of her reach. Was he playing keep-away for fun? His serious mood kept her from making the joke. Had she done something wrong? He'd been sweet all night. What had changed?

"You're making me nervous. Say something."

He looked worried. After his comments yesterday, he clearly didn't want her going, but this entire situation revolved around what they'd find out today. She needed answers.

Everly set her hand on Finnian's chest as he stepped to

her. His heart pounded rapidly under her palm.

With one finger and a subtle touch, he tilted her chin up.

Memories from yesterday spiked her blood better than any cup of coffee. Finnian's charm that usually sent butterflies dancing in her stomach didn't hold a candle to this intensity he watched her with now.

He licked his lips.

Oh God, did her legs almost give out?

"We should talk about this." Everly's whispered statement didn't stop his advancement, however slow he went.

"We will. Later." His harsh voice tingled up her spine.

He brushed his lips over hers before settling as if they belonged there.

He did. The taste of coffee was still warm on his tongue. Kiss after kiss, slow and controlled, pulled her further away from reality. From their struggles.

She guided her hand down his chest, over the soft, cotton T-shirt and abs, to rest on his belt buckle. He was her rock throughout this entire ordeal. She'd trusted him last night, and she wanted to do the same today.

But this wasn't like yesterday's explosion. She had time to think and consider the risks. Her hip bumped into the countertop. In an easy motion, he sat her up on the counter, stepping between her legs, never breaking the kiss.

Finnian glided his hands over her bare thighs to the edge of her shorts, his thumbs trailing high enough her breath caught in her throat.

"A little morning sexy time."

Everly scrambled off the counter, smiling at whatever Finnian muttered in French.

In her neon blue bathing suit with a sarong in a matching color tied around her hips, Claudia didn't look fazed by walking in on them kissing. "I like it. Very outside the box, I assume, for Miss Apple Pie. You struck me as a lights-off, one-position kinda woman."

Everly's face warmed.

Finnian stepped away. "Jealousy isn't a pretty color on you, Claudia. We'll be back later. The cab should be waiting downstairs by now."

Claudia sent him an air kiss.

Finnian mumbled something under his breath and motioned to the door.

Everly left ahead of him, a small part of her wishing for the coffee he'd poured. Her morning coffee would have to wait. The less she saw of Claudia, the better.

But something was on Finnian's mind. For most of the ride, he stared out of the window of the cab, one hand resting on Everly's knee, his lips pressed together in a tight line. No explanation of the kiss or his foul mood. He simply gave the driver the address, and off they went, remaining silent for the fifteen-minute ride.

The sunlight glinted off the chrome sign hanging over the door to the small office.

JOHN HARRIMAN, LEGAL SERVICES AND REGISTERED AGENT

Fancy office for a man with no professional license. He wasn't a lawyer, a CPA, or an actuary. Only a guy that understood paperwork and probably charged outrageous fees to the unsuspecting public. Why had Charles used him?

Finnian tried the door with a hard jerk. The metal clanged, but it didn't open. He looked across the street behind them. She'd seen that look before. Why did he think they were in danger? Was that his problem? He'd asked her yesterday not to come to the visit, but she'd blown him off.

Everly touched his lower back, feeling the lump of his gun underneath his untucked shirt. "What is it? What's wrong?"

He lifted a shoulder as he turned back around. "You know I didn't want to bring you here."

"I know, but why?"

"Your safety. Look. There's someone coming."

Everly studied Finnian another moment. "It'll be alright."

He grunted in response.

The deadbolt unlocked with a loud click. "Yes?" A thin guy in a dark burgundy suit opened the door a fraction of an inch. "Can I help you?"

He'd dismissed Everly with a mere glance. Not that she blamed him. Finnian commanded everyone's attention when those deadly vibes rolled off of him.

"John Harriman," Finnian said as a statement, not a question. How well did he know him?

John watched Finnian another second before he nodded. "You look familiar." John opened the door fully. "That may or may not be a good thing in my profession."

"That depends entirely on you." Finnian's lethal tone of voice sent a chill through Everly. Charm or strength. Those were the only two ways Finnian used to get what he wanted. She should have asked him more about John Harriman, so she understood the history. It meant something if he reverted to intimidation tactics immediately.

John's mouth twisted into something similar to a sneer. "Now, I remember you. You're that English bodyguard for Clarke and Wellington. Without them here, I can't discuss any of their business ventures with you." He started to close the door, but Finnian blocked it with an arm.

It had to hurt, to have the metal door close on his

forearm, but his face didn't reveal anything. "I wouldn't do that."

John pushed again.

Finnian's forearm muscles jumped. Again, he didn't budge. "I'm not here for them."

"Are you needing my services for yourself?" John asked, still squishing Finnian's arm in the door.

Finnian jerked his head. "This is Everly Clarke."

John's eyes shifted between Finnian and Everly. With a subtle nod of his head, he released the door and walked back to his desk.

Finnian stepped to the side and motioned Everly in first.

She ran a hand over his forearm, red from the door, before interlacing her hand with his and stepping into the small office.

The smell of freesia hit her hard, sickening her stomach. The culprit was a candle burning on a nearby shelf. How could the man stand it? It smelled like a funeral parlor.

Finnian squeezed her hand, tugging her forward as she stalled in the middle of the floor. "I'm here. Don't worry," he said, his voice barely audible. The only thing he could do for her right then was open a window.

"So, you're the famous Everly Clarke." John pulled out the high-back leather chair and sat. "I hadn't heard from Tripp since Charles's death, so I wasn't sure if you were aware of the trust." John linked his hands behind his head as he leaned back in the chair. "I was going to reach out to you once everything settled down."

Really? Seemed like a lame excuse since he'd died six months ago. "I'm sure you did. I had a couple of questions. Charles didn't discuss the trust with me."

"Yes. He told me you'd find out at his death."

That part came true. Now for the *why*. "Do you know why he didn't just leave the condo to me in his will?"

John sucked his teeth, shaking his head. "Charles never elaborated on why he wanted to shift legal ownership of the condo. I'm sure Tripp already told you that they owned the condo fifty-fifty. Until last March."

"Of course," Everly replied, even though Tripp hadn't said a damn word about anything.

"What happened last March?" Finnian asked.

John smirked. "Charles came in with new ownership papers to the condo. I figured it was because of Claudia. Wanted to make sure she was taken care of and nobody really trusts Tripp."

"You know about Claudia?" The question escaped before Everly could clamp her mouth shut.

"Yes." He looked at Finnian as if he shared some special male secret. "Everyone knows Claudia. Speaking of the past, have you seen Little Ray lately?"

Finnian sat back but didn't take his eyes off John. "No." The tips of Finnian's ears turned pink. What was the story between him and these people that he hadn't told her? She hated the secrets.

John sucked at his front teeth again. "Ray was a little put out how everything ended between him and your employers."

"I know. I was paid to protect them."

Everly crossed her legs and arms, hoping her "what-the-hell" look stayed off her face.

"Yes." John nodded. "But Ray thinks he's entitled to revenge. Lorenzo called him off before he jumped on a plane to Atlanta after you guys."

Finnian's hand covered hers. She'd twisted her fingers in the bottom seam of her shirt. He didn't look away from John but kept his hand firmly in place. She relaxed a fraction with his touch.

"So, Ray hasn't left Miami?" Finnian asked.

"Not that I'm aware of."

Finnian squeezed Everly's hand before dropping it.

Everly smiled at John, wanting to get back on topic. "Did Charles do anything else with the trust? Put any other properties in it? We found the bank account already."

John studied Finnian a moment longer before turning to Everly. "He asked several questions about the transfer of stock and keeping it from entering into his estate. At the time, I assumed he didn't want you to inherit ATL and it would all go to Claudia, including the condo and the stock. I gave him the paperwork to fill out for his half of ATL. A week later, I received the information to change it to the Everly Clarke Family Trust, and all of the ownership of the condo. It was a little bit of a shock." John's serious tone surprised her. "A week after that, he died."

"And what happened to his half of ATL?" Finnian asked.

John shifted in his seat. "I'm unaware of what happened to the stock. He never brought that up to me."

Everly sat back, crossing her legs. The main question buzzing in her brain was how had Charles timed it all so well? He managed to get the condo into a trust only a week before his death.

The information Tripp provided her stated he'd died in a car accident. If what Finnian said was true of his partying down here, which she had no reason to distrust him, maybe the drugs had caused some type of heart attack. Everly hadn't questioned anything at the time, her emotions so mixed between grief and disappointment. They hadn't resolved their own relationship, one way or another before they'd lost the chance.

"You don't have any idea what else is in the trust?" Finnian held that same ready-to-fight look on his face since they'd walked into John's office. Every tense muscle in Finnian's shoulders jumped as John stood and walked to a file cabinet.

Flicking through hanging files, John pulled out a thin folder. "No, I don't. Since a family member"—his eyes darted to Finnian for a brief moment—"referred Charles to me, his activities may not be of the highest moral standard." He sat down and slid the folder to her. "But in this instance, all I have is the condo. These are the legal documents on the trust."

So far, nothing Charles had done appeared to have any moral standards.

"Do you think Lorenzo would know more about what Charles did?" Finnian's question hung in the air as John resumed his position in the chair with his hands behind his head and leaned back.

"Possibly. You run the risk of meeting Ray." He grinned, showing two rows of obscenely white teeth. "Or his fists. I'd stay away if I were you."

Good idea. Finnian didn't need to get hurt on her account. Everly sat up straighter. "There's no reason for you to go and get in a fight over something Charles did. I should be the one to talk to them."

Finnian answered "no" as John laughed softly.

"Listen, doll, there's a reason I'm not involved with the family business anymore. I'd suggest you keep clear. They still consider what Charles did a punishable offense, even after he's dead. I'd hate to see it taken out on you."

Everly opened the file, wishing it had all the answers. "But I won't let them take it out on Finnian."

"They have their own beef with Finnian."

Finnian ran a hand over his hair. "We can talk about this later, Everly."

"But—"

"Later." The quiet command overrode Everly's newfound determination to avoid being a doormat. Even Nora would bite her tongue to get what she wanted later, and Everly wanted answers before he met with Lorenzo or whatever the man's name was.

"Too bad Charles didn't listen to you as well as his wife does. You might not have had to save his ass so many times."

"Charles didn't listen to anyone but himself," Finnian said.

"And Tripp. He always listened to Tripp." John tapped the file. "I think our meeting is over."

Everly closed the folder. She'd have to open it once their vague conversation wasn't a distraction.

There was one more thing she needed to ask. "If you set up the trust, then do you have the trust document?"

John pointed to the file in her lap. "It's in there. I charge a fee, of course, for managing the trust. You don't have a thing to worry about." He smiled in a placating way that burned Everly up. He wouldn't be the first man to underestimate her business intelligence. A fee for what?

"How exactly did you manage it? I was never notified of the trust's existence. You let the trust's only asset slip into foreclosure. There's more than enough funds to cover the mortgage." Everly flipped open the file. Right there, John Harriman was listed as the Trust Manager in charge of handling the assets.

"I, ah, well—"

"You haven't done a damn thing, have you?" Everly huffed and flipped to the next page. "How are you drawing money from the account for your fees? How did you happen to pay yourself money but failed to make a payment on the condo?"

He wiped his hands on his pants, his eyes shifting to Finnian. "When Charles set up the account, he provided a checkbook in the trust's name."

"I want the checkbook. You're no longer the manager." Everly stood and held out her hand.

"You need to rethink that decision." His smile looked a little crazed. "Before you make the same mistakes Charles did."

Finnian's chair fell over backward as he leaned across the desk, wrapping John's tie around his fist twice before hauling him partway out of the chair.

John's eyes bugged out either from fear or lack of oxygen the longer Finnian held him up.

"Do not threaten her. If she wants you gone, then you're gone. I'll make sure of it. Hand over the checkbook."

"My fees," he croaked out as he fumbled for the drawer. Finnian shoved him back into his chair. John gasped for breath as he found the checkbook and tossed it across the desk. "I'm still entitled to my fees."

Everly picked it up, thumbing through the carbon check copies remaining in the book. Every check was written to himself. "Over two-hundred thousand dollars! You've paid yourself a hefty commission over six months. For what?" She stepped to the edge of the desk. "You've done nothing but steal money. First from Charles and now from me." She slapped her hand down on his desk as her outrage gained traction. "You stuck a fancy sign outside your office and pretended to know what the hell you're doing, but you don't. Anyone with half a brain could make a payment on a mortgage and prevent foreclosure. Unless you want the FBI to start prying into your personal activities, I suggest you nicely agree to stop having anything to do with this trust or me." Everly drew herself up straight. "Or else you'll hear from my lawyer." Hopefully, poor Mr. Randolf was up for the job.

John rose, oddly calm after all his earlier bluster, and motioned at the door. "I look forward to it."

She was more than ready to leave. "One more thing." Everly turned back. "Be sure to include that income on your tax return this year. You wouldn't want a second visit from the government." She held up the checkbook. "I'm sure the IRS would be very interested in a lowlife like you." She strode out ahead of Finnian and turned on the sidewalk, heading in the direction of the mortgage lender a few blocks down. John Harriman should be thrown in jail for fraud. Her jaw hurt from grinding her teeth together. She wiggled it to release the tension.

Finnian caught up to her. "That was a lot of fancy talk back there."

"You threaten him your way, I'll threaten him mine." She pulled out her phone. While the trust document still showed John as manager of the assets, he had full access to the bank account and could take legal action on the condo.

She stopped at a crosswalk, waiting on the light to change. Finnian began to massage her shoulders, her eyes slowly drifting closed until Mr. Randolf answered.

"Mr. Randolf? Everly Clarke. I just met with the lying, underhanded trust manager." Finnian nudged her to walk when the light changed. He took her hand, and she let him direct her down the sidewalk, weaving in and out of people.

"Oh, really?" Mr. Randolf laughed lightly. "Judging by your tone, it didn't go too well."

"No." Everly sighed. "It didn't. The man's a thief. Please

tell me you handle trusts and understand what I need to do next."

"No, I don't. But I will advise you against using the first lawyer you find. Trust law is a rather lucrative business when most arrangements are straightforward."

Back to the beginning. "Alright. Thanks."

"Let me know what you decide."

"I will." She hung up. Managing the trust, for one condo, wasn't the issue. She could do that just fine, but editing the legal documents worried her. After everything they'd been through, she didn't want any hiccups and for John Harriman to remain the manager. She needed to change the bank account immediately before he tried to get any more money from it.

Finnian stopped in front of the mortgage office. "This is it." He shifted on his feet, his confidence wavering. Why the flip from anger to insecurity?

She laid her hand on his shoulder. "What's wrong? The truth this time."

"I had an idea." His brown eyes reflected the midmorning sun, highlighting a thin outline of gold. "But I'm not sure how you'll take it."

Trying for a joke, she smiled. "Did you want to volunteer to be the trust manager?"

He grimaced.

"Oh, Finnian, I'm sorry. I didn't mean . . ." She hadn't meant to hurt his feelings.

"No, I don't want to be the manager. But my brother could help you. The only thing is . . ." He narrowed his eyes and looked over her head. "If he assisted you with the documents, even after this situation has settled down, we might be, you know, in contact with each other."

So that was it. He didn't want her to feel trapped. Or was

he worried about being trapped? She needed to stop reading into everything. He offered for his brother to help. She should at least hear him out. A future without Finnian had become hard to imagine, even after only a week.

She linked her hand with his. "Which brother?"

"Brady. He's a lawyer in London."

"Does he deal with trusts?"

Finnian shrugged like a little kid. "He handles contracts all over the world. I don't know about trusts, but I know he wouldn't lie to you. Or steal. He's quite the straitlaced lawyer type. Couldn't wait to get away from the country and the farm. He studied at Cambridge. Will it matter if he's in England?"

Everly bit her lip. "It might. But even if he couldn't be the trustee, I'd like some advice. I'd rather take his suggestion than walk into some random office. You've seen the contacts in my phone. I don't have very many people on that list."

Finnian cradled her head, pressing a kiss to her forehead. "You have me."

She did. And she had confidence in his brother if he did. "Do you mind calling him and asking? Maybe I can call him once we're back in Atlanta and everything settles down." Would it ever settle down?

He pulled out his phone. "I can call him now while you handle the foreclosure." Making a big display of peeking in the window, he lowered his voice. "I don't see any need for me."

"No need for the muscle." She squeezed his bicep. He grinned down at her, happy with his title even though the anxiety, or was it anger, still flowed just underneath his skin.

"I'll stand out here and be your muscle." He tried to give her his charming smile. "You go be the brains."

11

_____

Everly held up the bathing suit she'd purchased on a whim on their walk back from the bank. They'd passed one of those souvenir shops that half the inventory is spilling onto the sidewalk. Thinking she'd buy something silly for Cade, she'd stepped into the store.

Finnian cleared his throat from the doorway. "I know you're against the ocean, but they have a rooftop pool. We can go if you'd like. Might help you relax."

She glanced at the window. "It's nearly dark."

He smirked. "People swim at night. The pool has lights."

"Do you have a suit?"

"Yes." A shred of excitement lit his eyes. "Are we going, then?"

She held up the yellow bikini top. "As long as you promise not to compare me to Claudia."

"If you're wearing that, there's not another female I'll be thinking about. I promise you. Get changed, darling. I'll be right back."

She walked to the bathroom, avoided the mirror, and slipped into the yellow bikini. After the past months spent in isolation, the exposure of wearing nothing but a swimsuit in front of someone should have wrecked her. It didn't. This was Finnian. She twisted in the mirror. Would he think she looked sexy? Would he want to touch her?

She pulled her hair down from her ponytail, shaking it out. "That looks like crap." She brushed it out, somehow making it even flatter against her head and highlighting the uneven ends from her at-home haircut.

Screw it. She pulled it back into a ponytail. She slipped into a pair of shorts and left her room, refusing to overanalyze herself any longer.

He held two towels in one hand and wore a bright blue and red swimsuit without a shirt. He slowly flipped through the pages of the trust folder.

"Find anything interesting?"

He continued to stare down at the paper in his hand, a line of concern between his brows. "Maybe."

"What is it?" Had he found a clue to Charles's purpose behind this stupid trust? "We don't have to go swim—"

He flipped the folder closed and barked out a laugh. "No way I'm letting this shit get in the way of a swim with you, darling." He looked up, his eyes darkening as he ran his gaze down her body. His throat moved as he swallowed. "Let's go."

"It's been nearly three years since I swam." Everly followed him into the elevator. "Don't let me drown."

"Oh, I won't." He draped a heavy arm across her shoulders. "You stay with me."

She wrapped a hand around his waist, enjoying the smooth muscle under her fingers. His body held so much power that she loved. That strength had saved her. Hopefully, that was the last time he'd have to risk anything for her.

The pool area was empty. Everly exhaled as Finnian set the towels on the bench near the shallow end of the pool. No one to judge her. No one to watch her.

Except him.

He waited patiently by the steps, looking out over the Miami skyline. "I've never enjoyed being down here, but it is pretty all lit up at night."

It was nearly full dark now. The pool, bright green from the underwater lights, cast a strange glow across Finnian's body.

With a huff and a lot of determination, she pulled off her shorts and haphazardly threw them on the same bench as the towels.

She crossed the pool deck and stepped onto the first step.

Finnian didn't follow. He watched her enter the rest of the way alone. She closed her eyes, taking in each detail of the moment, grounding herself instead of giving over to her anxiety.

The warm water caressed her skin one inch at a time until she stood waist deep. The smell of chlorine overtook the faint scent of the ocean. Music played in the distance, a mix of a live band and various car stereos.

She opened her eyes and turned. "This feels amazing. Are you getting in?"

He nodded. "Eventually. Just admiring you."

"There's nothing—"

"Stop." He walked down the steps and through the shallow end. "You aren't allowed to tell me what I see." He met her in the middle of the pool, pausing a few inches away. "I don't believe you have any idea how gorgeous you are, Everly."

"I still like the way you say my name." His accent made her sound unique.

Finnian touched her waist, his hand warmer than the water. "You look like the Lady of the Lake." His fingers skimmed underneath the edge of her bikini bottoms. "Not sure she wore a yellow swimsuit."

Everly raised her eyebrows as he glided his hands up the side of her ribcage. "I was going to suggest a round of Marco Polo." Her breath caught when he brushed his thumbs over her breasts. "You don't seem to be in the mood for that."

"Not at the moment, no." He walked her backward, the water getting deeper until it covered her chest. Without effort, he picked her up.

She wrapped her legs around his waist. The depth of the deep end stopped at Finnian's shoulders. "Hold your breath." He dunked them both under the water for a moment before reemerging.

She wiped the water from her face and pushed back her hair. "That feels great."

His shifted his hands, cupping her face with one and her bottom with the other. The intimacy of his hands on her body pushed her into initiating a kiss. That sexual energy needed an outlet.

He kissed her back. Slow, languid kisses that did their job in scrambling her brain. She held onto his shoulders, her body pressed against his, thinking of the dozens of reasons they shouldn't go any further.

But she had a dozen reasons why she wanted to experience this with him.

"You're beautiful," he said as his hand left her face and trailed down her neck. After a slight hesitation, he continued, caressing her breast, a throaty moan punctuating his movement. "Perfect."

She arched into his hand, not realizing it until cool water rushed between their bodies.

He swapped hands, the other molding over her breast while holding her up with the other. "The feel of you has stayed in my mind since last night."

Her body flared to life with the same memory.

The concrete and tile wall pressed gently against her back, his body weight pinning her there.

He moved both hands to her chest.

Her body bowed back on its own, breaking the kiss. Her thighs tightened, keeping their bodies anchored together.

Finnian studied her before trailing his focus to her breasts, hidden underneath the water. Mostly.

His fingers ran down the middle of her swimsuit, expertly parting the triangle cups to either side.

Her eyes flicked to the entrance of the pool area, relaxing when she realized Finnian's back would block anything someone might see.

He didn't seem to care about their location as he lifted her up slightly from the water as his mouth closed over one breast.

"Finnian!" His name was the only thing her foggy mind could say.

Finnian chuckled. "I love the way you say my name." He kissed the side of her breast. "I love the way you feel in my arms." He slipped a finger underneath the back edge of her bikini, tracing the curve of her bottom before pausing.

She stiffened but didn't pull away.

"I love your body." He lifted her a little, her breasts emerging from the water again.

But he didn't kiss her again.

His dark eyes were even sexier in the lighting. Slowly, he

pushed a finger into her. He pulled out and immediately replaced it with two.

Everly let her head drop back to the concrete edge of the pool as he worked his fingers in and out the same way as last night.

When his mouth returned to her breast, it shot her over the edge. Her body stiffened.

Finnian murmured something before dragging her back to him, his mouth crushing against hers.

She didn't know how long he kissed her, but she was wiggling against him, wanting that same release again.

And again.

And more.

"Let's go back," she managed in between his next deep kiss.

In a half-second, he'd slid her top back together, picked her up by the waist, and sat her out of the pool.

She laughed. "I'll take that as a yes?"

He hauled himself out next. "Hell, yes." He tugged her to her feet before hauling her up and over his shoulder.

She squealed and kicked her feet. "Put me down!"

He smacked her butt, his wet hand loud against her skin. "I'll toss you back in the pool if you don't stop wiggling."

"I doubt that." She held onto his shoulders as he set her down next to the bench with their towels. "That would prolong the trip back downstairs, and I might change my mind."

"You've always the right to change your mind, darling." He caught her around the waist, capturing her lips with his again. His hand snaked up her ribcage, but she pushed it down and stepped back. "And I'll be right there to persuade you once again until you tell me to sod off."

"No need to make the extra effort. My mind is made up.

Downstairs." She threw a towel at him and wrapped one around herself, grabbing her shorts as they walked back to the elevator.

Everly maintained her distance in the elevator. The way Finnian stared at her was enough to keep her ready and wishing they were in the privacy of a bedroom.

They opened the door to the condo. Claudia, luckily, was still gone.

He scooped Everly up into his arms and took long strides to her bedroom, kicking the door closed behind him before depositing her on the bed.

Finnian gripped the towel, still partway covering her body, and jerked it away.

She laughed. "We don't have anywhere to go. You can slow down."

He glanced at the clock on the nightstand. "Right."

HE'D LIED. He did have somewhere to go. Later. Right then, Everly in that tiny, yellow bikini was laid out before him, and he had a serious decision to make on how to get her out of it.

"How much do you like this bathing suit?"

Her eyebrows pulled down. "Why?"

"Because ripping it from your body is my first option." Hell, that sounded like fun. He reached down.

Her eyes widened. "Just wait a second." She kneeled on the bed and lifted up her arms. "Just pull it off. Don't tear anything. I like it."

He did as she asked, dragging the string and fabric up over her head.

She reached down, touching him over his wet swim shorts. "But that means you need to take these off."

"I think I like you bossy." He pulled his wet shorts off before tugging her bikini bottoms down to her knees. "But now's not the time. Lie down, darling."

A flicker of insecurity in her eyes as her head touched the pillow pushed him into action. Finnian could sit back and admire her all damn day, but that obviously made her uncomfortable. He covered her body with his, kissing his way from her ribcage to her lips. She smelled like the pool chemicals except for that faint scent of apples from her pillows.

God created perfection in Everly. Smooth, creamy, soft skin covered her body. He ran a hand from her ankle to her hip, along the curve of her waist, to cup her breast, finally exhaling a long breath.

Finnian kissed her throat, chest, and stomach, wanting to give her more pleasure before taking his own. He'd never questioned his own virility when it came to the bedroom, but watching Everly's climax in the pool, and now his first taste, would push any man to the limit.

But it was worth the torture. With their lives on the line and everything so chaotic, he wasn't going to leave a shred of her wants, or his needs, unfulfilled tonight.

She fisted her hands in the sheets as another orgasm ran through her body. "Finnian!"

He could listen to her voice saying his name for the rest of his life. If only she'd consider forever as an option.

When she relaxed back, drained and satisfied, he reached to the side, pulling a condom out of the side table.

Everly cocked her head back to see what he did. "When did you put those in there?"

"When you changed in the bathroom earlier."

Her eyes widened. "That was optimistic."

"I like being prepared and always plan for a favorable outcome." He fell back on top of her, the sound of her laughter making him smile. He sat the condom to the side. "And this is the best outcome there is." He kissed her mouth, his hands touching her everywhere until her body wrapped around his and her breathing signaled another orgasm.

He held his bodyweight up on his forearms, her legs intertwined with his, as he touched her body until she stiffened beneath him. She was so receptive. Sensitive.

"I feel like a limp noodle." She kissed from his shoulder to his ear. "But that was amazing."

"I'm not done, yet." He rolled over, dragging her on top of him. He nudged her hips back until a small smile curled her lips. She sat up, taking him in with one fluid motion.

His eyes closed on their own as his body shuddered at the feeling of her. Everly. No one but her made him feel this way.

Her body moved. His eyes flew open with the sensation, gaze locking with hers.

She rolled her hips again, a moan escaping her lips as they parted. He could watch her all day long. And she seemed inclined to let him.

For now, this body, this woman, was his as he was hers. Their future wasn't a given, not with the threats circling around them, with his own past still yet to come to light, but right then, he saw nothing but the two of them.

She threw her head back, her body tightening. He finally let himself go. Sex would never be the same.

He caught her weight as she fell forward.

Both of them were "limp noodles," as she'd called it earlier. And he loved the feeling. More so, he loved the feeling of Everly laid out across his body.

Finnian brought her fingertips to his lips and kissed them. "You're incredible."

Everly rested her chin on his chest. "That was nothing compared to all those things you just did."

He jack-knifed up, picking her up into his arms, and sweeping back the covers before laying her back down. He kissed her forehead. "I wasn't talking about sex."

"Oh," she murmured as he pulled the white comforter over her body. He walked to the bathroom and cleaned up, returning as quickly as possible to find her asleep.

Quietly, he set his phone alarm to vibrate and placed it underneath his pillow. He had a little time to stay in bed, hold her, but he couldn't risk falling asleep.

She rolled to him. She rested a leg over his thigh, nestling her cheek where his shoulder met his chest as if that one spot were created just for her.

"Thank you," she mumbled. The streetlights and restaurants along A1A brought in enough light to see her sleepy smile.

"Thank you, too." He sighed, needing to tell her so much more about the situation than he was ready to. But he could give her this. "You know how much I care for you, right? I realize that's crazy, having only known you a few days, but I'm serious."

Her body relaxed. "I know." She kissed his shoulder. "Me, too."

And that's why he'd leave tonight. He had to risk it to find out the truth for her. "I'm going to protect you. No matter what." He pressed his lips against her temple. "You've had a day of it. Get some sleep, darling."

"You, too."

Not yet.

12

Finnian stepped out of the cab in a section of town known as The Docks a little after midnight. The first three cabs had refused to take him to this side of town. The last driver, now lighting a cigarette, hadn't seemed fazed.

The danger didn't lurk in the light or in front of his face. Guards hid in shadows or on the roof. Closed-circuit video cameras captured his every move. Any time the members of Agosti Mafia saw him as a threat, his life would be over. He'd been in those shadows before. Watched through the cameras. His undercover work had prepared him better than an average person. Still, he didn't have the backup or authority he wanted when facing a group of men like this.

He kept his arms loose, hanging by his side. He wouldn't give anyone a legitimate reason to shoot him, not that any of these men needed another reason after what'd happened with Ray. He headed toward the unmarked metal building.

Eddie and Donavon guarded the steel door at the edge of the warehouse. Both were the same height as Finnian, although they had him by at least fifty pounds. Italian cooking agreed with these men.

If Lorenzo Agosti was involved with Charles or the men trying to attack Everly, the police were pointless. Sean's memory pressed down on him. Finnian had been the police in a similar situation, and he still hadn't been able to save the kid.

He blinked. *Focus.* He was useless to Everly dead, and Sean's memory was a distraction.

"I'm here to see Lorenzo." He held up his hands and turned around. Eddie patted him, pulling Finnian's cell phone out of his pocket.

"He's clear," Donavon called into a wrist microphone. The door opened. "Nice to see you. Can't say you'll leave in one piece, though. Ray's obsession with kicking your ass hasn't lessened since you've been gone."

"Oh, I'll leave in one piece." Finnian cocked a smile at the two men. "I might be a little sore and bloodied, but I suspect all the bits and pieces will be there."

Six more men guarded the inner rooms. A woman dressed in a short, red sequined dress blew him a kiss as he passed. A prostitute. Nothing more than sideline business for Lorenzo.

The dark hallway opened into a large room. Finnian's boots echoed on the concrete floor. His heartrate remained steady. He'd survive with a clear head.

Kyle, another guard posted near Lorenzo's office, looked Finnian up and down before nodding his head in greeting. They knew him here. Because of Charles's activities, they'd had to deal with Finnian, back when he was allowed to carry a gun.

Carrying one now was pointless. They'd shoot the second he reached for it.

He walked into Lorenzo's office. It was eerily similar to the one that he'd left Sean in that night. And like usual, the gut-wrenching memory of the gunshot that ended his life reemerged. That 'Boss' had surrounded himself with men willing to steal, cheat, and die for him. If only Finnian had stayed and fought or grabbed Sean on his way by, it might have ended differently. He'd been so close to getting the kid out.

But those regrets didn't have room here. All the people in Lorenzo's office were adults who were aware and capable of choosing this life for themselves. At sixteen, born to a prostitute, Sean never had a choice.

"Englishman!" Lorenzo laughed and motioned away the woman lounging on his desk. She wore the same red sequin dress as the first woman. "I didn't expect to see you again with Charles gone and Tripp no longer on speaking terms with me."

"I just couldn't stay away." Finnian shook hands with him.

A side door slammed open, hitting the concrete wall with a loud bang.

Ray headed right toward Finnian. "I saw you come in."

Here it came. Finnian's stomach tightened as Ray's fist pounded into his gut.

Finnian took it. As soon as he fought back, the men around them would draw their guns. Showing aggression lowered his chance of leaving alive. Or in one piece. That meant leaving Everly alone to deal with these guys herself.

Another punch jabbed into his ribcage. He grunted, gritting his teeth together. These were the consequences of showing his face here again. He'd take the beating. Lorenzo was the only person who could tell him about Charles.

He had to find a way to get Everly out of this situation before she got hurt.

He'd risk a few broken bones for her.

Ray shook out his hand. "It's like punching a damn brick wall." The men around him laughed.

Finnian attempted a smile as he straightened to his full height, although his stomach ached deep from the impact. His bruised ribs screamed in protest at the movement.

"I'll take the compliment."

Ray punched him across the jaw.

Finnian kept his footing. His neck twisted and cracked with the impact.

Bloody hell, that one hurt.

He tested his jaw. Still moving. It might not in the morning, but it wasn't dislocated. Ray barely reached Finnian's shoulders, but sharp, defined muscle covered his wiry frame.

"That's enough for now, Ray. Take a seat, Hayes." Lorenzo motioned him to sit across the table. Finnian considered walking sideways to avoid turning his back on Ray. Keeping his eyes trained on Lorenzo, he made it two steps before Ray landed a kidney shot to his lower back.

Shit. Finnian stumbled into the chair.

"We hadn't heard you were back in town. Where are you staying?" Lorenzo asked.

No use in lying. "At the condo."

"With Claudia? First, Charles steals her, and now you're sleeping with her?" Ray paced behind the chair. "I knew it." He popped the side of Finnian's head. "You took her for yourself."

Finnian held his ground as pain radiated into his temple. Pummeling his fists into Ray wasn't an option. His soft olive skin would end up covered black and blue if Finnian had any chance to get away with it. Someday, he'd get his moment. With Everly's life on the line, now wasn't the time.

"I'm not sleeping with Claudia. She lives in the condo that belonged to Charles, and I'm staying there for now."

"And you expect me to believe you aren't screwing Claudia?"

Lorenzo waved his son away to the side. "Who the hell cares? Why are you here, Finnian?"

"I'm in Miami with Everly Clarke. She's Charles's widow."

"And you're both staying with Claudia?" Lorenzo chuckled. "I can't believe Claudia let you in the condo. I've always been curious. From what Tripp said, Mrs. Clarke is a mousy little thing. Is that true?"

A third woman, in the same uniformed red sequined dress, stood off to the side. Whether these women were here by choice or by force, he would keep Everly far away from this lifestyle.

"I might not call her mousy." Gorgeous. Beautiful. Finnian nodded toward the woman in red. "She's pretty. Nothing that compares to the women you surround yourself with, Lorenzo."

Lorenzo nodded, his interest in Everly obviously casual. "I still don't know how you convinced Claudia to let you use the condo."

"She didn't have a choice. Mrs. Clarke owns the condo."

The room fell into silence. Ray and Lorenzo's eyes flicked toward each other, then back at Finnian. He'd kept Everly in the dark about his whereabouts for this very reason. Discussing the condo and Charles put Ray's temperament to the test and Everly's life on the line.

Finnian understood the danger. He'd made one brief call with his brother, Brady, waking him early in the morning in London to ensure he would take care of Everly's safety. If

Finnian didn't check in by the morning, Miami time, then Brady would arrange for the local FBI to protect her until he could fly over. Did Everly have a passport? Could he get her back to England and away from the immediate danger?

"Is the condo still owned by ATL?" Ray leaned over the desk, the muscles rippling up his sinewy arms. "Does Mrs. Clarke own ATL, now?"

At this point, there was no other way but to admit it. "Charles transferred the condo into a trust fund for Mrs. Clarke."

"What about the stock of ATL? Did he put that in a trust for her as well?"

"We don't know what he did with his half. It wasn't in the will. Tripp doesn't have it, either." Finnian waited while Ray's face turned red. "What does that mean?"

"Damn it." Ray pushed away, pacing the expansive office. "I'm gonna kill him."

Finnian glanced between Ray and Lorenzo. What had he said? "That would be a wasted effort since Charles is already dead."

"Tripp." Ray punched a wall, leaving a splintered hole in the plaster. "This is the second time he's lost my ownership. He'll end up the same way as Clarke if he's not careful. Accidents happen to people who cross me." Ray continued to storm back and forth.

Lorenzo watched his son before studying his own hands, resting on the desk. "You know, Hayes," Lorenzo began. "I don't like dealing with people I can't trust. I don't trust Tripp Wellington."

"I don't blame you. That distrust for Tripp shouldn't extend to me. We've never had any direct business dealings before."

"Why did you visit me? I thought you only took orders from Tripp. I presumed you were here on his business."

Finnian shrugged, hoping to look nonchalant. "Not anymore. I'm looking for answers for Mrs. Clarke. Neither Charles nor Tripp would ever discuss whatever happened here that night of your fight. Or afterward." And maybe he'd find out the "why" behind the trust fund.

"I don't suppose it matters any longer to keep it a secret. Charles owned all of the stock for ATL when he died."

That . . . was new. "All of it? Are you sure?" No wonder Tripp was hellbent on finding out who had it.

"Yes." Lorenzo looked to Ray for a brief moment before refocusing on Finnian. "Tripp failed to make good on some money that he'd guaranteed to us. He claimed that the construction contract's profit margin proved less than anticipated, and we never received our kickback. After delaying several months, he finally offered a small share of the business. We naturally accepted." Lorenzo spun a gold ring around his middle finger. "ATLighting is a highly profitable business. Charles promised that he would make things right. Instead, he took Claudia and, it appears, he gave the company away."

Ray kicked the trashcan, sending a few paper pieces and an empty fast-food cup flying out of the small basket. "Charles told me not to worry, that the stock for ATL would be safe with the only person he trusted. I assumed that was Tripp. And Tripp would either hand over my share or suffer the consequences."

"But Tripp didn't get the stock. Neither did Claudia." The breath rushed out of Finnian's body. "You think it's in the trust?"

Lorenzo cocked a half-smile. "The only person left we know of would be his wife."

Finnian shook his head. Impossible. Everly owned ATLighting? The entire thing? He swallowed, trying to think clearly through the shock. Tripp knew. He had to know. "She was left the condo and that's it. John Harriman said so."

"Since when does anyone believe a damn thing Harriman says? Have you looked through the trust documents to make sure it's not in there?"

"Shit." Finnian let his head drop forward.

What he'd seen earlier . . . that was it.

"Damn it, Charles." That put Everly right in the middle of danger. God, no wonder someone was after her. He'd scanned through the paperwork earlier, while she'd changed for the pool, trying to understand the legal jargon. There was one form, stapled behind some others, that had listed the condo, the bank account, a car, and then, at the bottom, ATLighting Inc.

When Everly entered the kitchen, already nervous about going for a swim, his concern over the paper was lost. Thinking back, it made sense. That had to be what they were looking for.

Shit. And that's what the people hellbent on kidnapping Everly wanted as well.

"Where is Mrs. Clarke now?" Ray crossed his arms as he looked down at Finnian. "We might persuade her to fulfill her obligation."

Finnian shot to his feet, towering over Ray as the sound of guns chambering a round echoed in the room.

"She has nothing to do with anything underhanded you and Charles were involved in. She doesn't even know she owns ATL at this point. Leave her out of this." Finnian had planned to keep his protection over Everly a secret. Too late for that. She was his weakness.

Ray held a hand in the air, and the guns pointed at Finnian lowered. "I don't want any woman that reminds me of Charles Clarke." Ray laughed once. "But, I do want the business."

"No."

"Is that your call to make? You don't own the stock."

It wasn't, but hopefully, Everly would listen to him. "How much did you expect to receive from the contract?"

He cocked his chin out. "One million."

Finnian kept his position as Ray began to circle around him.

Finnian could snap his thin body in two without an effort. He wouldn't pull Everly into this. If she paid him what they were owed, would they leave her alone?

"One question that has plagued me is why did you help Charles steal Claudia from me?"

Ray had considered Claudia his property. She'd worn one of those same red dresses as the other women in the room, but he'd kept her for himself.

Until he'd offered her up in a poker game.

"Charles directed me." Finnian braced himself. "He wanted her out of this situation."

"You make it sound as though Charles loved her."

"He did in his own way."

"No!" Ray stepped away and slammed his fist into Lorenzo's desk. Lorenzo didn't jump from the unexpected impact. He neatly folded his hands in front of him and kept watching the interaction.

Ray rocked back on his heels, his face twisting into rage. "I *loved* Claudia. Everyone knew I was going to win that hand. Until Charles cheated."

Charles had cheated, or so Finnian overheard him

telling Tripp on their ride home. Ray had tossed the card table across the room, refusing to let Claudia leave.

Charles, severely calm, had left without his prize.

Until the next day, when he'd directed Finnian to retrieve Claudia from The Docks. Charles had offered her a way out of her life, and she'd taken it in a heartbeat.

Finnian addressed Lorenzo. "Have you sent anyone after Mrs. Clarke? She's had some rather disturbing situations lately, and that's why I'm here."

"Until now, we didn't know anything about the trust. The only person we've sent to Atlanta is Donnie, my nephew, to keep an eye on Tripp and Ray's interest." Lorenzo rubbed a hand over his chin. "I haven't heard from him in the past couple of weeks."

"Lizard, Donnie's friend, tried to kidnap Everly."

Lorenzo smirked. "Idiot. Tripp knows, obviously, that Mrs. Clarke owns all of ATL." He leaned his head to the side at Finnian's silence. "Doesn't he?"

With the topic finally moved away from Claudia, Finnian eased himself back into the chair. Ray's eyes still held a murderous glare, but he seemed content for the moment.

"No. I don't think he's aware that Everly owns all of it. Not yet, at least. Charles left it completely out of the will. Tripp hired his own lawyer to look into the matter." Which means it wouldn't be too long before he found out.

"Your disloyalty to Tripp surprises me."

That caught Finnian off guard. "Is that really a question? You've met Tripp. He doesn't exactly inspire devotion in a man. I hate to admit it, but money is the only thing that kept me loyal to him in the first place. But now, he's not even worth that."

Lorenzo motioned to the guards around him. "If you've

decided to leave Tripp, remember that we've always a need for someone with your background. I'm curious about infiltrating the English market. Someone with your knowledge would be useful."

A job? After everything that Finnian had seen and done, the man offered him a job. Finnian wanted to find his way back to the right side of the law, not sink further into their underworld.

"I appreciate the offer, but I'm looking at all my options at the moment." There, that sounded like a diplomatic answer. "What do you know of the last few days Charles was alive?"

Lorenzo sat back, his gaze flicking to Ray.

Ray's anger left for a brief moment. "We have our theories on that. It looks like our work, but we didn't order it."

"Work? Didn't he die in an accident at the warehouse? He transferred all his ownership to Everly shortly before he died. I was curious about the timing."

"I say you start by asking Tripp. He'd have the biggest motivation for doing him in."

Finnian looked down at his hands, needing a second to gather his thoughts. Charles murdered? Of course, with all the shit he'd done, all the people pissed off with him, it was a possibility. Still, it was hard to fathom.

Tripp might have many issues, but would he be ruthless enough to kill his partner and best friend? No. He'd never get his hands that dirty.

But did he order it?

He needed more information. "You said you sent Donnie to watch Tripp. Why?"

"I wanted payment." Lorenzo drummed his fingers on the desk. "I didn't care if it came from that project or another, but I wanted my payment. I want either my million or my ownership."

"What if he didn't pay?"

Lorenzo smiled slow and motioned to the men around him.

Then there'd be trouble. "Right. Did Charles know about the money Tripp owed?"

"No," Ray replied. "I didn't deal with Charles in contracting kickbacks. He didn't have Tripp's flair for making deals and getting bids."

Lorenzo leaned to the side and pulled out a bottom drawer. He rummaged around for a moment before he set a folder on the desk. "I can tell you're having a hard time coming to grips with this. Believe me. Charles didn't have an accident. He was killed before he fell."

He flipped it open to colorful 3×5 pictures taken by the police of Charles's body. Finnian didn't have to wonder how Lorenzo would obtain internal police pictures. Half the police department was in his pocket.

"Look how he landed. And right here," Lorenzo said, pointing again. "Hardly any blood. I bet if the body was examined close enough, they'd have found the primary wound."

Finnian rubbed his temples. *Bloody hell.* Everly thought Charles died in a car wreck.

"I don't guess I need to wonder why an investigation wasn't opened."

"Money buys a lot of things, Englishman. At the time, it was a mess for ATL. The CEO died at a worksite from a fall. There's not a doubt in my head that the autopsy would've revealed the primary cause of death. It also would've revealed exactly how many drugs Charles had in his system at the time. Both of which needed to stay out of the news for the sake of the company."

How would Everly take it? At the time, he'd appreciated Tripp's connections to change the entire story for the press release. Now, he regretted the lack of an autopsy.

He'd shown up looking for answers about ATL. How had the big question became *who* killed Charles Clarke? Claudia didn't have much of a motive to kill Charles. He provided her a lifeline to stay off the streets and out of the reach of Ray. Ray had a reason to go after Tripp, but Charles? Would Ray kill Charles over Claudia? Is it the same person going after Everly now? The answers they'd given him only raised more questions.

Lorenzo waved his hand. "That's all I'm gonna say on the subject. The offer still stands to work for us if you're not interested in going back to England."

Finnian rose and shook Lorenzo's hand. "Thanks, but I'm content in Atlanta for now."

Lorenzo tightened his grip and didn't release his hand immediately. "ATL still owes us the million in my book. I'll trust you to give Mrs. Clarke that message on our behalf once she takes over. That'll clear ATL's debt. But I'll give you a heads-up that Novoa has several unsettled deals with ATL. He may be your next visitor."

Carlos Novoa was another incredibly rich lowlife that ran the real estate side of Miami. Finnian sighed. He'd deal with him later. One threat at a time.

"Thank you." Finnian nodded to Ray and left. Three of the men along the far wall moved to follow him out. He glanced back.

Ray followed the group, the sharp edge of murder gleaming in his eyes once again.

At least Finnian *had* hoped to make it out alive.

13

Finnian Hayes left in the middle of the night. The bed shifted with his exit and the soft click of the condo door closing a few minutes afterward confirmed that he hadn't made a quick trip to the restroom. But where had he gone? And without his gun? She hated being out of the loop. He'd asked her to trust him, and she did, but that didn't give him permission to keep her in the dark.

Everly eyed herself in the mirror as she piled her shorter hair on top of her head in her usual haphazard knot. She wasn't sure what they were doing today, so she finally tore the tags off her new clothes and dressed appropriately for Florida weather.

She slowly opened the door and peeked out. The couch looked untouched. The coffee pot sat empty. Did he ever come back?

The door to Claudia's room opened, and she emerged, laughing, with an impossibly short, purple silk robe wrapped around her and leaving nothing to the imagination.

Finnian walked out next.

Everly's stomach sank. She stepped out into the living room, making her presence known.

A towel hung over his shoulder, covering a corner of his bare chest. Claudia bit her lip and touched his shoulder as he laughed.

Oh, he was a double dead man to lead her on this way.

"Everly." His voice, husky from probably having sex with Claudia half the night, amplified her anger. She'd trusted him. She'd slept with him. How could she have been so stupid?

He reached out, but she jumped away.

"Don't you dare touch me." Her voice broke on the last word. "You don't get to sleep with her and then come back to me." She narrowed her eyes toward Claudia. "I didn't work like that with Charles, and I'm not going to work like that with you."

"Oh, honey." Claudia began as she leaned against the edge of the couch. "You've jumped off a tall bridge with that assumption."

Her stomach cramped. She'd gotten ill the first time she'd learned about Claudia and Charles, and her body now threatened a repeat performance. Why didn't she kick the woman out when she first arrived in Miami?

"Everly, darling." He blocked her view of Claudia's pleased smile. "Claudia helped me this morning. That's it. I didn't want you to deal with it."

She leaned to the side to see Claudia again. "Ha! Helping you and every other man that she ensnares."

Finnian glanced over at her. "I'm sorry, Claudia. Thanks again for your help." He laid both hands on Everly's shoulders, trapping her from moving. "Can you give us a moment?"

Claudia winked at Everly. "No problem. I think I'm starting to like the new Miss Apple Pie. She's feisty."

"You seem to think I care!" Everly ended on a shout as the bedroom door shut. She swallowed down the lump in her throat. No tears. She would *not* cry.

"I can't believe you assumed I slept with Claudia." He looked a little hurt. "I wouldn't do that to you. You should know that about me by now."

Everly crossed her arms, staring straight ahead at his chest but not seeing anything. "I would have said the same thing about Charles before he left me for her." Her lower lip started to tremble. She bit it hard.

"You continue to assume that I'm going to let you down each way Charles did. Have I let you down yet?" He paused, his lips pressing together. "Have I?"

"No." Everly snapped out the word. "She's rather pretty when she's not all made up. And anyone who has seen her knows her body is perfect."

He used a finger under Everly's chin to tilt her head up. "And I can confirm that she's slept with half the men in Miami."

"Since when does that matter to a man." As soon as the words left her mouth, she regretted them. Irritation replaced the flash of hurt she'd seen in his eyes.

"It matters to this man. You are the only woman in this condo, in Miami, in the world that I want to be with. Sex or no sex."

Her eyes refocused on his at his declaration. She blinked at what she saw. "Finnian!" A deep blue bruise covered his chin, and a fainter one circled his eye. A few cuts, covered with bandages, spotted down his arms. Butterfly strips taped shut one long gash along his stomach.

She explored his body. "What happened?" His back looked worse, covered in cuts and bruises. Everly ran her finger, as light as possible, along the long, stick-shaped bruise on his lower back. He sucked air in through his teeth and arched away.

"This is what Claudia helped with. I didn't want you to deal with the blood. I know you can't stand the sight."

"Blood?" She whispered. She looked up, pulling him down and laying a light kiss on his lips. "I'm so sorry, Finnian. I realize I have trust issues. You don't deserve them." She was a Grade A idiot.

He brushed her hair back. "Just try to wait for an explanation before you jump to the worst possible conclusion about me. I'm not Charles. I'm not perfect, Everly, but I'll never cheat on you. That's a promise I can make."

She closed her eyes, soaking in the unexpected feeling of love. He didn't mean it that way. She skimmed her fingers across his jaw. "Where did you go last night, and why didn't you tell me?"

"Remember that I have to keep you safe, and sometimes the less you know, the better." He raked a hand through his hair, grimacing when it hit the back of his head. "I went to visit Lorenzo and Ray, his son. Ray was still a little angry about Claudia."

"What about Claudia?" Why could she never get rid of the woman?

"Claudia used to belong to him."

"Belong?"

"Yup. And it was as terrible as it sounds. One night, Ray bet her, well, her services in a poker game against Charles. Charles won. Claudia was livid with Ray, so she agreed to go live with Charles until she could figure out what to do."

"Oh." She always envisioned her husband and Claudia

meeting at a strip club. Or a street corner. Turns out, she wasn't too far off.

"Charles had me go back and get her and her things the next day. Ray has never forgiven Charles or me, but Claudia wanted out and took the opportunity. Anything to get away from the drugs and prostitution."

All the insults aimed at Claudia soured in Everly's stomach. Charles rescuing her from prostitution still didn't give him a right to sleep with her.

Finnian rubbed his lower back and cringed. "Ray got some of his vengeance out last night. He still blames me for Claudia leaving him."

"Why did you let him do this?" Everly picked up Finnian's hands. Not a mark. No cracked knuckles or broken skin. Did he fight back?

"I knew they'd have some answers about Charles for you. I had to go to find out."

He'd sacrificed his body to find answers. She kissed him again, the rush of love for him unmistakable this time.

Finnian brushed her hair back from her face, cupping both cheeks. "I need to get dressed." He moved past her to his suitcase in the corner of the living room. He pulled the new tags off before he slipped his arms into a slightly rumpled white dress shirt. He buttoned up his shirt, covering cuts and bruises.

How could a man look sexy while putting *on* clothes? Because he's taking a beating to help her. He didn't get anything out of this situation.

His brows knit together. "We need to visit the warehouse at the Port of Miami." He waited, probably for a response, but she didn't know what he meant. Why did they need to go to a warehouse?

Finnian grabbed his wallet and phone and slipped them

into his pocket as he stepped to her. He pressed his lips lightly on her forehead. "I'm going to go get a cab. Grab your purse and meet me downstairs in a few minutes. I have more things to talk to you about. Things I found out last night." He left, grabbing the folder of trust documents still sitting on the counter and leaving her heart pounding. Regret from her accusations earlier poured through her. She'd never known another man like him. She had to do better.

"Finnian is something else, isn't he?" Claudia sauntered into the kitchen. Did she walk like that when she was alone? Like she had to strut down a catwalk for an audience?

The warmth of the moment rushed away at her entrance. "Were you listening to us?"

She laughed as she made the coffee. "No, but I know that look anywhere. Worn it myself a few times."

Everly crossed her arms. She didn't enjoy being analyzed. "And what look is that?"

"Falling in love, of course." She leaned against the counter and watched Everly as the scent of coffee filled the kitchen. "I admire your choice."

"I don't think I asked for your opinion."

Claudia's eyebrows rose. "I don't think Charlie gave you enough credit."

"I know he didn't."

"He used to tell me—"

"Stop." She held up her hand. "I don't care what he told you." Each time she started to push away from the painful past and think about her future, something always showed up and knocked her back two steps.

Not this time. Too bad Claudia didn't cooperate with anything.

"Charlie said he loved you enough to let you go before

you got hurt. That's why he made Finnian write the email to you. Charlie just couldn't do it himself. Helping you now is giving him a little bit of closure."

The world tilted. Everly grabbed the back of the chair, needing something tangible for support. "Wait!" Every word from the email ending her marriage rushed through her mind. "*Finnian* wrote the email?"

EVERLY SAT beside him in the back of the taxi, pensive and rigid. Different from the woman he'd held in his arms a few minutes earlier. Was she still upset about Claudia? Her immediate conclusion that he'd slept with Claudia had bruised his ego. Everything he'd done since they first met was for her protection.

Because he cared for her. Deeply.

But they had more pressing matters than proving his dedication. Finnian needed to explain Charles's death. About ATLighting's ownership. About Lorenzo's warning for payment.

He laid an arm around her shoulders. She didn't pull away, but her half-smile didn't push away the sadness from her eyes. He rested his hand on top of the folder, wanting the press her about the documents inside. But something bothered her.

"What is it?"

She shrugged. It was the same answer she'd given him the first time he'd asked. The taxi exited the freeway.

"Alright. If you won't talk, then will you listen to me?"

Again, she lifted a shoulder.

"Everly, we need to talk about Charles."

"I'm not in the mood to talk about him. Not right now."

Frustration finally overtook his patience. "You're not going to have a choice in another fifteen seconds. I found out some details last night. That's why we're here today." He held up the folder. "This is important."

She narrowed her eyes as the taxi came to a stop. "Why don't you send them to me in an email?"

What?

She climbed out of the taxi before Finnian could ask her to explain.

"Women problems?" The taxi driver asked. "They're not worth it, bud."

Finnian dug out a twenty and passed it to him. "This one is." He climbed out and walked to where Everly stood, staring at the large warehouse perched along the edge of the Atlantic.

Enormous metal containers of shipments from all over the world were stacked six high outside the building. Inside, more of the same but on a smaller scale. A ship in the distance looked to be headed right at the dock.

"Let's go." He took Everly gently by the arm. He stepped, but she didn't.

Finnian closed his eyes, breathing in and trying for patience. They were so close to getting even more answers about Charles's death and potential murder, and she had to do this now.

"Dear, these men came to meet us today. I don't know why you're riled up, but you can tell me to piss-off right after this appointment." He held up the folder, trying his damnedest to get her to listen. "And after we go through this."

Her shoulders slumped. "I'm not going to tell you to piss-off." She rose on her toes and kissed his cheek. "That would be pretty shitty of me after you got your ass beat to help me out."

He half-laughed, glad she retained a little humor. He'd approach the topic of ATL ownership later. Right then, she needed to cooperate so they could find out the truth. "That's good to know. Do you think you can meet with them?"

She lifted her chin. "Fine. I'll be 'happy Everly' for you."

He kissed the top of her head. "Don't strain yourself trying." His joke went unacknowledged, and he gave up for the time being.

They crossed the pavement from the taxi to the warehouse. Two men in hardhats met them at the door. "You must be Finnian," the younger man said, offering his hand. "I'm Jake Beasley. This is Marcus Travers."

"Nice to meet you." Finnian shook Marcus's hand next.

Marcus nodded. "We're happy to show you around." His smooth voice reminded him of the Kenyans he'd met during his first undercover operation.

"This is Everly." Everly stepped up and smiled as she shook their hands. Didn't bat an eyelash. In fact, Finnian thought she smiled a little too warmly at Jake Beasley.

"You'll both need to wear a hard hat." Jake set one on her head.

She tilted her head back, trying to see from under it. "I think it's a bit too big, Mr. Beasley."

"Please call me Jake." He adjusted the hat for her. His eyes took on a light that Finnian didn't appreciate. The boy might have been fresh out of college, but any man with half a brain would recognize her wide, friendly smile.

Finnian's teeth ground together, letting the pain in his jaw add to his darkening mood. Last night, taking her to bed, changed everything for him. He was falling in love with Everly.

And she was smiling at Jake Beasley.

"Where did you want to start?" Marcus motioned for them to walk inside. Finnian rolled his sore shoulders and pushed aside the urge to grab Jake by his shirt collar and toss him off the dock.

Refocusing on why they were there, he followed Marcus into the building. He left Everly to flirt with the eager puppy. If that's what she needed to do, not twenty minutes after he'd flat out told her he wanted to be with her, then she could go right ahead.

She didn't have a clue that they stood near where the police found Charles dead. And because of her unexplained mood swing, he didn't have a chance to prep her.

"How complete was the warehouse when it happened?" Exposed metal rafters ran throughout the long warehouse. The massive industrial lights were the ones that ATLighting had installed. That was the reason that Charles was there, to begin with.

"It was done except for the office walls hadn't been built yet." Marcus pointed at the concrete ground in front of him. "This is where they found him. I think about it every time I come to this end. I don't believe in ghosts, but it's still unnerving."

Finnian turned to Everly. "This is where—"

"Let me get your number," Jake said as though Finnian hadn't even made a sound. "If I make it to Atlanta, you could show me around." He sat his hand on Everly's shoulder. "I'd enjoy getting a chance to talk more in private."

Finnian cracked his neck. Now wasn't the time to go after the boy brave enough to run his hand down Everly's back.

She stepped to the side, but Jake didn't look the least bit deterred.

Finnian looked back at Marcus. "Who is that kid?"

Marcus grunted. "That's my partner's son. Just graduated with his MBA. He thinks he can take on the world."

"He's about to take me on if he doesn't take his hand off of Everly." *My Everly.*

Marcus wiped away a smile. "I see. Jake?" He waited for the young guy to acknowledge him. "Finnian wanted to see the stairs that lead to the rafters."

Jake shrugged his shoulders. "Why don't you show him?" He smiled down at Everly. "I was explaining my expansion plans to her."

Everly waved her hand in the air. "You can tell me about them when you get back." She cut her eyes at Finnian. "Although, I'm not sure why Mr. Hayes has a sudden interest in climbing around on rafters."

"We need to talk."

"I agree. Why are we here?" She walked away from Jake, her gaze holding his.

Hell, this wasn't the time to try to explain it, but he didn't have a choice. "We're here about Charles."

Her mouth turned down in a slight frown as she walked across the concrete warehouse.

"This was where the police found Charles Clarke." Marcus crossed his arms. "Dead."

"Wait." She stopped. Still too far away for Finnian's taste. "Why would the police have found Charles here?"

Finnian stepped to her side as the swirl of confusion moved over her face. "I told you before that we needed to talk." He narrowed his eyes at the boy. Jake stood straighter under the glare. "Alone."

Marcus nodded and stepped away.

The *boy* decided to move a little slower than necessary.

Finnian could always offer to box his ears so he couldn't hear their conversation.

Instead, Finnian stared him down and cracked his knuckles. Jake's exit speed noticeably increased.

"Why are you scaring Jake? And what are you talking about?" She dropped her voice. "Why are we here?"

Finnian closed his eyes and rubbed his hand over his face. "Charles didn't die in a car accident. He fell here. From the rafters."

"But . . . the news. All the press."

"Tripp paid off a lot of people to keep it from the public." He tilted his head toward Marcus. "They knew because they own the building, but it was kept under wraps."

"And you knew?" She shook her head. "This whole time?"

Finnian wouldn't lie. "Yes. But with everything else you've gone through, I hadn't gotten around to telling you. I would've, though. Please believe me."

"I do." She set her hand on his forearm. "He's dead. I don't know why it would make me upset." She sniffed and looked up at the rafters again. "Why was he up there? Did he normally go to worksites and climb around? ATL has never had an accident like that."

"It might not have been an accident." Might as well tell her everything. "Lorenzo thinks that the fall didn't kill him. That's what I found out last night. He was already dead."

She snapped her head around. "What do you mean 'already dead?'"

"Someone carried him to the top and dropped him, trying to make it look like an accident. Might've been poison, but there's no way to know since the entire thing was covered up." He ran a hand up and down her arm. "Are you okay? I wanted to prep you—"

"I know. Sorry." She leaned closer to him, her hip brushing his as she looked around. "I'll be okay. Just a shock."

And she would be. That hidden strength would surface again.

"I'm trying to understand how someone could haul him up there," Finnian said. "I'm strong, but it would be a struggle to climb a ladder that high with a full-grown man slung over my shoulder."

"It is very high." She craned her head back. "But when they are installing the lights, they usually use scissor lifts and cranes. Someone could have lifted him up and dropped him off the top." She scanned the area as she walked. "But you said he was already dead, right?"

"Yes."

"That's good that he didn't suffer until someone found him."

Marcus approached them. "I'm afraid I have a shipment that just docked I need to attend to. Do you have any more questions?"

"Everly wondered if they would have used scissor lifts during the construction."

"Yes. I hadn't thought of that. I was too confused by the report in the paper about a car accident." He held his hands out. "But this is Miami. Questions can lead to trouble."

Finnian thought back to what Lorenzo said. The police report was paid to rule his death accidental. The news reported it as a car accident. Someone with some significant power had orchestrated the entire thing.

Jake shoved his hands in his pockets and gave Finnian a challenging look. "Scissor lifts have keys. Only the crew leader would have access to the keys."

Marcus agreed. "Yes, that's right." His radio crackled, and he answered it.

Tripp's secretary would know which crew leader worked on this project. "I think we're through. Thank you for your time." Finnian and Marcus shook hands. Jake didn't even start to hold out his hand. Instead, he pulled out his phone.

"I meant what I said earlier, Everly. I'd love to see you again if I come to Atlanta." He typed in her name. "What's your last name?"

Everly's eyebrows raised a touch. "Clarke. Everly Clarke. Charles was my husband."

Jake's fingers froze a moment before he pocketed his phone. "I'm sorry, Mrs. Clarke. I had no idea you were here about your husband's death."

"It's fine."

Finnian placed his hand along her lower back. "C'mon, Everly, *dear*, the taxi is waiting."

Jake crossed his arms, trying his best to look down his nose even though Finnian still had a few inches on him.

"Marcus said you were a security guard for ATL. We have a few of those on the payroll." Jake smirked. "I understand your protection over Everly now. Being paid a salary to be here."

The disdain in that statement struck at Finnian's ego. Every muscle snapped tight as he looked into Jake's privileged face.

He stepped close to the kid, ignoring Everly's tug on his hand to back away. His body still ached from the beating he'd taken, but he'd never walk away from a stuck up guy like Jake. "I was paid to protect Tripp Wellington. I protect Everly because she's *mine* to protect."

He led her out of the warehouse and into the taxi. At least, he'd kept Jake from getting Everly's number.

Everly sagged in the seat, her elbow propped on the window.

"Are you interested in Jake Beasley?" He snapped out the question, unable to contain the jealousy.

She frowned. "I was trying to be nice."

Nice? He leaned down, capturing her lips in an urgent kiss, breaking it off just as quick. "I will always be jealous of any man that touches you."

She grazed her fingers along his bruised jaw. "I understand the feeling." She kissed him again, softer this time, the sadness in her eyes still there when she pulled back.

Finnian set a possessive hand on her thigh. "I wish you'd tell me what's wrong."

She shook her head, the hair on top wobbling back and forth. "Later. Do you know who was the crew chief for that project, Finnian?"

"No, but I'll find out." He fired off a text to Shelley, the secretary at ATL. "Everly?" He waited until she looked at him. "We have more to talk about." Charles's death was just the beginning. He held up the folder.

"About Charles?" Taking it from him. She opened it, picking up the paper where he'd left off. "What is it? Do you think there's *another* condo with *another* mistress?"

He didn't laugh, although she'd meant it as a joke. "I think you own ATLighting."

Her mouth dropped open. "Impossible." She looked down at the paper, her eyes lingering at the bottom. Slowly, she turned the page, her eyes widening. "Wait? *All* of ATLighting? How?"

"Charles obtained all of the stock before he died." Finnian smiled at the disbelief floating over her features. "If that plays out to be true, you're the new owner of this business."

She looked out the window. What was she thinking? Upset? Worried?

"You don't think Tripp had anything to do with Charles's death, do you? They were best friends. Had been for almost fifteen years. He was the best man at our wedding. How far would he go to keep control of the company?"

"The only issue with that theory is that Tripp wasn't in Miami when Charles died. It doesn't take away the motivation." He interlaced his fingers with hers. "Honestly, I have no idea, but I'll help you figure it out."

"There's something else you can help me figure out."

He kissed the back of her hand. "Anything."

She met his eyes, her blue eyes still somber. "Why did you write the email to end my marriage?"

14

Turquoise blue waves ran along the sandy shore of South Beach in uneven lines. It was a beautiful, panoramic view of one of the world's most iconic beaches. Instead of the rolling waves and scent of the ocean relaxing her, it represented the most significant decision of her life. Had she made a mistake by staying in Atlanta when Charles moved to Miami? Would she have liked it here? Could she have saved him?

No. To everything. This fancy lifestyle suited thousands of people calling Miami their home, but not her. She wanted a simple house in a little neighborhood where she'd have kids and a dog. Even with Charles's death, accident or not, that small dream didn't change.

The sliding glass doors muffled Finnian's telephone conversation with various employees of ATL. He'd been trying to put the pieces of the puzzle together since they came home from the warehouse. Everly lacked the energy to help. The longer she stayed in Miami, the more Charles's ghost sucked the life out of her.

Her phone rang with "Mom" displayed across the

screen. Canceling the call would only lead to more questions from her mom later.

"Hi," Everly said with as much happiness as she could force into her voice.

"I can't believe you didn't call and tell me about Charles leaving you. And Miami. *And* the mistress!" Her mom's voice rose higher with each accusation. "I had to hear it from Cade, and you know how horrible he is about giving details. He announced it as he walked out the door to catch his flight back to California. Just dropped the bomb on me and left."

Yup that sounded like Cade. God, telling her was like pulling the pin out of a grenade and setting it on a ledge. But maybe it was time to explain. Or explode.

"I guess you want the details."

"You're damn right I want the details. Especially since Tripp called me a few minutes ago. He's very concerned about the men that broke into your house last weekend. You know, that break-in you didn't tell me about."

"Look, Mom—"

"And *then*," she shouted. "Someone tried to kidnap you at the mall! You leave me no choice, Everly Ann Fischer."

No.

She wouldn't.

"You're coming home to Indiana, or else I'm flying down to stay with you."

And there went the grenade. Everly dropped her head against the balcony railing. "That's really not necessary."

"I can't believe you just said that. It is most definitely necessary. You're not living alone until this is figured out. I don't want you sleeping one more night without protection."

"And you're going to protect me, Nora?"

"You'd be surprised about what a mom can do when it comes to protecting their children."

"Don't go buying a rocket launcher yet." Everly tilted her head up, staring at the sky and wishing she knew something to mutter in French. It always seemed to help Finnian.

"Cade almost postponed his interviews to fly down to Miami to be with you. That's how serious he took it. The only thing stopping him was Finnian. Tripp mentioned him too. Turns out, you're in a relationship with a thief. Tripp filed a police report because that handyman of yours stole from the company."

Now, that was just plain ridiculous. Finnian had too much pride to ever steal. "He's not a thief."

"You don't know that."

"Yes. I do. I know *him*." She pressed her lips together before declaring her love. Defending him had a way of bringing those emotions clear to the surface. He was an incredible man that didn't deserve her mistrust.

"If you don't fly back to Indiana tonight, then I'm flying to Miami. Your choice."

"Then, I'm going with the third option where you stay in Indiana, and I stay here." Dragging her into this situation would be a disaster. What if they decided to target her mom instead of her? What if she got hurt?

It was safer for Nora to stay where she was. "I'm okay. Finnian's a good guy. A great guy. I know he didn't steal anything from Tripp. Tripp's just mad about Charles's will. Charles made a mess of everything."

"Tripp said you'd defend this Finnian. I don't want some con man taking advantage of you."

Everly shook her head, exhaustion pressing down harder than before. "No one is taking advantage of me.

We're flying back to Atlanta tomorrow, so there's no need for you to leave Indiana."

"Will Finnian be with you when go home?"

No point in lying. "Yes."

"That solves it. I'll meet you in Atlanta. Tripp said that Finnian was a playboy. I don't want you taken advantage of again."

Again. Damn, that hurt. Was the situation with Charles her fault? Her lack of judgment?

The sliding glass door opened and closed. She started to turn, but Finnian boxed her in, propping his hands on either side of her. His aftershave mixed with the fresh ocean air.

A hum vibrated in his chest as he pressed his lips against the side of her neck.

She closed her eyes and leaned back into his warmth.

"Tripp's worried about you," her mom continued. "You know he always thought of you as a sister. He cares, and I think you should listen to him."

Strange, she never remembered Cade insulting her sex life the way Tripp had at the airport.

"There's more to this situation than you understand, Mom. Stay home. Don't fly to Atlanta. I mean it. I'm fine."

Finnian kissed her neck again and murmured, "You're perfect."

She was far from perfect, but he made her feel that way. "Finnian will keep me safe. Everything will work out. Promise. I need to go."

"I'm not happy about this," she grumbled. "You are to call me every night."

Everly grimaced, swallowing down her refusal. It would just prolong the conversation. "I'll try to text you. Goodnight, Mom."

"I'll talk to you *tomorrow*."

Everly ended the call and slid her phone into her back pocket. She'd deal with that later.

"I will die before I let anything happen to you. I'm glad you understand that." He slid his hand across her stomach. "Is your mum doing okay?" He nipped at the edge of her ear. "Are you doing okay?"

She barely noticed his accent anymore until he said the little words like mum that highlighted it. "She's threatening to come to Miami or Atlanta to protect me."

"We'll call her in if we need back up." He wrapped his other arm around her, holding her against his chest. He pressed his cheek against hers, staring at the ocean. "Are you ready to talk about the email?"

Where to start? It'd be easier to pretend it all didn't exist and stand there, staring at the ocean as the sun faded, loving him. But this wouldn't last. Not if Tripp went through with his threat and had him arrested. She needed her feelings for him resolved.

"Why did you write it?"

His arms tightened. Another set of waves rolled in before he finally answered. "I didn't want to. I quit when Tripp gave me the ultimatum. But it was shit timing. As soon as I made it to the airport to fly back to Atlanta, my oldest brother called begging for money for the farm. I immediately asked for my job back and wrote the email. I hated every second of it, Everly. I hope you'll believe me."

"Is that why you're helping me? Guilt for writing it?" She held her breath, waiting for his answer. When none came, she turned.

He brushed the back of his fingers along her cheek. "Aye, I suffer from guilt. Guilt from being the person to end what was left of your marriage. Guilt from not preventing a senseless death when I had the chance. Both of those things influence how I live my life. Every inch of my soul has to protect you, Everly."

She immediately regretted asking him. The pain in his voice broke her heart. She cupped his face, bringing his head down. "Neither my marriage ending nor Charles's death was your fault." She kissed him, wanting to forget about it all, but he pulled back.

"I wasn't referring to Charles. It's Sean's death I have on my hands."

"Who is Sean?" He'd never mentioned someone named Sean before.

"A kid I failed. He was sixteen and living with the mob I went undercover with back in London. I became close to him. First, to get information. Then, because he deserved a better life." He swallowed, the muscles in his arms tensing. "He'd agreed to leave the life and go work on the farm. He didn't have any family. His mother had already died of an overdose the year before, and there was no father in the picture." A faint smile touched his lips. "Sean was excited about moving out of the city. He'd ask me all sorts of questions whenever he got a chance. My mum was excited as well. She had a room all done for him."

Everly stroked the tense cords along the side of his neck. "What happened?"

"Our undercover team got sloppy. We figured out that one of the boss's guards spotted him talking with a uniformed officer and relaying information. Sean was supposed to meet me the next day at this little pub on the outskirts of town, but the entire plan changed that night."

Was this why he had such a deep need to protect her? He stared over her head at the ocean, his dark eyes haunted.

"When it was nearly time to leave, that same guard

who'd seen us earlier strolled into the boss's office. Sean came flying into the room, stopping at the first of my agents and letting him know about the discovery. With close to forty armed men in the room, we were toast once they blew our identity." Finnian shoved his hands in his pockets. "Sean looked at me, took a deep breath, and then walked right into the room. I heard him shout and yell, causing a distraction, and giving us more time to ease our way out of the warehouse without causing too much suspicion. When the boss shouted the orders for us to be killed, I ran with the last few of our team. One gunshot brought me to a standstill. The echo of Sean's scream wakes me up every day of my life."

Everly covered her mouth. "Oh no, Finnian."

"Sean tried to protect me when I should have been the one to protect him. I swore I'd never let that happen again." He locked eyes with her. "It will never happen again. Not while I'm alive. I'll not live with that regret again."

She ran her hand through his already messed up hair, resting her hand at the back of his neck. When Charles hurt her, she'd hidden away and refused to ever let anyone near her again.

Finnian's loss made him take on the world. It explained so much about him.

With the smallest of pressure, she pulled his head down and kissed him, offering as much support and compassion as she knew how.

His lips fit perfectly with hers. His tongue was cool, tasting faintly of beer. They both needed each other for different reasons. On the surface, it wasn't enough to sustain a relationship. Not without love to go along with the need.

She loved him. But did he love her? Could he tell the difference between that need for redemption and love?

Finnian pulled her tight against his body, although his kiss remained gentle. He fisted his hands in the back of her shirt. He didn't seem like a man who dealt with his emotions often. Having to live with the daily reminder, the nightmare of losing Sean must be torture.

"I'm sorry I kept the email from you." He rested his forehead against hers. "I wasn't sure how to approach you with it. But I promise you that I'm not standing here, holding you out of guilt. I've told you that already. I care for you, Everly. Deeply."

She kissed him again, urging him faster.

It didn't take much for the kiss to turn hot, the urgency from last night reemerging so naturally between them. His teeth dragged her bottom lip.

"Take me to bed," she mumbled. "All of this goes away." And she could pretend they had a normal future ahead of them. That they loved each other and could live happily ever after.

The sliding glass door opened.

Claudia cleared her throat.

Perfectly crappy timing, like always.

"Go away," Finnian snapped before tilting his head and continuing the kiss.

Claudia's light laugh destroyed the moment. "Sorry to ruin your chances at second—oh, my, make that third base, but we have a problem."

"What's the problem?" He faced Claudia, pulling Everly under his arm.

"No biggie. The police just arrived to arrest you."

POLICE? "Why do they want to arrest me?"

Everly's head snapped up. "I didn't get a chance to tell you. Tripp called my mom and told her that he turned you in for stealing from the company."

He jerked away from Everly, pacing down the balcony, his movements jerky from the rush of anger. Unbelievable. The last time he'd stolen something was when he was eight and didn't have enough money to buy candy at his town's small store. The beating he'd suffered from his mum still lingered in his memory.

A policeman, shorter than Everly, came to the door behind Claudia.

Claudia turned and looked down at the man. "I don't think I invited you in."

He tipped his chin in Finnian's direction. "I didn't want him to try and make a run for it."

Finnian narrowed his eyes. "That's ridiculous. We're at least nine stories up."

"I've seen some crazy things in my time." He motioned Finnian forward. "We have a warrant for your arrest."

"So, I've heard." How had Tripp managed it so quickly? What did he even claim he stole?

"Then I hope you'll come along peacefully. Are you Everly Clarke? I'm Officer Singletary." He pulled out a picture from his pocket. "We have a missing person case out on you."

Everly crossed her arms. "Funny, last time I checked, I wasn't missing."

Claudia snickered.

"Your family reported you missing."

Finnian clamped his hands down on Everly's shoulders. "She just spoke with her mum. Which 'family' reported her missing?"

"I'm not sure. Regardless, we need you to come down to the station and meet with an officer for a well-being check."

"Tripp managed to do all of this in a couple of days." Everly shook her head. "Ridiculous. He's lost his damn mind."

Officer Singletary pointed his pen at Finnian. "After you're booked downtown, you'll meet with Immigration."

The balcony felt as though it fell out from under him. Tripp would have him deported. Was it because of his protection over Everly?

"Immigration?" Everly aimed the question at Finnian.

"I'm sure it's just standard procedure." He rubbed his hand up and down along her back. He'd cross that bridge if needed. Flying to England and leaving her unprotected wasn't an option.

"C'mon now, let's get going." The officer motioned for Finnian to turn around. "Hands behind your back. I assume you know the procedure."

"Aye."

"Finnian?" Everly pleaded with him like he had any ability to sway the men. He didn't want to leave any more than she wanted him to because she'd be alone. As soon as he left the apartment with the police, she'd be alone and defenseless against everyone.

He thought fast. "Everly needs to come down to the station with us until I can speak with your Superintendent. She needs to stay with us."

"Our who?" Officer Singletary asked.

Finnian shook his head. "The man or woman in charge of the station. I need to speak to them. We have an unusual situation." He had to try to persuade someone to watch out for her. At least if she sat in the waiting room at the station, she wouldn't be alone. Hopefully, even crooked cops on

Tripp's payroll wouldn't attempt a kidnapping in the middle of the day.

He dangled the handcuffs in the air. "I don't think you're in a position to make demands."

Everly stepped in front of Finnian. He had to pull up at the last second to keep from trampling over her. He hadn't even realized he'd made a step toward the insipid police officer.

"Then I would like to talk to him," Everly called over her shoulder. She patted Finnian's chest. "Calm down. That won't help."

No, but it would feel good to lay into the officer, work off some frustration.

"Yeah, yeah," Officer Singletary said, waving them off. "You can make your requests once we get there. You have the right to remain silent."

He mumbled through reading Finnian the rest of his rights.

Finnian closed his eyes briefly at the mention of having an attorney. Brady. He didn't have a damn choice. No matter the strained relationship between his brother and the rest of the family, he needed to be here.

"Everly, darling," he tried to sound as lighthearted as possible. "Take my phone and call Brady, will you. Tell him what's happened. Let him know that I'll give him a call once I'm out."

"How can he help you? You need someone here. Now."

"Aye. I know that, darling. But he knows a lot more people than I do when it comes to this sort of thing. I'll need him to wire the money to bail me out—"

"I'll bail you out."

Finnian rolled his shoulders as his hands were cuffed. "I'll not have you bailing me out of jail."

"I'm the reason you're in jail." A quick glint of amusement reflected in her eyes. "I'll use company money. Just pretend Tripp is bailing you out." She rose on her toes and kissed him firmly on the lips. "I'll send you some cigarettes as soon as I can. I hear they can buy you protection. You're too pretty to be in jail without allies."

His lips twitched.

Officer Singletary tugged at his arm. "C'mon. You two love birds can ride in the backseat together down to the station."

"Wait." She held onto Finnian's arm as the policeman began to pull him toward the door. "Lovebird."

The officer tugged again. "Yeah, you know, the two birds that like to sit close together—"

"No, no." She fluttered her hand in the air. "That's the password. It has to be. I can't believe I didn't think of it before. *Agapornis*. That's the genus of the lovebird. Charles was a bird watcher."

Claudia, standing just inside the living room, grunted. "That makes sense. I used to tune him out when he began rambling on about birds and their migration habits. He almost lost it when he saw some red bird land on the balcony last winter."

"Wasn't it annoying?" The two women smiled at one another. "Anyway," Everly continued. "I bet that's his password. Let me grab his laptop. I can try on the way. Do you mind, Officer?"

"I don't care if you pack a picnic, as long as we get going. My shift ends soon."

She disappeared into the bedroom as Finnian followed Officer Singletary to the front door. His partner stood outside, checking his phone. Not really Miami's finest.

"Got it." Everly linked one arm through Finnian's. "I hope this laptop gives us a clue about Charles's death."

Finnian kept his thoughts to himself about the murder until they were seated together in the backseat of the patrol car.

"If Charles knew of someone that wanted him dead, he kept it to himself. He never let me know. The man had dozens of bad qualities, but I'd never let him die that way." He leaned toward her, keeping the physical connection between them. With deportation a real possibility, he didn't know when, or if, he'd get to see Everly again.

"I know you wouldn't." She kissed his cheek.

Finnian knew in his heart that this thing between them was real, but did she? He'd expressed to her twice that he cared for her. Hopefully, she believed him. "Everly we need to talk—"

Officer Singletary sat down in the front seat. "Let's get this show on the road."

Everly patted Finnian's thigh. "Later." She popped open the laptop and typed in the scientific word. The screen opened to his desktop. "That was it. I can't believe I'm in." She linked the laptop to her phone for the internet. Quickly, she clicked through different programs, going too fast for Finnian to catch anything important. Until she opened Charles's email.

"Wait a second." Finnian nodded toward the screen. "Open that second one. Mr. Novoa." It was what Lorenzo had warned him about. Lorenzo and Ray were the kiddie pool compared to Carlos Novoa's connections, both above and below-board.

"What type of business did he have with ATL? Was he a builder?"

"No." Finnian shifted in his seat as the tips of his fingers began to tingle from the restricted blood flow from the handcuffs. "He ships in the inventory for ATLighting for the Miami projects. He's, um, not the most upstanding person in Miami."

"He and Charles probably got along great, then." Everly clicked through a few more programs. "Strange. He's not on any of the payroll or vendor records. ATLighting's bank account doesn't show any payments associated with contracts, or else it would go through the accounting system."

That did sound strange. Handling the bookkeeping and bank accounts didn't fall under Finnian's job duties. Paying someone like Novoa under the table wasn't too far-fetched. That just meant that his association with ATL wasn't something Everly should involve herself with.

Because if Novoa had a hand in Charles's murder, Finnian would try every tactic possible to get Everly out of the country until someone else resolved it.

"Wait." Everly gripped Finnian's knee. "This is an email from Tripp the day before Charles died. He wrote, 'I don't feel comfortable with you owning it all. What if something were to happen?' That's odd." Everly shivered, and Finnian wanted nothing more than to put his arm around her. She clicked to Charles's response. "'I told you before the stock is safe. If something happens to me before you buy your half back, then it goes to Everly, where it"—she took a deep breath—"where it belongs.' He expected Tripp to do something."

"And Tripp knows you have the stock. He just doesn't know how you got it."

"That's why Tripp was borderline crazy when Charles's will didn't list it as an asset."

Finnian leaned his head back and stared at the ceiling. If

Tripp was behind this, the last place he needed to spend time was in jail. The men Tripp sent after Everly could already be in Miami.

He squeezed his hands into fists. He didn't have a choice in the matter. "Darling, go ahead and call Brady so I can speak with him. He needs to find a way to get me released. Tonight."

Or he needed to get his ass on a plane and come to America. Brady was the next best person he knew to protect Everly. As long as his stuffy, Cambridge-bred brother hadn't forgotten how to throw a punch or two.

15

"What did Brady say?" Finnian scribbled his signature on another piece of paper.

Everly drummed her fingers on the stainless-steel counter as the conversation with his brother buzzed around her mind. Posting bail had been easy, and Brady wasn't too worried about the charges pending, but something he'd said stuck with her.

She fell in step beside him as they exited the police station. "He said if what you'd mentioned was true, then he'd better head this way. What does that mean?"

Finnian stopped when they reached the sidewalk. "Good. It means my brother remembers that family comes first."

"And . . ."

"Brady is coming to America."

"Does he have to? It's not like he's driving to Atlanta from Nashville or something. It's a long, expensive flight. I can't imagine he's able to practice law here."

"He's not coming to practice law." Finnian threw his arm out, and a taxi stopped in front of them. "It means he recognizes the same threat I do. He's coming to protect you."

No. She didn't need anyone else to risk their lives for her. "I don't need his help."

"Please, don't tell me we're back to that again." Finnian held the door open for her. "After everything that's happened since we first met. Someone is still after you. And it looks like we've confirmed Tripp is behind it all."

Even after all the years acting like Charles's friend, Everly had to agree. Tripp was the only person left that could stage this entire thing.

As the taxi pulled away, Finnian grew silent. He remained bent over his phone the rest of the ride. When it stopped in front of the condo, he looked up with an apology already in his eyes.

"We need to go back to Atlanta."

"I know."

Relief washed over his features. "Good. I just booked our flight. It leaves in a couple hours."

She nodded and climbed out of the taxi. They needed to get back. There wasn't anything else to find out about Charles in Miami. The only oddity she found was the relationship with Novoa. After an internet search of the man, she'd agreed with Finnian's assessment that he was shady. And dangerous.

Everly tilted her head back to see to the top of the sky-high condo. "Let's get the tearful goodbye with Claudia over." But there was one thing left to do. "Will you do a favor for me?"

Finnian ran his hand over her hair and rested it on her shoulder. "Do you even have to ask?"

No. She didn't have to ask. He'd done everything he could to keep her safe. She'd never take it for granted. At any point, he could change his mind and walk away. This wasn't his fight.

She interlaced her fingers with his. "Do we have time to go for a walk on the beach? I think I'd like that before we left."

His slow smile spread across his lips. "Follow me."

He led her around the side of the condo and to the main highway. Expensive cars, most with music blaring, sat bumper to bumper along A1A. The noise and lights reaffirmed her desire for a quiet subdivision, not this rich, party lifestyle.

Everly paused at the crosswalk, waiting as a Ferrari with the top down eased past. Finnian tugged her farther down the sidewalk. "Come this way." He guided her down a short flight of stairs. "These tunnels are handy. Keeps you from being roadkill on A1A."

"I doubt any of those luxury cars want me as a hood ornament." The cool ocean breeze hit her face as they emerged from the tunnel. "So this is it?" She paused where the sidewalk met the sand.

This was the beach from her nightmares.

"Are you okay?"

She kicked her shoes off and wiggled her toes in the sand. "Yes." She looked up at him. "It's a relief to have new memories of this place. I'm glad those memories include you."

He kissed the back of her hand. "Me too."

They moved closer to the water and away from the lights of the bars, restaurants, and high rises. The world around them faded.

"Would you ever consider leaving Atlanta? Moving away?"

The question threw her off. Two weeks ago, she'd said

no out of fear. And now, with everything that'd happened, she still had to say no. She owned one hundred percent of a massive business. While Finnian was in jail, she'd combed through the business's books on Charles's computer. After a few hours of running reports, she pushed past her self-doubt that she couldn't run the company.

She'd help start it. She could run it.

"I can't. Not now. Why?" She shifted to see his face and caught a glimpse of worry before he covered it.

He drew her close to him, his large hand almost spanned her lower back as their bodies pressed together. She expected a kiss, but he stepped to the side. Then swayed to the other side.

They were dancing.

And there was music. Faintly, it sounded like a band playing a soft, blues song that drifted back to them on the breeze from a bar down the way. He rested her hand against his chest. The strong beat of his heart thumped against her palm.

His fingers trailed slowly up and down her lower back. "What do you want in life?"

"That's complicated because I don't know anymore." That was the truth. "I used to want to be left alone. But then you came along and changed that. Now, after finding out I own this business, everything is different. What do you want?"

Their swaying slowed a fraction, and he looked out at the ocean for a brief moment. "To keep everyone that I care for safe. You and my family." He tightened his hold on her and resumed the dance. "If you could go anywhere in the world, where would it be?"

Anywhere with you. But the words wouldn't leave her lips. That put them in a different category, beyond some uncomplicated fling. At every turn, he'd found a way to be there for her. He'd opened her heart that she'd shut down so long ago.

She loved him and losing him would suck.

But she refused to lose herself again, either. Handing over her heart and trust scared the hell out of her.

"I've never traveled." She rested her cheek against his shoulder, and the sweet ocean breeze eased her nerves. "More of a homebody. What about you? Have you traveled all around the world?" Women everywhere would probably fall over themselves for him. She traced the outline of his shoulders with the palm of her hands before settling on his biceps.

"I've gone to a few countries. Ireland. Scotland. Spain. Canada. Nowhere exotic."

A couple stumbled past them, laughing and clinging to each other. Would their relationship ever be that simple? "Are those men going to be waiting for us when we get back?" The wind blew through her hair, gooseflesh rising along the back of her neck.

Finnian tightened his hold on her by a fraction. "Yes. They wouldn't have given up just because we left town. They're probably watching both our houses."

"Are we headed to a hotel again?" She almost wished he'd say yes, give them a few days alone in a bubble as if they'd met under different circumstances. She blinked as she looked up at the bright moon. That seemed like a lifetime ago.

"I figured we'd go to my place. Your house is too wide-open. You have too many entrances and exits, whereas I only use my front door. I've already arranged for the repairs to be made to my house from the break-in. It's safest. The backdoor stays bolted. The windows are nailed shut except for the bedroom."

"So, when someone tries to get in, they'll have to kick in the front door like they did mine the first time? Seems scary to only have one entrance and exit."

"I also have four guns."

She smiled. "Of course, you do. For all four of your hands."

His eyebrows furrowed. "I hope you trust me to keep you safe, Everly. I will. I swear it."

She hugged him, wishing she could take away that responsibility. He didn't need to shoulder everything. "Yes. I trust you." She gave him a quick kiss to make her point. Sighing, she stepped back. "I think it's time to go face reality."

He cupped her cheek, stopping her retreat. "This could be our reality. You and me, darling. I want that."

He did? "Here?"

"Anywhere."

She wanted it—a real relationship. Not something forced because men were after her. She pulled his hand down and threaded her fingers through his. "Someday."

HE SLID the three-inch deadbolt into place and set his alarm. The dark car parked on the other side of the street would inform Tripp they were back. The two men watching the house failed in their attempt to hide as their taxi drove past. Sorry idiots. But that didn't change the gravity of Everly's situation.

Finnian had served as a pillow for Everly for most of the flight, trying to figure out his next move. After going over the facts, Tripp looked one hundred percent guilty. No one else had the motivation or the capability to pull it all off.

He typed up his theory, the situation, everything that'd happened since someone first broke into her house, and he sent it in an email to Brady. If he was deported or killed, his brother would know the circumstances and hopefully pass it along to the authorities.

Finnian expected Everly to fall into bed after the hard, fitful sleep she'd had on the plane. Instead, she set her bag on the floor next to the sofa and strode to the nearest wall. Dozens of pictures covered the wall. All of them were taken by Megan.

"What are these?" She leaned closer to the picture of the farmhouse. "Pictures from England?"

The undeniable pull to her wrestled with his inner conscience. He should tell her about the risk of deportation, but her answer of 'someday' when he'd hinted at their future stuck with him. When he left for England, he needed Everly with him. But how did he get her to go along with his plan?

Standing behind her, he rested both hands on her shoulders. "That's my house where I grew up."

She looked back at him. "Did you even fit in there? It looks as tiny as a dollhouse."

"It helped that by the time I left for the police force, only Megan and our mum remained. As long as I gave Meg as much time as she required preening in front of the mirror, we got along."

Everly laughed. "You said that you were the second youngest of twelve, right? Tell me about your family. Do they all live near you?"

Finnian pointed to the hill in another picture. "Elliot lives over that hill, about a mile down, I'd say." He moved to the next scene in the countryside. "Aislinn lives just over there, on the other edge of the property. She's due to have her first baby next spring. John and William each live a few miles away and closer to town. They manage our small store in town, and if you ever meet them, you'll know why they haven't found a wife yet. They're both rough."

"And Megan?"

"My Meg. The only one I can call my baby sister. Went to school in Edinburgh, and now she's wandering from place to place, drawing and painting, and taking pictures. Part of the money I sent home went to her schooling. Now, Brady and I help to support an unemployed, amazing artist. She's somewhere in Northern California right now."

"Sounds like Cade. It's taken him far too long to graduate because he took a couple 'gap years' right out of high school to help my parents. He finished his MBA in August and has been interviewing the past few months." She motioned to the pictures. "You have so many siblings. Who are we missing?"

"Let's see." He wrapped his arms around her shoulders, placing a kiss behind her ear. "Oliver and Leo work on the farm, but they live about thirty miles away in opposite directions. Six kids between the two of them. You already know that Brady works in London."

She rested her head on his shoulder. "You all seem really close."

"Aside from Brady, we are." He trailed a finger down the side of her throat. Her skin was so soft.

"What about the others?"

It was a fairly remarkable feat that his family, living over six thousand kilometers away, managed to block his attempt to seduce Everly to his bed. He wanted her there. Once. He needed to have her be *his* for one more night. The peace wouldn't last long.

"Finnian?" She glanced up at him.

He sighed. "Right. Rebecca, another sister that's somewhere in the middle of the pack, lives a good drive away near Liverpool. Bridget is a schoolteacher, has three children, and lives up near Gretna Green." He moved his lips lower on her neck. Her head tilted to the side, giving him better access. That one move of consent almost made him lose his focus. "Katherine is still single, living in Dublin, working herself to the bone as a chef." There. That was all of them. He had more important things to focus on.

"A chef? Does she have her own restaurant?"

"Yes. Brady invested in a restaurant for her last year," he mumbled against her skin. He couldn't resist much longer.

"What kind of food does she cook?"

His lips pressed against the soft rhythm of her pulse. He held perfection in his arms. Her strength mixed with the softness she let him sample now. It baffled him that Charles let this woman slip through his fingers. But Finnian was thankful. She was too precious of a woman to treat carelessly.

"Finnian?"

"Hmmm?" He turned her in his arms, his lips never leaving her skin.

"Your sister?"

He grazed his teeth over her earlobe as he ran his hands up her back, pulling her even closer. She snaked her arms around his neck. Finnian's lips hovered above her own. The restraint he'd worked so hard to maintain stretched to the breaking point.

"What kind of food does she cook?"

"Everly." He rested his forehead against hers and

squeezed his eyes shut. "Be a sweetheart and pretend I'm an only child or an orphan for the next little bit."

"I was wondering how long I could keep you distracted." She smirked and rose on her toes. "You lasted longer than I thought."

He kissed her, lingering over each kiss, making each one longer and deeper until she clung to him. In this dizzying torment, he belonged here where the desire to take met the need for a slow seduction.

Finnian moved her backward until he pinned her against the wall with his body.

Everly fisted her hands in his shirt as her mouth moved quicker.

No. Not this time. They both needed this.

Slow.

Intimate.

Intense.

He shifted his arms, accidentally knocking a picture off the wall. They both jumped to the side, away from the glass as it shattered.

"I'm so sorry—"

Finnian picked her up, her legs wrapping around his waist. "Just kiss me."

Everly threaded her fingers through his hair. "Gladly."

As she launched into a kiss, he carried her to his room. She leaned back, stripping out of her shirt and tossing it away. Her bra went next.

"Everly," he growled, setting her down on the bed. He tugged off his shirt and pants as she wiggled out of her jeans.

He pulled her jeans off her feet and threw them away as he crawled on top of her. She giggled and wrapped her arms around his neck. He'd miss this. When they sent him back

to England, he'd miss her. Everything about her. Her smile.
Laugh. Her strength.

Finnian kissed her, long and deep, the feeling of real
love for a woman for the first time in his life shredding his
heart.

He'd hold her tonight. All night. Because right then, he
loved Everly. And tomorrow, he'd leave everything behind.

No matter how much he prepped, he wasn't ready to
leave.

EVERLY'S SOFT breath ran across his chest, the even rhythm a
sign of her deep sleep. Good. She needed the rest.

But Finnian couldn't sleep. He climbed from the bed,
careful not to wake her, and grabbed a beer before falling on
the sofa. After scanning his missed text messages, he
checked the time. Meg was in California, still a few hours
behind him.

"Hey there, beautiful," he said when she picked up.

Her light laugh eased his worry away. "Hallo, handsome.
I was wondering if I'd hear from you. Been keeping a pretty
American busy, I heard."

"I'm surprised Brady called you, but the girls in the
family are the only people Brady seems inclined to speak
with."

She sighed. "He seems concerned about you and Everly.
More than just the big brother routine he usually dishes out.
What trouble have you gotten yourself into this time? I
always thought you were a little too rebellious to be a cop."

"No trouble our slick-talking brother can't get me out of,
I'm sure. Darling, I'm actually calling to ask for some
advice." He opened the top of his beer, enjoying his first,

long drink. He sure as hell needed some help when it came to Everly.

"Legal advice or female advice?" Meg asked.

"Female." He drained half of his beer while she finished laughing. "There's a chance I'm going to be sent back home. At least until this thing gets straightened out, and I apply for a new work visa. How do I get Everly to come with me?"

Her laugh stopped abruptly. "Oh my. The situation is that serious, huh?"

"Yes. I was arrested—"

"No. I meant you're that serious with Everly. I had no idea. When did you fall in love with her?"

He stood and walked to the front window to peek out at the car, still sitting across the street. He finished his beer. "I didn't say I did."

Megan snorted. "You just said you wanted her to come home with you."

"I want to keep her safe."

"Fin . . ."

When did Megan start sounding like their mum? A shadow shifted in the car, and he let the blinds drop back into place. "Fine. I'm in love with her, but she's not at that point yet."

"How do you know?"

"'Cause when I mentioned having a future together, she replied with 'someday.' Not exactly the words of a woman in love. I even tried to hint at her traveling to England with me. She said she was a homebody." He looked at the bedroom door. He should've checked that window again. Did he lock it? The alarm was set.

"I don't want to hurt my big brother's ego, but maybe she's really not at that stage yet."

"But I need her to come with me. I need her safe."

"That's not exactly the most romantic reason to invite someone to leave the country with you."

He sighed. That wasn't the point. "I won't be able to rest knowing she's over here unprotected."

"Isn't that why you called Brady?"

A car door closed outside. Finnian's insides twisted into a tight coil.

"Yes. Listen, those people that have been after Everly are headed to my house right now." He leaned against the blinds, able to see the shadow of two figures walking across the pavement. At least he was ready for them.

"Gotcha. Love you, sweetie. Stay safe. Go be a cop now." She hung up with a click as he pocketed his phone. He reached under the sofa's seat cushion in two steps, and his SIG Sauer P226 9mm was warming in his hand. Leave it to Meg to keep a cool head in the face of danger. But she always trusted him without a blink.

At least Everly had finally put that kind of trust in him.

He rolled his eyes at the mumbling taking place outside his house. An elephant could sneak up to the watering hole better than these scrubs.

The kitchen window blinds were open so he'd have to crawl to get to Everly. As if she heard him think her name, the door opened.

"Finnian," she yawned and stepped one foot into the living room.

"Stop!" He yelled in a whisper. Her eyes widened as they landed on the gun in his hand. He raised his finger to his lips. Then pointed at the door.

She nodded in understanding and moved back into his room. Going on the offense always ended better than waiting for someone to strike, but he didn't have that luxury with Everly in the house. It would leave her unprotected. He gripped the gun tighter.

The back doorknob rattled loudly. These men were idiots.

Maybe there was a way to go on the offense.

He dropped to the ground and belly-crawled across the living room to Everly. She wrapped her arms around him when he stood. "Shh," he whispered as he reached out and punched in his code to the alarm pad on the wall in his bedroom. No sense in sirens blaring a warning when he wanted a good look at the men after them.

"What are we going to do?"

"I'm going outside." And keep them outside. "Here." He pressed the gun into her hand. "This is the safety. This little latch. It's off right now. Shoot anyone that comes through that door." He kissed her hard on the mouth. "Except me. Try not to shoot me."

He didn't leave her any time to ask questions. He pushed up his window and looked around. It opened into a narrow gap between his and the neighbor's wooden fence. Those men wouldn't know what hit them.

16

The gun dropped by her side as Finnian's head disappeared out the window. Shouldn't he have taken the gun with him if he was going to fight them off? They probably had guns. He had what? Brute strength? It wasn't a damn *Popeye* cartoon.

She gripped the gun tighter with both hands as they began to shake. The doorknob in the back of the house rattled again, causing a familiar surge of panic.

Her body jerked with the first loud bang. Finnian said it was bolted shut, but that didn't mean they couldn't break a window like before.

Someone shouted one short intelligible burst that made her jump again.

She stepped to the bedroom window, sneaking a glance at the ground. Empty. She looked back and forth as well as she could and didn't see anyone. Did they get Finnian or the other way around?

Everly walked to the living room and leaned against the wall, listening. The absence of gunshots didn't mean he was okay. Silencers were made for this sort of thing.

A shadow passed in front of the window, crouched low. Something hit the front door with a dull thud.

Her hands tightened around the handle of the gun. If the door flew open and it wasn't Finnian, she'd shoot. Her throat squeezed shut, but she pushed away from the doubt. She'd just have to deal with the sight of blood. She had nowhere to run and hide. It was her or them.

She wouldn't be the victim.

"Everly."

The breath she'd been holding rushed out with the sound of his voice.

"Open the door."

Everly set the gun on the sofa as pure relief washed over her. Was it over? Did he catch whoever was after her?

She unbolted the door, and a man fell into the house between her feet. His face smeared with what must be blood. His head rolled to the side as he moaned.

Her stomach revolted, but she clamped her mouth shut. She would not get sick because Finnian had broken the guy's nose.

"I'm going to go put these men back in their car while we wait for the police." She tore her eyes away from the man at her feet. Blood splattered across Finnian's white shirt. His knuckles were covered with it. His eyes held a feral gleam in the small shred of light from the streetlight as he looked down at the man.

She stumbled past him and lost the contents of her stomach in the bushes. Okay, maybe she couldn't control her reaction. It wasn't Finnian's blood. He was okay.

Finnian's hand rubbed her back. He held out a bottle of water, his hands now clean. "I'm sorry. I should've made better preparations. Are you better?"

She nodded and swished the water around in her

mouth. And he'd expected her to shoot someone? Impossible.

The man on the ground moaned again.

"Do you recognize him?" She managed to ask in between gulping the water.

Finnian walked back over and pulled him up to a sitting position. In one motion, he hauled him up and across his shoulders like a caveman.

"This one's name is Donnie. He's the nephew of Lorenzo, the man I met in Miami. I figured he'd have something to do with this. I need you to open the car door for me. Use something, so your fingerprints aren't traceable."

"Got it." She ran back inside and grabbed a dishtowel from the kitchen before meeting him in the middle of the empty street. "Isn't he heavy?"

Finnian adjusted his grip on the man still hanging like a limp rag doll off his shoulder. "Not really. The other one is bigger."

The scent of stale cigarettes, body odor, and old fast food hit her the second she opened the car door. Dozens of empty beer cans littered the floor.

And a picture of her sat on the dashboard.

It was of her in a sundress at Tripp's birthday party maybe three years ago. A shiver crawled up her spine. Who had taken that?

A second photo was taken at the food court with Finnian last Sunday. She shoved them in her pocket. "Creeps," she muttered.

Finnian tugged at her elbow. "C'mon, I need to get the other one." He hesitated at the edge of the house. "Better wait here. The next one is a little worse."

Her imagination didn't help with her nausea, but she kept her head down and waited for him to return. He approached with the man hanging over his shoulder the same way as the first. She turned and opened the car door before the streetlight shone on the man's face.

Finnian ungracefully let the man fall into the backseat, and she shut the door without looking.

"What will you tell the police?" She asked, her mind still racing over the photos. How long had someone stalked her?

"I'll tell them the truth. I heard something and saw a suspicious car sitting out front. I noticed it'd been there all night."

"What will you tell them if they ask for your ID and link you to the arrest in Miami?"

Finnian shoved his hands into his jeans as they headed back into the house. "I hadn't thought of that. Not used to having a rap sheet, I guess." He closed the door and returned the deadbolt to its place. "I'm a little surprised you thought of that."

"Hey, one point for Everly."

"You get a million points for as much as you've put up with over the past week." He switched on a lamp. The second man must have been pouring blood because Finnian's shirt had a dark red streak down the back from where he'd carried him.

He turned. More blood covered his shirt from his shoulder to his waist. He picked his shirt away from his skin before pulling it off. "I need a shower."

"Yeah." Her gaze trailed over his chest, down to his abs. "Me too."

His eyes shifted to that dark look she loved. Warmth ran down her arms. She dragged her mind out of the gutter, or shower, and spotted a long, dark red mark already turning into a bruise that crossed over his ribcage. It was the second beating he'd taken in two days for her.

"What the hell happened this time?"

A half-laugh escaped. "The one in the back of the house had a crowbar."

She bit her cheek as she traced the mark. "That had to hurt when he hit you with it."

"Yes." His eyes met hers. "But I hit him harder."

"I guess you did," she mumbled. That explained the blood. "I don't like seeing you get hurt because of me."

"I have to protect you, Everly."

She understood that now. His nature was to protect. The power and heat from his body almost scalded her. She glided her hand down to his hip. "Thank you."

He whispered "Everly" as he shifted in front of her. "I wish we weren't in this situation. I wish we met some other time."

"Me, too. Just the two of us." But wishes didn't come true. Those men might be knocked out for tonight, but they'd be back.

EVERLY STRETCHED her arms over her head. She didn't know the last time she'd slept so well. She snuggled down deeper into Finnian's sheets, reaching for him, looking forward to a lazy start to the morning.

But his side was cold.

The clock read ten fifty. Brady was due to land around two. She'd have to evict herself from the bed sooner than later. No use in staying there alone.

This was the first time that she met someone from Finnian's family. A big step if she let herself dwell on it. Brady had seemed nice enough on the phone when he wasn't shouting about something Finnian had done.

Braving the chilly house, she slipped on a pair of socks and headed to the bathroom. Washing her face in ice cold water pushed the rest of the sleep away. They had a lot of decisions to make. About their next step with Tripp.

About their next step together.

Although their relationship seemed to be headed in a good direction, jumping in without some reservations wouldn't happen. Everly leaned on the bathroom sink, watching herself in the mirror. She needed time to stand on her own. This time, with Finnian, she wouldn't settle.

The smell of freshly brewed coffee drifted into the bathroom before Finnian's footsteps approached the door.

"Everly?" He knocked.

"Yes?" She brushed her teeth in record time and ran a hairbrush through her hair.

"Are you okay? Did you sleep well?"

She rubbed lotion over her face. "Yes. Even with the break-in, it was some of the deepest sleep I've had in a long time." Because he'd been beside her. "What happened to those guys?"

"The police picked them up about six this morning. Someone else must have called and reported it. From what I could tell, the men were still knocked out cold."

He sounded so proud of himself. She opened the door, as glad for the coffee as she was the good morning kiss he gave her. She could get used to this.

"I think I'm going to let Brady take a taxi here. I don't want to risk leaving you here alone, and I don't want to take you out in public."

She smiled and leaned her shoulder against the door. "Awe. Somehow that sounds sweet and insulting all rolled into one sentence."

He laughed. "You know what I mean."

She sipped her coffee and turned back to face the mirror. After her late-night, her skin and dark circles needed a little help. She shook the foundation she'd purchased from the nice lady at the mall and unscrewed the top.

She paused. "Are you going to watch me do my makeup?"

He shrugged and shoved his hands in his jeans. "It's been a while since I watched a woman doing makeup."

"Oh, and which of your past loves was that?" She tried to keep her voice light, but they'd never even discussed his past girlfriends. A man like him was bound to have a few in his history.

"She's a current love. Megan. She used to take up the bathroom for hours. She turned fifteen, and suddenly she was glued to the mirror."

"That sounds like every fifteen-year-old girl around the world."

He ran a finger through her hair, twisting the end. "Were you like that?"

"I suppose I was. Fifteen was so long ago. I remember feeling like everyone was watching me all the time."

"You're so pretty. I'm sure they were." He continued to twirl her hair.

If she was stronger, she would declare her love to him and see what happened. But that was major risk. Maybe in a few weeks, if everything calmed down, it would be easier. Did he love her?

She turned to face him. "For someone who's body has been beaten and bruised, you sure did wake up in a good mood." She skimmed her fingers along the light pink cut on his side, the butterfly strips still holding in place. "This looks good."

He wrapped his arms around her waist. "I'm not

worried about it. Any of it. Not when I had a beautiful woman sleeping in my bed, her glorious legs tangled with mine."

She arched an eyebrow at him. "Are you sure you're not just excited to see Brady?"

"Absolutely." He kissed her, long and slow. "My brother's legs are not nearly as sexy as yours." He released her. "But I'm happy enough to see him, I suppose. We haven't always been close, but it's still nice to see someone from my family. Meg was supposed to come to visit in a few months." He trailed off, a worry line forming between his eyebrows for a moment before he straightened and pushed it away. "But Brady will have to do."

"How old is he? Where does he fall among the dozen of Hayes children?"

"Fancy number nine."

"Oh." She rubbed her hands up and down his arms, hating the sudden switch in his mood. "I thought he'd be older for some reason."

"Did he sound like an old man on the phone? I'll be happy to tell him so."

She shook her head. "I've only heard you talk about being the youngest besides Meg."

"He's two years older than me."

She waited until she couldn't stand it. "How old are you?"

"Thirty-four."

"So, he's thirty-six."

He kissed her forehead. "That accounting degree sure does come in handy, doesn't it?"

She slapped at his arm. "Shut up." Waving her hand in the air, she made herself let go of him. "Let me finish getting ready and enjoy my coffee. Then maybe we can rummage through your kitchen, and I'll find something to cook us for lunch."

"Oh, there are so many culinary possibilities, I don't think you'll be able to choose." He laughed and flicked her hair. "Frozen pizza it is." He darted back into the bathroom and planted a kiss on her cheek, winking at her in the mirror before he left.

Her heart stumbled. The reflection in the mirror confirmed it. She was insanely in love with him. Although everything on the surface suggested he had some feelings for her, she would never know for sure until she was safe. Until she was confident that he wasn't acting this way because he had to protect her.

She needed more than his protection.

By the time she emerged, dressed in the pink sweater she'd bought that first night at the mall with him, he was sliding the pizza into the oven.

"Make yourself at home. I'm going to change." He closed his bedroom door, and she looked around the room. Neat. Clean. Not a book out of place. No evidence of anything from the night before.

Everly sat down and turned on the TV, flipping through the channels until she landed on a comedy, but it only served as a minor distraction. Waiting for Brady to arrive was killing her. If he was coming to help keep her safe, did that mean Finnian thought there was more trouble out there? What exactly could a lawyer do?

Finnian walked to a fake plant on the far side of the room, withdrawing a gun and holstering it under his pant leg.

"Because everyone hides their guns in fake plants."

"Did you know it was there?" He waited for her answer, a serious expression covering his face.

"No."

"Then I guess it works." He kissed the top of her head as he passed.

Did he ever relax in his own home? Not that she blamed him with the recent events. He checked the doors and then the window locks. Twice.

Finally, he brought the pizza out, setting it on the cardboard box it came in on the coffee table. With him beside her, the nerves she'd felt about Brady and the situation with Tripp disappeared. Snuggled up against his side, she laid her head on his shoulder. This was how it should be. Taking it slow. Getting to know everything about each other.

She studied his profile. Someday, maybe, she'd be at a place where she'd want to get married again.

Tires crunched over acorns as it sounded like a car pulled into the driveway. Finnian shot to his feet, gun already in his hand, this one from underneath the sofa.

The shadow of a car pulling into the driveway passed in front of the window. He peered around the edge of the blinds, and his shoulders relaxed. Everly released the breath she'd held.

"Brady's here." Finnian holstered his gun and opened the door. She came to stand beside him. "Of course, he wouldn't take a lowly taxi."

Brady unfolded himself from a gleaming black Porsche wearing a perfectly tailored dark gray three-piece suit. His hair was dark, nearly black, and trimmed neatly. A chrome tie pin that held his cobalt blue tie in place winked in the sun. The two men favored each other, but Brady's overall appearance held a certain gloss that Finnian's didn't. She decided right then that she wanted the T-shirt and blue jeans over the fancy suit and car.

Finnian met him at the edge of the small porch.

Brady climbed the steps, shaking his head until Finnian embraced him in a quick hug. Finnian's shoulders were broader, but Brady matched him in height. There wasn't a shortage of good looks in their family.

Brady moved past Finnian, a smile that wasn't quite warm sliding into place. "Everly Clarke, nice to meet you." He held out his hand.

"Hi." How was a man like this supposed to help keep her safe? She didn't see him crawling out the window at one in the morning to take on two men with his bare hands.

"Did you rent the Porsche or buy it?" Finnian asked as he passed them both.

He shrugged a shoulder, casting a glance back at the sports car. "Rent. I always try something different whenever I travel."

Finnian set Brady's bag down on the sofa and closed the door behind them, sliding the bolt into place.

"A little much in broad daylight." Brady indicated his head toward the lock. "Although you do look like you've had the shit beaten out of you a few times. Sorry I missed it."

Finnian glanced at Everly as he relayed the story from last night.

Brady's face hardened. "They attacked, *knowing* you were home with her. I hope you gave those bastards a taste of what it means to mess with us."

Finnian's quick smile, full of boyish charm, told her everything she needed to know. This easy, high-class lawyer image Brady Hayes portrayed shouldn't be underestimated. A thirst for fights ran in the family.

"Knocked them both out cold and then returned them to their vehicle. Someone else in the neighborhood reported them to the police this morning." He drew his brows together. "Ruined a perfectly good shirt too."

"They didn't even land a punch and disfigure that pretty face of yours. Those bruises will heal." Brady leaned close to Everly and dropped his voice into a mock whisper. "A crooked nose or broken tooth might help with the ego we've had to deal with since he was a baby."

"Okay, I didn't invite you here to insult me."

"Don't I get to be your lawyer *and* insult you? I thought that's what being your brother allowed me to do. I'm sure you'll toss one my way eventually. I can't help it that you can't call me 'baby Brady' like the rest of the family. You know how much I hate that."

Everly pressed her lips together to keep from laughing. "Did they ever call you baby Finnian?"

"Him?" Brady rested a hand on Finnian's shoulder. "He came out the same size I was at two. No one ever thought of him as a baby. Meg got a little bit of the teasing, but our mum always took up for her. You didn't argue with a wooden spoon to the back of your thighs."

"Ouch!" Everly said. "I'll be sure to remember that if you ever get out of line."

They all laughed for a moment, but Brady cleared his throat, and his smile fell away. "I need to understand everything from the beginning. Both of your relationships with Tripp. The information you learned about Charles and why you think Tripp paid off someone at the Miami police station. When your deportation hearing is scheduled—"

"Wait!" Everly held up a hand as her blood turned to ice. "You're being deported? When did you find out about that?"

Finnian sighed. "In Miami while in jail. The deportation officer said he'd been ordered to expedite the matter as soon as possible. Tripp must have spent a chunk of money to pull it off."

Brady crossed his arms and looked down his nose at Finnian. "I can't believe you didn't tell her."

Finnian shoved his hands in his pockets. "I hadn't gotten around to that yet."

Everly poked her finger at his bicep. "Don't give me that. You had almost twenty-four hours to tell me."

The apology on Finnian's face didn't make up for his deception. How could he leave right now? She needed him.

"Well, we're out of time now. I stopped by the police station on the way here." Brady looked between the two of them, but Everly had zeroed in on Finnian. After everything they'd been through, why did he keep it from her?

"You said you'd include me in decisions."

"This isn't my decision," Finnian shot back.

She crossed her arms. "No. But it affects me. Us. You've got to stop keeping me out of the loop."

"I think I need to talk to Finnian alone. If you'll excuse us, Everly." Brady grabbed his folder and pushed past Finnian, unlocking the door and stepping outside.

Finnian held out his hands. "Everly, darling—"

"Go." She leaned away from him. "Just go talk to Brady. See what he can do." Maybe he'd tell his brother everything since he obviously didn't feel the need to discuss it with her.

"We'll talk about this later."

"Before or after you're kicked back to England?"

"Before."

She walked back into the bedroom as her hopes of making a future with him disappeared. He was being deported, and that left her . . . alone. Again.

17

Everly peeked out of the blinds, the same way she'd done for the past fifteen minutes. Brady paced, his shouts carrying into the house, although she couldn't tell what he was saying. The window turned the display into a dramatic silent film starring two angry Englishmen. Finnian returned the shouts, gesturing at the house and then back at Brady. Judging by Brady's reaction, Finnian's deportation was imminent.

Brady shook a packet of papers at Finnian before he popped the back of his hand across Finnian's chest. He leaned in close and pointed between the paper in his hand and the house, again. How had she ever thought Brady was a calm, cool lawyer?

Finnian used both hands and shoved him away.

The hard push scattered Brady's papers on the ground. Brady lunged back at Finnian, swinging his fist.

Finnian ducked to the side, and the blow landed on his shoulder. Once he righted himself, he charged at Brady.

Men.

Everly ran outside. "Stop it!" She clamored between

them and pushed Finnian away with two hands. "Stop, Finnian." She couldn't control Brady, but Finnian's eyes focused on her. His heart pounded under her fingers.

Brady shifted around Everly and landed a solid punch along Finnian's already bruised jaw.

The smack of flesh caused Everly to squeal. She elbowed Brady in the ribs, pleased when he grunted in pain. He deserved it after his cheap shot.

"I said, 'stop.'" Everly held her hands up between them. "I don't know what's going on between you two but beating the crap out of each other isn't helping."

"You're wrong about that, darling. It's helping quite a bit." Finnian rubbed his jaw. "You've lost your touch, Brady." His accent sounded thick, and his voice strained.

"I wasn't trying to knock you out. Your flight leaves this afternoon."

Her stomach dropped. It was happening. "Flight?" Her dry throat made swallowing difficult. "Today?"

A sudden softness in his eyes transformed Brady from a man ready to brawl back into the sophisticated lawyer. "If he doesn't leave voluntarily, then there's a chance they won't let him back in the country for ten years. If what you've said is true about Tripp, he has some high-ranking officials in his back pocket to be able to pull this off without the actual hearing taking place. He's convinced someone that Finnian is a significant threat to society if he remains here."

Finnian shouted something completely unintelligible that caused Brady to chuckle.

He stopped pacing in front of her. "Come with me."

Everly blinked. "To the airport?"

"To England." He grabbed both her hands and held them to his chest, which was a good thing since her knees felt like they could buckle at any moment. "Come live with me there. At least until we get all of this figured out."

"Live with you," she repeated. "I can't just leave, Finnian."

"Nothing is stopping you." The pleading in his eyes almost changed her mind. God, she wanted to go with him. Not to England but anywhere.

Did he love her? She waited, but at his silence, she tried to make him see her side. "Finnian, my family is here. And the business—"

"I don't want you to stay here without me."

Did he love her?

"Tripp is still out there. You're not safe. I'll marry you if that's what it takes."

Brady whistled low and moved away.

Her stomach turned to lead. No matter how many times she'd told herself to believe him, that she wasn't just an obligation, he'd just declared it. She loved him, and he only wanted to keep her safe.

"Please, Everly." He kissed the back of her hands. "You know how I feel about you. I don't want us to be separated."

"Oh, yes, you've made that very clear. You have an unwavering need to protect me." She paused, wishing there were some other way around it. Wishing she could ignore that voice in her head. "I'm not going to give up my life again for a man when all he's offering in return is protection. It's not enough. I could buy a dog and a gun and get protection."

He paced away and shouted in French before returning, grabbing her by the shoulders. "You know that's not what I meant."

Every inch of her rebelled at the idea of taking that leap of faith when he'd not given her anything else to rely on.

Her imagination must have filled in the gaps in their relationship for her to have thought there was more. She'd wanted so much more.

"I . . . I can't give up my freedom again, Finnian."

"It's not like I'm throwing you into a damn prison. I'm asking you to come to England with me to stay out of harm's way." The look of pain and frustration on his face broke her heart. Hurting him was the last thing she wanted to do.

He was so wrapped up in his world of guilt over Sean that he didn't even see her. A part of him cared for her. That was reflected in his eyes, even now. But she wasn't going to love another man that didn't love her just as much in return. That mistake would not happen again.

Everly slipped her hands from under his. Her feet felt unsteady on the solid ground as she moved away. She had to put some space between them. She just . . . she couldn't leave. Not with him. Not like this.

"Don't worry about me. I'll find someone to keep a watch on the house until I figure out this thing with Tripp."

"I'm staying with you." Brady rested a hand on her shoulder. "Fly home, Fin. I'll set up an appointment for you to meet with someone at my firm's location in London. We can handle the case without having to extradite you back."

"I can't leave," Finnian muttered between clenched teeth. Every defined muscle down his arm popped out as he balled up his fists. The cords along his neck strained. His brown eyes darkened.

Even though she caused his unshed tears, Everly ran a gentle hand up and down his arm, trying to offer comfort through her own pain.

Brady checked his watch. "The next flight leaves in three hours. You need to pack. I'll take Everly home and then come back to get you."

"No." His eyes didn't waver from hers. "Stay with her. Whatever you do, stay with her and keep her safe. Promise me, Brady."

Brady held out his hand. "I promise."

Finnian shook it, the muscles of his forearm popping. "I'll get myself to the airport." He walked away with slow controlled steps.

Had she done the right thing? She gasped, sucking in a deep breath as his front door closed. A panic attack waited to overtake her.

"Don't do this here." Brady motioned her to walk to his car. "If we don't leave, he'll never go to the airport."

Everly jumped at a loud bang and then the sound of glass breaking. She turned back to the house, needing to see him, but Brady caught her arm.

"Leave him."

"But—"

"No. Get in the car, Everly."

Her blood thumped in her ears. Her skin turned to ice and then fire. Finnian had been with her since the beginning of this. And now she was alone.

"Everly." The command in Brady's voice pushed her down the driveway and into his car.

He typed her address into the GPS.

"I should have said yes." The words tumbled from her mouth before they even made it out of the neighborhood.

Brady's smile didn't reach his eyes. "No, you shouldn't have. It was poorly executed on his part, but he couldn't help it. He's never forgiven himself for . . ."

Everly waited, but Brady remained quiet.

"Sean?" She finally finished for him.

He sighed. "I wasn't sure if he'd told you about that. Besides our mum and me, and maybe Meg, he's never told anyone else in our family. Didn't want the sympathy. But maybe you understand the protective side."

"I do. That's one reason I didn't go. It's hard for him to split me away from his past." She leaned her head against the window. "I don't want to leave him like that. What if he doesn't forgive me?"

What if he decides to never come back? She'd have been safe in England. They could have taken the time then to get to know each other without this mess following them. It might have been her only shot. She stared out the window as her familiar city passed by. She'd just thrown her chance away with the best man she'd ever known.

"He needs to be alone. Maybe on the long flight home, he can figure out why you wouldn't marry him." Brady turned onto her street. "His proposal could've used a little more flowers and candlelight, and less marry me, so you don't die."

"The mention of love would've been nice." She twisted the bottom of her sweater. "I love him."

Brady pulled into the driveway and shut the car off but didn't move to get out. He faced her, his eyes the same brown as Finnian's. He placed a hand over hers. "Do you really doubt he loves you?"

"He's never said it."

"Finnian's told me a little of your past. Did your ex-husband tell you he loved you?"

Everly glanced at the house they'd lived in together. "Yes." He'd told her nonstop when they first got married. Even when he'd stay late at the office or jet down to Miami, he'd end his phone calls with the three words. Three empty words.

"I hope you see what I'm getting at. Remember that old adage that actions speak louder than words. Finnian's guilt over Sean drives him to protect everyone, but it wouldn't drive him this far. Sean wasn't just some kid down on his luck. Finnian was with him for close to three months. Night and day before he died. Finnian loved Sean like a brother."

Everly closed her eyes, squeezing out the pain for him.

"Finnian loves you, Everly, even if he doesn't know how to say it or even realize it himself yet."

Brady made it look so simple. Her stomach cramped as the reality of her life hit again. He was leaving, and she couldn't go. She couldn't trust what Brady said was true if Finnian couldn't even utter the words.

Brady got out and jogged around to open her door.

She stood, looking up at her house full of memories. She was content only a week ago. Not happy but coping. The little accounting business she'd neglected since Finnian arrived gave her enough money so that she didn't have to spend what little Charles had left to her in his will.

But she would sell this house. Too many memories of Charles and what she was before the world opened up again. Before Finnian walked into her life.

"Should we go in?" Brady glanced at the sky. "I'm not sure those storm clouds will hold much longer."

A piece of plywood covered over her front door from the last break-in. "I look like I live on a different side of town."

Brady chuckled. "I suppose it does. Do you have a hammer or crowbar?"

Everly patted her jeans. "Fresh out."

He rolled his eyes and walked to the trunk of his car. She leaned against the side of the house, crossing her arms as she stared up at the dark clouds. Why was everything so screwed up?

"I don't have a crowbar, but I think a hanger will work."

Crowbar. The blood on Finnian's shirt flashed in her

mind. "Did you know that Finnian beat one of those men with a crowbar? He took a hit across his ribs and then took the crowbar from him. And before that, he went to see some drug dealer guys, knowing he'd get the crap kicked out of him just by showing up. All to protect me."

Brady shut the trunk. Taking long, slow, deliberate steps, he began to unwind a metal hanger. "He was one of the top specialists in the drug unit. He's wasting his talent here in America, in my opinion. And since he doesn't give a shit about my opinion, I keep it to myself." He flipped over one of the empty terracotta planters set to the side. Standing on top, he straightened the metal wire, threading the hook end through the top crack of the garage door.

"What are you doing?" Everly flinched as the first few drops of cold rain fell. "I don't think you can reach the toolbox that way."

"Do you always have such a smart mouth?"

"Only when I'm irritated."

Something inside the garage gave way with a click, and the entire door settled. "There." He tossed the destroyed hanger to the side and, without any effort, lifted the garage door. "The emergency release lever."

"Ah. Nice to know that after living here for so long." She never locked the house door leading from her garage into the laundry room. If Brady could get in that easily, anyone else could as well.

She groaned as she walked into her kitchen. She'd expected the house to be trashed based on what the police had said before she left Miami, but did they really need to break everything she owned? It's not like she was hiding important documents where she kept her cereal bowls. Brady touched her arm.

"Stay here. Let me check it out."

"You and Finnian are too much alike."

Brady grunted and moved inside. He checked out each of the rooms, even venturing upstairs. "Clear," he called from the top landing.

She moved to her bedroom. The dresser drawers hung open, most of her clothes scattered around on the ground. Her bed sat at an odd angle as if they'd checked under her mattress.

Brady leaned into the room. "I think we need to stay at Finnian's house."

That wouldn't help his memory to leave her alone. Neither would hearing Brady's accent and subconsciously comparing everything he did to his brother.

"My house is perfectly safe."

Brady glanced around her room. "If by safe, you mean not safe at all, then I agree with you." His eyes narrowed. "It will be much easier to protect you there. At least Finnian has working doors. Any idea about what they were searching for?"

"I think it was information about the ownership of the company. There's nothing here. Everything I have is sitting in my suitcase at Finnian's."

"Pack a bag if you need it. We'll stay here until I'm sure Finnian has made it to the airport. I don't know if I can get him to leave if he sees you again."

"Tell me the truth. How hard will it be for him to come back?" Everly sat down on the edge of her bed.

"If we can find a judge that won't be paid off, not too hard, I suspect. They don't have anything other than Tripp's word about the theft."

"What did they say he stole?"

"Money. He took money from Tripp's personal safe in the office."

"That's stupid. Can he be deported for that? I thought it took years to deport even criminals."

"Anything can happen if you give a judge enough money. Tripp seems to want Finnian out of the way. After hearing the whole story, I think we all know if Finnian's out of the way, Tripp can get to you. That's why we need to go back to his place. It's easier to keep you safe. A two bedroom house like his is smaller to protect than a big thing like this."

She pushed herself up and grabbed a bag from the closet. If Brady was anything like Finnian, and he seemed worse being a lawyer, she'd never win the argument when it came to her safety and where she would stay. Besides, Brady seemed like he would enjoy the verbal fight even more than Finnian.

How long would she have to stay at Finnian's? A few nights? Weeks? Weeks of living with Brady Hayes worried her.

Finnian's small house didn't leave much room for separation. She'd hardly been away from Finnian since this all began, but it'd never bothered her. But now, she wanted her space. Somehow, she needed to settle this with Tripp as soon as possible. Then, maybe, she could put her life back together and figure out if she could salvage her future with Finnian.

FINNIAN CARRIED a light duffel bag through security. He'd left his guns and most personal items at home. He'd be back. As soon as the judge cleared him, he'd return to Everly and set everything right. Brady's blunt announcement about the deportation hadn't helped. He couldn't blame his brother. It was his own fault for not discussing it with her sooner.

He hadn't planned on asking her to marry him, either. She seemed so reluctant to drop everything to be with him that he'd assumed that she'd wanted something more permanent before leaving everything.

So, like he'd always heard, he spoke from his heart when he asked her to marry him.

He was never doing that again.

He couldn't help it if that fear to keep her safe overrode every other emotion. Even now, if someone nearby needed help, he'd go to them without a second thought. But she wanted more from him. There was more to give her, but he knew as soon as he said the words 'I love you' she'd run.

Appealing to her logical side had made the most sense at the time. He handed over his passport and ticket to the TSA Agent. How would he possibly get her back now? Did she really think he wanted her to come home with him only because he wanted to protect her?

"Idiot," he muttered. The TSA agent looked at him over his glasses. "Not you. Me."

The man glanced at his passport and handed it back. The easy trip through security gave him a few minutes to spare at the gate. The airport, without Everly, was the last place he wanted to be. Or needed to be. His place was beside her. Either in America or England. He'd always dreamed of returning home, helping on the farm, and maybe starting back with the local police. But those plans disappeared the minute she'd kissed him in this same airport.

He pulled out his phone, shoving away the urge to call her. He called Megan instead.

"Whoa, big brother, two calls in two days. I'm beginning to think you like me."

Finnian relaxed back into the small plastic seat. "You know you're my favorite baby sister."

A female's voice came over the loudspeaker and announced that the plane would be departing on time.

"Wait, are you at the airport?"

"Yes."

The long pause worried him for a moment.

"Is Everly with you?" Megan asked.

If only his answer were different. "No."

"Idiot."

"I've already declared myself as such, but it never hurts to have your baby sister to really dig in the knife."

She barked a laugh. "That bad, huh? What happened?"

He relayed the conversation, grimacing at his own words. It was a horrible proposal.

"I'm going to pretend that you are paraphrasing, and you really didn't say 'I'll marry you if that's what it takes'?" Meg sighed into the phone. "I'm begging for you to tell me you didn't say that."

"It sounds a lot worse when it's said back to you, okay, but it made sense in my head at the time. Look, I wasn't even thinking of being romantic. I needed her to come with me. Stay safe. I won't be able to live with myself if anything happens to her."

"I know, honey. You've both been through a lot. Do you want me to fly home? We can intrude at Katherine's flat in Dublin and force her to cook us crepes and crème brûlée until our stomachs burst. It's the least she can do since she only cooks for us on holidays."

"No." He half-laughed. "I don't want to pay for your ticket home."

The boarding instructions for his flight began.

"I have to let you go, Meg. The executioner has spoken."

"Don't be so hard on yourself, Fin. It will work out. You'll come back and sweep her off her feet. I promise. Then you'll have to pay to fly me to your wedding."

"I hope so. Do me a favor and call our mother and let her know I need someone to pick me up tomorrow. I'll text you my flight number."

"Will do. Talk to you later."

He hung up. The long flight to England should give him plenty of time to figure out what to say next time he talked to Everly. How could he make it up to her an ocean away? She didn't seem like a woman who would accept flowers or jewelry as an apology. She needed the words.

He shifted the phone to turn it off, but Brady's number lit up the screen.

"What now?"

18

E verly finished packing her bag, shoving a sweatshirt and exercise pants into it at the last second. No need to try to dress nicely for Brady. He moved so easily in his suit, he probably slept in one. She walked into the living room. The desk sat empty, her laptop missing. All her files were backed up, but it still annoyed her when she typed in the command in her phone to remotely erase the hard drive.

"You know you have no food in this house. Not a single biscuit or bag of crisps." Brady stopped in the doorway. "What's wrong?"

"You sound like Finnian."

"Impossible. There's not a bloodthirsty bone in my body."

Everly quirked up the edge of her mouth. "I think that's a little off-target after you sucker-punched Finnian in the face."

"That's not being bloodthirsty. That's just strategy. Finnian can bend a steal bar in half with his hands. I learned a long time ago to attack when I can." He crossed the room, surveying the mess around them. "Can you tell if everything is here?"

"My laptop was stolen. It's not a big deal since I wiped it remotely, but I hate knowing someone took my belongings."

"I hate it when someone takes something that belongs to me as well." Tripp appeared in the doorway from the garage.

Everly froze, her blood feeling as though it stopped pumping.

"How was Miami, Everly? Too bad you didn't manage to grab a few hours by the beach, get a nice golden tan while you were down there. It would've served you better than running around town, messing everything up."

She clasped her hands together. Shaking was her body's way of reminding her she was weak, and she hated it. The heat from Brady's hand as it squeezed her shoulder helped. She wasn't alone, but the wrong man stood next to her.

"It was enlightening." Her voice didn't shake. "Don't people usually knock before they enter someone's house?"

Tripp's shirt was half-untucked, his khaki pants smeared with dirt on the knees, and his hair sticking in all directions. It matched the slightly crazed look in his eyes. "We're old friends."

"Friends is an unusual way to describe our relationship."

"It would be safer if you considered me a friend. And who do we have here?" Tripp moved into the room. Brady's grip on her tightened. "My, my, Everly, you have moved on quickly. Did you tire of poor Finnian already? My resources tell me he's on his way back to England as we speak. Too bad he's not here to protect you."

"Why do I need protection, Tripp? What do you want?" She motioned to her destroyed house. "You've already had someone destroy the place looking for something."

"You know what I want," he yelled. He shook his head

slightly, his voice calming down. "The stock ownership. I know you have it. Charles wouldn't have given the stock to anyone else. He told me you'd inherit it. He was in love with you to a fault."

"He had a lousy way of showing it. What makes you think I have the stock for ATLighting? Charles could've given it to someone else. You saw the will."

"Before Donnie ended up in jail this morning, he'd already discussed it with a few friends of mine down in Miami. Finnian was there, asking about it. I doubt your lover kept it to himself." Tripp sneered. "And sadly, you're too smart to just go along without asking a billion questions. How did he give you the stock? In your trust fund? I told Charles that was a stupid idea, but he was determined to leave you the condo."

She tipped her chin back. Fine. If he already knew, then she wouldn't play dumb any longer. "It doesn't matter how I own it. I do. But what makes you think I'm going to give you any part of the business? I may run ATL myself."

Tripp laughed, and two men stepped out from behind him. "That's cute. Little Everly thinks she can run this company?" Tripp's face contorted into a sneer. "Where's the stock information? You need to sign it over before anyone else gets hurt."

"I don't have it here."

Tripp scrubbed his hand over his head, back and forth, until his hair stuck out at all angles. "Then, where is it?"

"Finnian has it."

Brady squeezed her shoulder again. At least while he kept quiet, they wouldn't realize he was related to Finnian.

"Fine. We'll search Finnian's place. Or should I call up my friends across the ocean to search his mother's house when he arrives?"

How could Brady stand it? He rested his other hand on her shoulder, pulling her back against his chest. He was either trying to restrain her or himself. She didn't dare look up at him. It probably took every ounce of his control not to charge at a man threatening his mother. Especially if he was anything like Finnian.

But Brady already said he played with strategy. Hopefully, that's what he did now because she didn't have a damn clue what to do next. Run? Fight? Play along?

Tripp stepped back and to the side. "We're going to Finnian's. Let's go, Everly."

She picked up her duffel bag. The legal papers for the stock sat in her suitcase in Finnian's bedroom. Along with Charles's computer. Her mind went to the gun hidden in the fake plant. Did Finnian leave it there?

Tripp stomped his foot, and she jerked. "Get a move on!"

Brady rested an arm over her shoulders.

"Not you." Tripp raised a gun she hadn't noticed before.

Everly stepped in front of Brady. "You'll have to kill me too. Then you won't get the stock."

"Get out of the way," Brady whispered. Unless that thousand-dollar suit came with a bulletproof liner, she didn't plan to move an inch. Tripp needed her. She had the upper hand.

Tripp's hand began to shake before he lowered the gun. "If you need your new boyfriend along, fine. Just get going."

Brady nudged Everly. She kept herself between Tripp and Brady as they passed by him. Somehow, she could get through this. She needed to keep a level head and think.

A four-door stretch sedan with tinted windows waited in the driveway. Tripp and one of the men climbed in the front. Brady shielded her from the other guy and helped her into the seat. His phone gripped in the palm of his other hand.

His fingers tapped a pattern onto his phone screen, and a second later, a faint phone ring began.

"Tripp," she tried to talk over the noise, give whoever Brady called time to answer, but it was no use.

The guard shouted as he slid into the seat across from them. "Hey!" The ringing stopped. The guard swung his big fist at Brady's head, but he ducked.

Brady shouted something in French as he and the guard wrestled in the small area.

Everly curled up against the door, glued to the fight, praying Brady knew what the hell he was doing as the two men wrestled in the confined space.

The guard's foot kicked her thigh, and she pulled into a tighter ball.

Brady gained the upper hand and pinned the guard against the seat with his forearm pressed into his throat. The guard gasped and kicked for air. Brady pressed harder. And shifted his knee into the guy's groin, earning a new, raspy protest.

He twisted in his seat. He smashed the end of a gun across the back of Brady's head.

Brady slumped to the floor.

Everly screamed and fell beside Brady. She grabbed the phone. *Number Eleven* displayed on the screen. It had to be Finnian since he was the eleventh child. Had he answered or did it go to voicemail? What had Brady yelled?

She ended the call and locked the screen before the guard snatched it from her hand. They'd never know who he called.

She rested her hand on Brady's back. His breathing was deep and steady, but no other movement. "Brady." She shook him. Blood trickled down the back of his neck in a thin line. She looked away.

"Don't try anything fancy, little Everly. I'm not above smashing this over your head as well." Tripp pointed the gun at her until she sat back. He adjusted himself in the front seat and directed the air conditioning vents in his direction.

A bead of sweat rolled down his temple. He looked horrible. Claudia had mentioned Tripp's drug habit. Great, let's add an addict in need of a fix into the mix of Tripp's insanity.

She leaned forward to check on Brady again, but the guard kicked her hand away. It stung, bringing tears to her eyes, but she didn't utter a sound. She wouldn't utter a sound from here on out that let Tripp know he scared her. He wanted the stock. She wanted to stay alive and keep Brady safe.

"You okay, Leo?"

Leo, with bright red marks covering his throat, grabbed Brady's cellphone and broke it into two pieces. Maybe Finnian would get the message. In the end, she couldn't rely on that. Everything rested on her ability to stall Tripp until Brady recovered. Or else she had to handle it herself. For the first time in years, the thought didn't scare her.

Two men and Tripp are taking us back to your house for the stock. They all have guns. She's scared but fine for now. Hurry.

His brother's message ended with a loud thump and then the worst sound in the world: Everly's scream.

Finnian jerked his bag on his shoulder and slowly moved away from the gate before he burst into a steady jog. Any faster and he would have to answer to airport security. He apologized as he pushed through the crowd until he exited into the bright afternoon. He hailed a taxi and checked his watch. It'd be rush hour getting home right now. He shouted his address to the driver.

"Where? I didn't understand what you said, man."

Finnian took a deep, controlled breath and repeated his address. The echo of Everly's scream replayed in his mind. He had to get to her.

"That will take almost an hour in this traffic."

"I know," he gritted out between his teeth. Finnian typed his and Everly's address into his phone. With traffic, it would take about thirty minutes for Tripp to drive them back to his house. He can only hope that Brady's call hadn't cost him more than the price of his phone. Brady would die before he let something happen to Everly. But that commitment belonged to Finnian.

Should he try her phone? He didn't want to risk Tripp finding out that Brady called him. The more Tripp thought he'd get away with it, the less protected he'd be. That's *exactly* where Finnian wanted him.

Cocky and careless.

Finnian unlocked his phone again but let it fall into his lap. He needed to call the police. Have them show up and arrest Tripp. But what would happen then? If Tripp managed to pay off a judge, he probably had the police on the payroll as well. They hadn't been any help since the first burglary.

The stop and go traffic pushed Finnian's patience. He rolled down the window, trading the taxi's smell of a litter box with the exhaust of rush hour traffic.

He didn't have a gun. He didn't have a knife. Nothing but his bare hands. He itched to wrap those around Tripp's throat for everything he'd done to Everly, but he needed something. Whoever was guarding Finnian now probably had orders to shoot him on sight.

"I need to make a detour. Stop by the ATLighting building on Peachtree."

"You're the boss, man." The driver swung off at the next exit. In three short traffic lights, he pulled up in front of the building.

"Wait here." He jumped out and started for the front door. No. They'd probably have a watch out for him. He diverted to the left. There were only three external cameras on the left side of the building. He'd pointed out that lack of security several times, but no one had listened. Now he was glad for it.

He pulled out his wallet and slid his key card in the rear exit. It flashed red.

"Damn it." He paced short, quick steps in front of the door. What to do?

Shelley.

He dialed her office number.

"Good afternoon, ATLighting, Inc."

"Shelley."

"Well, aren't you a bold Englishman." She laughed. "I miss seeing that handsome face of yours around my office."

"I miss you too. Listen. I don't know what Tripp has told you about the theft—"

"That it's fake. He didn't exactly tell me, but I was here the afternoon he staged the entire thing. I wanted to come forward, but you know, I have six grandchildren that I'm raising with their mama being deployed."

"Well, good news is that Tripp no longer owns ATLighting, so you don't have to worry about the repercussions."

"What! I think you just made my year with that

statement." She rambled on for a moment and Finnian held his tongue.

"I'm in a hurry. Can you access the card reader access from your computer?"

"Yes. What ya needin'?"

"I need to get in the back door. There's a few things I need from my locker."

"One second ... done."

He swiped his card. Green. He pulled the door and took the stairs until he reached the elevators. He paced in the small elevator while the soothing music grated against his nerves. Shelley waited by the doors when he stepped off.

"What's the matter?" she asked.

"Tripp has lost it. Charles left the entire company to Everly." Finnian motioned her to follow him to the break room. "He's been sending men after Everly to try and kidnap her to force her to sign over the stock."

Shelley started fanning herself. "That sweet thing never hurt a fly. She's the one that's been stomped on by those two idiots since the company got so profitable."

"Tripp has her now."

Her hand flew to her throat. "No! Do you think he'll really hurt her? Did you call the cops?"

"Tripp has paid off so many people, I don't trust them." He rolled the numbers to his combination, and the lock popped open. He grabbed his gun.

"You don't mean to go rescue her yourself, do you?"

He patted Shelley on the shoulder. "You do remember I was a policeman back home, right?" She nodded, her eyes glued to the 9mm in his hand. "Good. But, yes, now is the time for the police to be involved. Do me a favor? If something happens to me, I want you to give this to Everly." He turned and scribbled on a sheet of paper lying on the break room table. Shelley read it. She smiled and folded it in half.

"You just make sure nothing happens." Her eyes misted. "I enjoy watching you prance in and out of my office too much for you to go and get yourself killed."

Finnian gave her a hug and shoved the gun in the back of his pants, untucking his shirt to make sure no one could see. He started to walk away but turned back to Shelley. "Prance?"

She laughed and pushed him out the door. At least, now, if something happened Everly would know the truth. She'd know that he loved her.

19

Everly stood on the porch while Derek, the man that drove the car, wrestled with Finnian's front door lock.

"Is there an alarm on this door?" Derek looked back to Everly, but she crossed her arms.

Tripp nudged her with a gun. His new favorite thing to wave around in the air since he knocked Brady unconscious. Thankfully, Brady had recovered before they'd made it to Finnian's house.

As if nothing happened, he'd blinked, sat back on the seat, adjusted his tie, and propped an arm on the back of Everly's seat. Pain radiated in his eyes with the one glance he'd given her, but to anyone else, he looked just fine. Now, Brady kept the side of his body in full contact with Everly.

"Yes." Everly sighed. "There is an alarm."

"Do you know the code?"

"No." That was the truth. She held her hands up when Tripp wheeled around with the gun. "I'm serious. I don't know the code."

"If this alarm goes off and the cops arrive, I won't have a

choice but to shoot your boy-toy here and drag you back to the car." Tripp pointed the gun at Brady's forehead.

Everly's breathing increased despite her attempt to control it.

"I know the code. Calm down." Brady set a hand on her shoulder. "Zero-four-sixteen." He leaned closer and dropped his voice to a whisper. "Our mum's birthday. We all use the same number."

The alarm beeped when the door opened. Derek punched in the code, a loud beep signaling the all-clear.

All signs of the mess she'd heard Finnian make was gone. Just as before, the room was neat and clean. The faint smell of their pizza still hung in the air. Only a few hours ago, she'd sat snuggled up to Finnian on the couch laughing and enjoying life. Even contemplating a future with him. Now, she didn't know if he was on the plane to England or on his way to her.

"Where are the papers?"

Everly pulled her shoulders back, glad for the support Brady gave her. She could do this. Stalling was her only option. "I want answers, Tripp."

"I don't have to give you anything." He waved the gun at her. "I will shoot you."

"My will states that all of my assets will be given to my brother should I die." She tilted her head to the side. "That would include the stock. You know how tenacious Cade is. I think you have a few minutes to explain yourself."

Tripp's face turned red. He pulled at the end of his hair. "Fine." He wiped the back of his hand over his glistening forehead. "What is your pathetic, little brain wondering?"

Everly crossed her arms, giving Tripp the best "eat shit" look she could. "Did you kill Charles?"

"No." His nasty smile heightened her anger. "I didn't kill Charles."

"*Who* killed Charles? I know he was murdered before the accident was staged."

Tripp's smile fell a little. "You found out more than I suspected while in Miami. Donnie did the job. But I ordered it."

The confession only confirmed what she'd suspected. "Why?" It was the biggest question that haunted her.

Tripp sat down on the sofa and leaned back, cocky as he ever was. "Charles owned my half of the stock and wouldn't give it back. We'd talked about our wills. When he said he'd planned on giving the stock to someone for safe-keeping, I was worried it was you. I know how to handle Claudia. But you—" He sat forward and slammed the butt end of his gun down on the glass coffee table.

The table shattered. His eyes glassed over, and his breathing became erratic. "You complicate the hell out of everything."

"What is wrong with you?" Everly wouldn't have customarily asked a man with a gun that question, but this was Tripp. He'd been the best man at her wedding. Her husband's best friend for nearly two decades.

"You!" He pointed the gun at her. "You're my problem. You've done nothing but cause me problems." He stood, ignoring the glass on the floor as it crunched under his shoes.

Everly stood her ground, more in fear than confidence as he stalked closer, his eyes locked on hers. "If you'd just given me the stock last week, none of this would have happened to you."

He raised his hand.

"Tripp—"

He backhanded her.

She staggered back and covered her face, the stinging almost unbearable.

Brady lunged at Tripp. He landed his punch, but Derek grabbed his arm before he threw the second one.

Tripp pulled the gun and cocked it at Brady.

Everly, arms out wide, plastered herself to the front of Brady. "Don't shoot! If you shoot him, you'll never get your stock back." She buried her face in his shirt. She wouldn't let something happen to Finnian's brother.

Brady wrapped his arms around her.

The pain in her face radiated from her cheekbone to her temple and behind her eyes. But she wouldn't cry now. Later. She'd sob like a baby, later.

"Damn it," Tripped mumbled. Slowly, she released Brady's waist, twisting so that she still blocked him, partly, from the gun.

Tripp scratched his cheek with the barrel of the pistol. "The stock, Everly. My patience is running low with you two."

Brady's hands rested on her shoulders. He leaned down. "Keep stalling."

Did Brady think Finnian was on the way? God, she prayed he was.

"I don't like whispering." Tripp motioned Brady to the side with his gun. "Separate."

Brady stepped away.

Everly edged toward the fake plant. Stalling was one option. The other was a heavy gun. She blinked, clearing the last of the haze from the hit to her face. Could she do it?

"Derek, get me some ice." Tripp sat down on the sofa again.

Stay strong. "I don't need ice."

Tripp flicked his hand. "I was talking about me. The English brute hits hard. I can tell you're from the same stock as Finnian."

The corner of Brady's mouth twitched. A light amusement shone in his eyes for a moment. He fisted and then relaxed his hand.

If they weren't in this situation, she'd have laughed.

It ran in the family. They enjoyed these things—even the prim lawyer whose suit was *still* unwrinkled enjoyed fighting.

Tripp leaned back when Derek handed him ice wrapped in a towel.

Everly inched closer to the plant.

"Tell me, Everly, how does screwing this brother compare to Finnian?" He laughed and opened his eye, the craziness back. "Or Charles? You really do get around. I hate it I never got in on the rotation."

The amusement vanished from Brady.

"Since I'm so dull and lifeless in bed, I doubt you would've enjoyed yourself," she tossed back, repeating his own words back to him.

Tripp chuckled, waving the gun at her. "Funny. You're right, I wouldn't have. Sign over the papers."

"Not yet." She crossed her arms. "How did Charles end up with your half of the stock?" He'd kill her one way or another. That was clear now. He had no intention of letting her go. Or Brady.

Tripp rolled his eyes, grimacing and replacing the ice. "You never stop, do you?"

She shook her head, the pain now a dull ache. "Nope."

"I owed some money to a man in Miami. Charles wouldn't let me pull it out of our general business accounts. He said that the side businesses we ran didn't ever need to mix with the main business. You know, didn't want the Feds catching on."

Oh, she knew. Charles was meticulous with his records when it came to taxes. That's why so many things didn't add up. The extra money pouring into that account in Miami didn't all come from ATL.

"So, Charles bailed you out, and you repaid him by having him killed?"

Tripp chewed on her words a moment before that mad gleam came back. "Yes. That sums it up nicely. I had him killed before he could screw things up. Turns out I was too late."

Another step and she'd be within an arm's reach of the fake plant.

"Give me the stock, Everly. Then we can both go our separate ways."

"I still have questions." Not many, but she'd have to come up with something. A trickle of sweat ran down her back. "What does Claudia have to do with everything?"

Tripp's eyebrows jetted down together. "Claudia? Charles didn't leave anything to her. She's not involved in this."

She exhaled slowly with her focus on Tripp. She'd thrown that out for no reason, really, but maybe he'd start talking about her and give them a little bit more time.

"But she's still living in the condo."

"True. Claudia loved Charles. She was interested in me too." He crossed his ankle over his knee. "I think she hoped something would become of us once Charles died. I dabbled there once or twice but decided to move on."

"Did she know your plan to kill Charles?" Everly took another step.

"No, but she didn't cry at the funeral. She assumed Ray

or someone else killed Charles. No one ever suspected me." He stood and walked over the broken glass and started pacing by the front window. He tapped the gun against his leg.

Brady watched him like a hawk zoned in on his prey.

Derek stood to the side, his eyes focused on Brady. Good. Maybe he wouldn't notice her. Leo passed by the window, keeping watch.

Derek and Tripp both had a gun. Who would she shoot first? How could she shoot anyone! Breathe. She could do this. She *had* to do this.

Tripp paused, turned, and punched the wall. "Where are the papers?" He screamed.

He rushed toward Everly, coming within an inch of her face.

Brady darted her direction, but Derek grabbed his arm, restraining him.

Tripp's spit hit Everly's cheek when he spoke. "Give it to me!" He pushed the gun up under her chin. "I'm tired of playing this game."

She stumbled to the side, toward the plant, as if she were frightened. It wasn't hard to pretend. If the gun were there, she'd use it. The cold steel pressing ruthlessly against her throat confirmed that.

"I can't give you back ATL if you kill me, Tripp."

"If the documents are in here, I'll find them after you're dead."

A harsh laugh escaped her lips and surprised her. "Too many people know that I own the company. If you suddenly show up with all the stock and I'm dead, they'll all point the finger at you. You can't kill everyone."

"Like who?"

"Uh, Ray. Lorenzo." She tried to think of others but those two made Tripp's pale face turn white. "Yeah. They both know," she continued. "Ray said he still has some score to settle."

With Derek's hand on his bicep, Brady looked ready to pounce, everything in him straining. His focus stayed on Tripp's gun.

"I'll handle Ray." Tripp's gun pressed harder against her throat. "Where. Is. It?"

She swallowed down the contents of her stomach. Her stalling had ended. "Finnian's bedroom. My"—she swallowed again—"suitcase."

Tripp cocked his head for Derek to go search.

"But what about this guy?" Derek shoved Brady.

Brady turned and swung for Derek. He caught the edge of his shoulder as he ducked.

Derek returned the punch.

Brady's head knocked back. He counter-punched.

A moan escaped as Derek stumbled to his knees.

Tripp fired his gun in the air.

Everly ducked, covering her ears as the ceiling plaster rained down.

"Stop!"

Both men had their hands up, ready to hit again.

Tripp cocked the gun at Brady. "Derek, go get her suitcase. I'll keep this one straight."

Brady shot Everly a hard look she couldn't interpret.

She bit the inside of her cheek, the metallic taste of blood filling her mouth. This shouldn't be happening. It'd be better if Finnian stayed away. At least he'd stay alive that way.

A sob escaped.

Tripp cut his eyes at her. "There's the fear." He laughed. "I knew it was there somewhere."

She filled her lungs with air. Focus on the gun. Everly caught Brady's attention. She purposefully looked to the plant and back.

He narrowed his eyes.

She did it again. He'd have no clue what she meant.

"Derek? Did you find it?" Tripp kept the gun pointed at Brady.

"Yeah." Derek emerged. "I had to get through all the girly things." His eyes landed on Everly's chest and slid down. "The papers were in the bottom."

She repressed a shiver. These men wouldn't have anything else to hold over her.

Tripp held out his hand. The folder contained everything she'd learned in Miami. It had her notes from what Finnian relayed Ray had said, what Claudia mentioned, down to what John said about the trust fund. Tripp flipped through the pages without pause.

"I don't see it." He shoved the folder at Everly. "Find it."

She turned away, just a little, pretending to set the folder on the edge of the flower planter.

There it was.

The edge of the gun lay below the fake moss. But how did she use it? She remembered what he said about the safety, but did she have to cock it or simply pull the trigger?

"Well?"

She searched through the papers. ATL's transfer document was attached to the back of the trust documents. Hoping this was the right move, she pulled it out.

"Here it is."

Tripp snatched it from her hand. "Finally."

Derek turned away. Tripp's head stayed bent over reading the document. Brady stared straight at her.

She reached in and pulled out the gun. It was now or never.

20

"Yes, I'm pulling up to my house. There's a man in there with a gun."

"Sir, do not enter your house." The ticking of the operator's typing on a computer increased. "Stay where you are."

"My fiancé and brother are in there." He didn't even think before naming Everly that. After today, she'd marry him one way or another. He'd beg her if necessary. "I'm a former police officer. Please tell the police to stay back. Do not use lights and sirens. The man in there will start shooting."

"Sir, I have to advise you again to stand down."

"I can't."

"Sir—"

"Listen." Finnian ignored the confused look on the cab driver's face. "I'm going in. I have a gun. I'm a trained SWAT member. Tell them to approach with caution." He opened the door. "Oh, and don't shoot the big Englishman. Either of them."

He hung up.

"Dude, you might want to listen to the 9-1-1 person."

Finnian threw three twenties at the man. "Unless you want to wait and have a front-row seat, leave."

"Gotcha." The cab drove off before the door was closed.

Finnian scrambled to the bushes three houses down. He had no idea how many men were in there with Tripp. Who was posted? Where? Did he know them?

A better question. Did they know him?

He crawled along the edge of the sidewalk until he reached the grass of his own yard. One man that he didn't recognize stood on the porch, his gun sticking out of the back of his pants.

Taking a rock, he threw it to the driveway.

The guy turned, and Finnian rushed between the houses to the backyard. He scaled the fence in a few moves and then looked at his bedroom window. "Please bloody work," he mumbled.

He reached up. The window gave way and opened. Still unlocked from when he'd crawled out this early morning. How had he forgotten to relock it? Didn't matter. It was the "in" he needed.

Pulling himself up, he slid inside, and dropped to the floor. Years of training came back. But this was a different situation. It meant more than his own life or death.

"You need to sign this." Tripp's voice carried from the living room.

"It still won't change anything if I end up dead. No one will believe you."

"I'll make it look like a lover's quarrel between Finnian and this guy."

"Not likely," Brady's voice boomed.

The pressure released a little. They were alive. Both of them.

He gripped his gun tighter. From this position, he'd enter the room blind, not knowing where either one of them stood.

"What the hell? Where'd you get a gun?"

Finnian pressed his body harder against the wall, forcing himself not to move. Who had a gun?

"Finnian leaves all sorts of thing lying around."

Damn it, Everly!

Finnian leaned into the open doorway. Everyone should be preoccupied with Everly and her gun. She stood near the fake plant, holding his Sig Sauer pointed straight at Tripp.

Both Tripp and his guy pointed a gun at her. Finnian's stomach tightened before relaxing. He'd done this before. It'd just never involved two people he loved.

Brady stepped in Everly's direction, but the guy closest grabbed his arm and yanked him back as he pressed the gun to his head.

"Drop the gun, little girl, or else he gets it."

The sunlight shifted, highlighting a sizeable blue bruise across Everly's face, from her cheek to her hairline.

Finnian growled.

Brady and the man beside him turned at the sound.

The moment Brady's eyes connected with his, Finnian rushed the room, keeping his gun down. He didn't have any jurisdiction to kill Tripp if he could diffuse the situation. He wanted Tripp to rot in prison. The minute he made a move to shoot Everly or Brady, he'd risk jail to save them.

Brady grabbed the guy's gun as he wheeled it at Finnian.

A shot discharged. Finnian flinched as shards of the wall exploded beside his head.

Brady kneed the guy in the groin, unarmed him, and hit him across the jaw.

One down. That left Tripp with a gun pointed at Everly.

Everly smiled. It was the oddest sensation to have the woman he loved to smile at him as Tripp roared, "Dammit!" He swung his gun toward Finnian. "You aren't supposed to be here."

The gun in Tripp's hand shook. Finnian shifted to the side, drawing it farther away from Everly. "Well, here I am."

Tripp fired.

He jumped to the side, but not quick enough. Pain and heat seared Finnian's leg. He stumbled forward as his free hand felt for the wound. Upper, outside of the thigh. Nothing major hit. He cocked his gun as Tripp pointed it at Everly again.

Everly looked down at her gun. She flipped the safety and pointed it back at Tripp. "Drop your gun, and I'll drop mine."

"Little Everly doesn't know when to quit, does she?" Tripp cocked his head to the side as he shifted his stance. Tripp's gun trembled harder. That wasn't a good sign.

"I'm not little, and I'll quit when you stop being an underhanded snake."

"Such harsh words." Tripp laughed with a dry bark. "I should call your bluff. You wouldn't shoot me."

"I don't want to shoot you, but I will. I will right between the eyes if you kill Finnian."

"What if I give him a matching limp on the other side?" Without pause, he pointed at Finnian's right leg and fired. "Oh, I like this."

Don't fall. His leg went numb before pain replaced the sensation, pulsating through his body in steady time with his heartbeat. He kept his feet and reached down. This was closer to the center. Could've hit something vital. They needed to wait for the cops. Let them arrest Tripp. Everly didn't need to watch him kill Tripp.

Everly's breath started in soft, quick intakes.

No. She could *not* have a panic attack right now. Their eyes met. "Focus, darling. I'm fine."

"Yes, he'll likely bleed to death before you have the nerve to do anything." Tripp cocked the hammer back on the pistol and raised it to Finnian's chest.

Everly fired.

Tripp slumped to the ground and screamed. His gun fell, discharging, putting another hole into the wall. His hands clutched over the blood spreading over the crotch of his pants.

Finnian dropped to a knee, wanting to go to her but the pain in his legs was too much. "Don't look, darling."

Everly ran to him. "Finnian!"

He took the gun from Everly's hand and set it on the sofa beside him. "I'm fine."

"You're not. You're bleeding." She helped him sit on the sofa. "We need to call an ambulance."

"Police will be here soon." He cupped her cheek. "Are *you* alright?"

Everly started to turn toward Tripp, but Finnian held her chin. "No. Don't look."

Brady kicked Tripp's gun away from him as he approached, blood smeared across his cheek. He tossed his coat to the side and began to unbutton his dress shirt soaked through with blood, some from his own bloody nose and a cut above his eye.

He wadded the shirt up and pressed it to his nose. "I doubt the cleaners want to try and deal with this one."

The man who'd held Brady lay unmoving on the floor with his face a mess. London hadn't made his big brother too soft after all.

"Are you alright?" Brady asked. "Your legs?"

Both legs had eased into a steady burn of pain but walking again was out of the question. "They hurt like hell right now, but I'm better off than Tripp."

"I think I'll have nightmares about that," Brady said as he motioned to Tripp. "Did you mean to hit him there?"

Everly nestled her head tighter on Finnian's chest and mumbled something.

Finnian leaned back. "What was that?"

"Yes." Her lips twitched as she looked up at him. "I split the difference in the shots you took."

"Split the difference?" Brady repeated before laughing and slapping Finnian on the shoulder. "You better get the next proposal right. We need to make sure she stays on our side."

"I'm going to propose every day for the rest of my life until she says 'yes.'" He pulled her close again, kissing the bruise along her cheek. "I love her too much to ever leave again."

"Oh, Finnian," she mumbled and began to cry. He didn't know if that was a good sign but holding her was the only thing he wanted to do.

The door kicked open.

"Freeze!" Three policemen bust through, guns drawn and pointed at Finnian and Brady. Finnian shielded Everly with his arm, a wave of nausea nearly toppling him over.

Brady held up the bloody shirt.

"I'm the one that called you." Finnian let the police take his gun. "This guy is the one that kidnapped these two."

"Yes, we got the message about your brother and fiancé being involved."

"Fiancé?" Everly's hands twisted the bottom of his shirt.

"I told you I wasn't going to stop asking." He kissed her, meaning for it to be short, but not wanting it to end.

"Sir, an ambulance is out front. We need to have you checked out."

Everly jerked away from him. "Please, go."

Brady and the paramedic supported him as he limped out of the house. A stretcher passed by for Tripp. The third man, the one he'd spotted outside, sat in the back of a patrol car.

They settled Finnian on the stretcher. "Thank you, Brady." Everly rose on her toes and kissed Brady's cheek. Finnian pulled her back after her lips barely touched. That was enough of that.

"You're welcome."

"I have another favor to ask you." She snuggled under Finnian's arm, her arms wrapping around his waist as the paramedic cut the jeans from his legs.

"Someone else you need me to beat up?"

Finnian laughed at the optimism in his voice.

"Not right now." She looked up at Finnian. "But do you mind coming back to America and staying for a few weeks?"

"I'm due for a holiday. Why?"

"I need someone here I trust to run the company while I'm on my honeymoon."

Finnian crushed his lips to hers. He tried to drag her across his lap, but the paramedic stopped him.

He cradled her face in his hands. "You're saying 'yes'?"

She nodded.

"I love you."

Her features softened. "I love you, too."

"You're coming with me, then? To England, until we can figure out my citizenship."

"A wedding on a farm in England sounds perfect."

He kissed her lips. "Spending the rest of my life with you sounds perfect."

EPILOGUE

Weddings weren't unusual for the Hayes family. Out of twelve kids, roughly half were married, with Finnian being the latest. It still remained a bloody mystery how in the hell he managed to convince a remarkable woman like Everly to become his bride.

Brady Hayes sat alone at a table outside his family's farmhouse, listening to the hum of the conversation around him, considering how to gracefully exit without causing too much attention. The toasts had been made. The cake cut. Now, everyone was dancing and drinking. He loved his family, but he enjoyed his life in London, away from the faint smell of goats and memories of growing up in the country.

Away from the painful memories of their father.

"Ready for your big American adventure?" Megan, the youngest of the Hayes dozen, plopped down in the chair beside him. Her brown hair was curly and wild from dancing, the same way it was when she was little. "Fin said you're leaving in two days."

"I am, and yes, I am ready. I've squared away everything

at work." Ready to step into the role of temporary CEO at ATLighting, Inc.

"And what about Layla?"

Brady kept his personal life personal for the most part. That'd included his relationship ending two months ago. "We're no longer together."

Megan's eyes widened to large, brown saucers. "You were going to propose. Wait!" She grabbed his arm. "Did you propose?"

He sighed, wishing to be back in his own flat with a drink. "Yes."

"Did she say yes?"

"Yes."

Megan huffed. "So, what happened."

"I broke it off." He looked off into the distance. "It wasn't right."

"When was this?"

His little sister was the nosiest of the group. "September."

Megan smiled. "Good."

He arched an eyebrow. "Good?"

"Yes. This is great timing. You can go to America without any worry of Layla back in England. Get away from it all. She wasn't right for you." She nudged him and winked. "Maybe find a pretty American, like Finnian?"

"I'm not interested in finding anyone pretty, American or not. I'm going to do a job. Based on my conversations with Everly and Finnian, it's not going to be an easy vacation. The bookkeeping is dirty. A lot of underhanded dealings went on with the prior owners." Dangerous dealings based on the fact that Finnian was cleared only last week to walk down the aisle after being shot in each leg.

"I know if anyone can do it, it's you." She messed up his

hair. He laughed and jerked away. "All those smart brains are hidden behind your pretty face."

"Same with you, my Meg." He picked up his beer. "Such talent. When will you settle down and give us an art show? I know those contacts of mine have reached out to you. Even without connections, the art world would welcome you, I'm sure."

Megan rolled her eyes. "I will. Promise. I'm just not ready yet. I told myself that by the time I reached thirty, I'd toss my arse into the ring and take the criticism. That gives me another month."

Everly approached the table, a bright smile that hadn't left her lips aimed at Megan. "I'm getting ready to throw the bouquet. I think you're required to come to fight over it." She bent down, pretending to whisper. "But watch out. If you don't catch the bouquet, my brother will be waiting to console the women who lost out."

"No." Finnian walked up, dropping his arm around Everly's shoulders. "I've seen Cade in action. You're not to go near him."

Megan wiggled her eyebrows and leaned around her brother. "I am single now. Which one is he?"

"The one I plan on following around the rest of the reception, ready to box his ears if he takes one sideways look at you. He's not for you, Meg."

Everly patted Finnian's chest. "He's not that bad. He's coming to work for the company. Said he'd be happy to help with our Miami office and do the legwork for Brady when he needs it down there. He finished up his MBA in August and already has some crazy degree in engineering. He'll be a great help on both sides."

"Sounds interesting." Megan leaned farther to the side until she nearly fell from the chair.

"Don't even think about it," Brady mumbled. "Maybe I do need to stick around. Keep an eye on you."

"I'm twenty-nine. Remember?"

Finnian patted her shoulder. "I think you're mistaken. You're only ten, and I'll not have you talking like that." He kissed Everly's temple. "Now, can you throw this bouquet so we can make our exit? I'm ready to have you to myself for the next six weeks."

"C'mon, Meg." Everly left with her arm hooked through Meg's, looking like sisters already.

"Don't know how you managed to find the perfect woman for you, but there she is." Brady stood and held his hand out, shaking Finnian's. "Congrats."

Finnian didn't release it right away. "I'm worried about what you may find once you start digging into ATL. I've personally seen a lot of what Tripp and Charles did, but not everything. I need you to promise me two things."

"What?" Brady hated that Finnian had any thoughts of that on his wedding day, but it may be the last time he saw his brother until the six weeks were up.

"First, I know I've asked this of you before, but I need for you to get some of the mess cleaned up before Everly returns. She'll say she can handle it, and I'm sure she's more than intelligent enough to run a multimillion dollar business legitimately. That's not what you'll find. The last thing I want is for her to be exposed to corruption and be endangered."

"You know I'll protect her. She's yours, and that makes her mine as well." His relationship with his family may have been strained for the past ten years, but that didn't mean he'd ever turn his back on them. Not for something like this.

He nodded once. "Thank you."

"What's the second thing?"

"Don't be stupid and get yourself killed."

Brady grinned. "Well, that's a hell of a thing to say. Not many other CEOs get that little pep talk when taking over a company. My fists are still sore from the fight. I doubt I'll be trying to find trouble." But he wouldn't back down from it either. Finnian knew that.

"Then, good luck. Try not to call me."

"I won't." Brady shook hands once more before leaving the party. He'd drive back from the hotel in the morning, say bye to his mum, and leave for America. Should be an adventurous six weeks.

The End

KEEP READING for a sample of the next book, *Forbidden Present!*

"WHAT THE HELL are you talking about, Finnian?" Brady Hayes paused outside the door to the coffee shop. Whatever he had to say needed to wait.

There she was. The woman he'd seen every morning over the past week since arriving in America stood in line, impatiently glancing at her watch. He felt the same way. If his brother would get off of the damn phone, he would finally introduce himself to her.

Finnian's voice grew louder. "I'm *trying* to explain that simply because Tripp Wellington is in jail doesn't make you safe. The company was involved in dozens of shady business dealings. If you keep digging—"

"I'm bound to strike gold. I know. You already warned me dozens of times." And now wasn't the time to get into the latest threat facing the company. Because he'd already discovered it. The more questions he asked, the less the employees seemed to know.

"This isn't a game, Brady."

No. It was definitely not a game. Not when both he and Finnian were nearly killed less than a month ago. But that worry needed to wait until *after* he had a coffee. No one was likely to kidnap him again while the mystery woman ordered a coffee at a small shop in the middle of downtown Atlanta.

Brady stepped out of the way of someone leaving. "I never said I thought it was a game. And I absolutely know the risk, but that's why you sent me here, isn't it? Clean up the company and get rid of the risks before Everly came back."

"Yes," Finnian began. "But not at the risk of you getting hurt. Or killed."

Finnian was being overprotective like usual. The woman stepped up to the counter to order. Now was his chance before she left. "I won't get killed." Brady pulled open the door, the warmth and scent dragging him in. "I need to go."

"Wait—one more thing. Everly has hired a PR specialist to help revive the company's image. Both with the public and with our employees. ATLighting's name has been through hell and back lately."

"Sounds great."

"You have a meeting with him at eight thirty this morning. Everly said his name is Keegan Richardson."

Brady glanced at his watch. "Thanks for the short notice. Bye." He ended the call before his brother trapped him on the phone, and he missed his opportunity.

The woman took out her credit card, oblivious to his interest. She'd dressed in a dark suit, with her dark hair pulled back. And like before, she'd worn a pair of heels that put her two inches taller and at least six feet. He wasn't in the habit of staring at a woman's body, but damn, her legs were hard to ignore.

Brady waited in the back of the line, pleased when she scanned the store and their eyes met.

He smiled.

And, after a week of Brady smiling and getting zero response, she finally smiled back before moving down the counter to wait on her drink.

If the two slow men in front of him would hurry with their orders before she left with hers, he might have a chance to ask her on a date.

Before he came to America, he had no intention of dating. He was here to do a job. His focus as the temporary CEO of ATLighting Inc was to handle the bloody mess that the prior owners had left. Everly Hayes, his newest sister-in-law, had asked him to tidy up things before returning from her honeymoon with Finnian, and that's what he intended to do.

But ATL was second on his priorities at the moment. Brady placed his order and moved toward the gorgeous woman still waiting for her coffee. His thoughts on the subject had changed. Leaving England to work in Atlanta didn't preclude him from dating. Especially if *this* was the woman he had the opportunity to date.

"Good morning," he began, stopping a few feet away.

"Good morning," she replied, picking up her coffee as the barista set the cup on the ledge.

"I'd hoped to see you this morning."

Her forehead creased. "Really?" She twisted her lips to the side in a cute smirk. "I hoped if I sat still long enough that Monday wouldn't see me and I could go back to bed."

She tapped her fingers on the side of her cup. "But that didn't work, so here I am." After a brief hesitation, she crossed the floor.

Brady followed, amused at her response. "Yes, here you are. Do you work nearby?"

"Yes." She pulled the lid off of her cup. "What about you? I've come here every morning for the past few years and never saw you before last week."

So, she'd noticed him. That was better than nothing.

"I work two blocks away in the ATLighting building. I just moved to Atlanta from London. I suppose I should thank my brother for his rotten coffee maker for sending me in search of my own."

"If he's anything like my brothers, he hid the good one just to make your life miserable."

Brady chuckled. "That is a good point. I'll have to check when I get back to his place."

She glanced at her watch. "I actually have a meeting in the ATL building this morning that I'll be late for if I don't hurry up."

This was his chance. "I'd hoped to ask you out to dinner."

She paused with the sugar shaker hovering over her coffee. "Oh," she said, setting the shaker down softly. She stirred her drink. "I can't say I typically go to dinner with men I don't know." She lifted her eyes, meeting his. They were the color of the ocean, a melting of blue and green together. "And since I don't know you, I'll have to decline the invitation."

"Fair enough." He leaned his hip against the counter beside her, studying her profile. Her smooth cheek looked soft, and he refrained from reaching out to check. He wanted a date with her, not to end up arrested.

"How about lunch?"

"Say Yes?" the barista called out, staring at the cup another second. "Say yes. Hey, did you mean to write this?" She asked, turning to the clerk.

The woman beside Brady looked at the barista and back to him. "Did you have them write that?"

Brady grinned. "Yes. Will you go to lunch with me? Today." He motioned toward a small cluster of tables in the corner. "Or we can sit right now?"

"Sir, I think this is yours," the young man called from the counter.

Brady held up his finger, never taking his eyes off of her. "I'd really enjoy the chance to get to know you."

She glanced at her watch again and winced. "Not right now. I didn't lie. I really do have a meeting I need to get to."

According to Finnian, he had a meeting as well, but he'd skip it for a chance with her.

"Then lunch," Brady said. "I don't care if you meet me at a hot dog stand somewhere. I'd really like to see you."

She seemed pleased by the admission. "Yes, I'll meet you for lunch." She snapped the top on her coffee and then sat her hand on her hip. "Only because your coffee cup told me to say yes."

"It's a smart coffee cup. There's a restaurant in the Ritz-Carlton on Peachtree. Noon?"

"I'll be there." She left before he remembered to ask for her name.

It didn't matter. He had a lunch date with a beautiful, funny woman. Brady retrieved his coffee and left the shop, his phone ringing.

Finnian. Again.

"What now?"

I'M SCREWED.

Keegan Richardson stared over her boss's left shoulder, tuning out his long list of her shortcomings. Her chance of getting the promotion inched farther and farther away with each of his coffee breath sighs and shakes of his shiny, bald head.

Mr. Stewart swooped his arm up to reveal his massive Rolex. "It's almost eight thirty. Your email stated you have a meeting with your new client"—he arched one eyebrow—"right now?"

"Yes, sir." She shifted an inch closer to the open elevator doors. "I probably need to get going, as you said."

Mr. Stewart crossed his arms, peering down his short, stubby nose, his square body still blocking her path. A sheen of sweat already glistened across his forehead even this early in the morning. Why did he seem perpetually sweaty?

"This is not the proper way to meet your clients. Especially one this high profile. If you want to be considered for the promotion, timeliness is a critical factor to being professional."

"I agree. Completely." She inched around him. "So, if you'll excuse me . . ."

Keegan lunged for the elevator, sticking an arm in before the door closed. She jumped inside, pressing the button until the doors closed.

She drank her coffee. What if Mr. Stewart passed her over for this promotion, again? She'd have even longer to wait before getting the managerial experience she wanted before moving on to her next job.

To her dream job.

Keegan stepped off the elevator, and a few seconds later, she walked out of the warm building and into the sharp November wind. It cut right through her pencil skirt and suit jacket. She came to a quick halt, remembering the long coat she'd worn into the office, currently hanging in her cubicle. No time to turn around or care about being cold. She wouldn't have a future if she didn't hustle right now and get to that meeting with Brady Hayes.

She quickened her pace and headed in the direction of ATLighting Inc, a multi-billion dollar business specializing in industrial and commercial lighting. She bent her head against a blast of frigid air. Five blocks seemed farther than she'd remembered with the cold wind blowing straight into her face.

This sucked for a day that started out so amazing. Keegan sipped her coffee. She had a date with a man. Her smile became uncontrollable. The man was charming and insanely attractive. Something had to be wrong with him, and lunch would be a letdown.

Keegan adjusted her navy blazer when she came to a stop at the crosswalk. "Positive thoughts," she said aloud and pulled her shoulders back, inhaling more car exhaust than positive energy.

She tilted her head up at the enormous building ahead. ATLighting's offices occupied the top four floors of the skyscraper. A dizzy feeling swam in her head. If she were lucky, the temporary CEO wouldn't suggest that she admire the view from that height.

Everly Hayes, ATLighting's owner, obviously trusted her new brother-in-law. But Keegan's potential promotion relied on the success of this one client. The Cambridge-educated Mr. Hayes would not get in her way. Good credentials didn't necessarily qualify him to run this company after the horrible publicity it had suffered.

She finished her coffee as she entered the building. It was a stupid thought to wonder if the man she met this morning knew Mr. Hayes just because they were both from England.

Focus. A critical meeting that had a direct impact on her career would begin in a few minutes. She stepped up to the receptionist, who wore a bright orange and green patterned headscarf. The entire area smelled of lavender from a small incense stick burning off to the side.

"Hi, I'm here to see Mr. Brady Hayes." Keegan didn't want any confusion between the brothers. However, she suspected Finnian Hayes hadn't returned from his honeymoon if Everly wasn't back yet.

The receptionist hesitated a little, her brown eyes darting over Keegan's shoulder.

"Who may I tell him is here?" The receptionist asked.

"Keegan Richardson."

The woman chuckled. "*You're* Keegan Richardson?"

"Yes, ma'am."

She shook her head. "This should be interesting. He'll be with you in a moment."

Brady Hayes was probably like every other owner of a large company she'd dealt with. Egos usually led the way into a room. Only their time was important and no one else's. And people usually jumped at their every command.

She rocked back on her heels. But she didn't have a choice but to cater to his schedule. If he were willing to give her ten minutes, she had a chance to pull this holiday party together.

And she would prove to Mr. Stewart that she deserved the promotion.

Keegan looked at her watch. Quarter till nine. He had every right to keep her waiting, but she wouldn't change any part of her morning. Except running into her boss. That she wished never happened.

"Ms. Richardson."

The deep rumble of a familiar English accent caused a shiver up her spine. She turned. "You!" She felt heat crawl up her cheeks.

"Me!" He mimicked her voice before smiling and motioning her into the office. "We can talk in here, Ms. Richardson."

She passed by him, that same light scent of aftershave in the air she'd noticed that morning. His suit fit him perfectly —the gray coordinated with the hint of violet in his tie. The feminine color highlighted his masculinity. Seeing him standing in such a big, open corner office with an incredible view of downtown Atlanta put him into perspective. He wasn't some random man. He wasn't like a staff accountant or manager at a chain restaurant. Right then, he had power in the office. Confidence that before then, Keegan had never known was so attractive.

"I'd expected a *Mr.* Richardson based on my rushed conversation with my brother." His sexy smile returned. "I'm pleased you're not a man."

"My mother is pleased, as well."

He closed the door. "Why is that?"

Keegan set her laptop bag in an empty chair. "I have three older brothers, so she was bound and determined to have a girl."

"Ah." Once she sat in the chair, he seated himself across the desk from her. "I understand large families. I'm toward the end of twelve myself."

"Twelve." She shook her head, trying to knock away the

picture of *that* family reunion if they all resembled him. "Here in America, that's enough to have your own reality show."

"So I've seen." He leaned forward, resting his elbows on the table.

Those intense eyes threw her for a moment. A long, pink scar ran across the top of his eyebrow. Was it new? The classy Cambridge lawyer's smooth, confident exterior suddenly took on a different undercurrent.

She pulled her focus back to the purpose of the meeting. "I've spoken over the phone with Everly a few times about changing the company's image. We decided on two projects. The first is changing the company's logo. I wasn't sure which colors or styles she had in mind, but I brought some examples."

"I work with contracts and numbers, Keegan, not with colors and butterflies."

Unexpected annoyance crawled through her body with his dismissive statement. "That may be so, *Mr. Hayes*," she emphasized to keep things professional. "But Everly instructed me to consult you. She gave you one hundred percent decision-making authority, and now, all I'm asking for is a decision."

"Fine. You have my undivided attention." He clasped his hands together. "Ask me a question."

She ignored his sarcasm and pulled out her tablet. She tapped the screen to bring up the new logo the advertising agency designed and set it in front of him.

"What do you think?"

"I don't like it." He watched her with that same interest from before without even a glance at the screen. "Is this meeting why you didn't stay and have a coffee with me?"

As much as she enjoyed the attention from a man like him, she needed his help if this would be a success.

She cleared her throat and kept the pleading out of her voice. "Yes. Now, do you like this?"

"No."

"C'mon, you barely looked at it."

He wrinkled his forehead and looked at the screen with obnoxious focus now. "I'm fully looking at it, and the answer is still a hard no. I don't even know what color that is. Green? Yellow?"

"It's chartreuse."

"Ugly."

"It's not ugly."

"If you have such strong opinions, then why are you asking me for mine?"

Was he being difficult on purpose? "Fine." She took the tablet back and flicked to the next picture. This was actually her favorite. The light blue and bold red was a subconscious salute to America. Patriotism draws in customers.

"I hate it."

She opened her mouth but snapped it shut instead of arguing. He was the client. She flicked to the next and last potential example. Black. The letters were black with a faint illuminating white highlight behind them. The script was in block letters. Boring.

"That's simple. Clean lines. I pick that one." His email chimed.

"Of course, you do," she mumbled. "Mr. Hayes—"

"Brady. If you're going to send murderous glances my way, please use my first name, so none of my siblings are in harm's way."

"Believe me, I could never confuse you with anyone else." She pulled out her laptop. Maybe she'd have more luck with the company event. "We need to discuss ideas for a holiday party."

"A party?" His email dinged again. His eyes shifted for a brief moment before settling back on her.

"It's not only a party. It's a chance to give your employees, customers, and the press a glimpse into a changed ATLighting. One that cares about the hundreds of employees that helped build the wealth of the company." The wealth that the two ex-owners, Tripp Wellington and Charles Clarke, nearly destroyed by their drugs and spending. She suspected more to the story, but the part that was already public knowledge didn't favor ATL's image.

At the next email alert, he grimaced. "I'm sorry, I need to check this."

She settled back into the chair as he turned to his computer. "Just think about it. We can tie the party into a charity. Maybe hold a silent auction for prizes benefiting the charity." Brady grunted in response as his eyes locked on the computer screen. She pushed on with her idea. "Maybe find a local shelter or children's hospital?" It was the perfect combination to weave into her resume for her next career move. Working for a children's hospital in their PR department was her dream job.

But Brady didn't answer. His focus seemed fully engulfed in work. Did he remember she was there? She wanted this opportunity.

She needed this promotion to get to the next level in her career.

Being bold, she reached over and set her hand over his that worked the small computer mouse.

He stilled, his eyes locking with hers at the contact. He didn't look surprised by her move, but his eyebrow ticked. Despite what he thought of her, she needed him to plan this party and give her a budget. She'd push him if that's what she needed to do.

Brady lightly brushed his thumb along the side of her fingers. "Your hand is freezing."

She pulled her offending hand away and covered it in her lap. "Well, it's cold outside."

Stay on track.

"If you don't want to help, then maybe you can see when Everly will have time. She and I can plan this remotely." Something. She needed some sort of approval to get the funding to start the process. They had four weeks until her planned date of the holiday party. Everyone thought she was insane to even try to pull it off.

But if she did, she'd get the promotion. It was a no-brainer.

Brady pushed his chair back and stood, turning around to stare out of the window at Atlanta.

She took her time studying his strong shoulders and back. It really was a shame that he ended up being the temporary CEO of ATLighting. Because, unfortunately, she wouldn't get to go on that lunch date after all.

"England is well over six thousand kilometers away, and that still isn't far enough to force Everly to relax. I've been here ten days since the wedding, and she's called me six times a day for the first half and sent me over four dozen emails. When they left for their honeymoon, my brother took her phone away. I agreed to stay an extra two weeks to give myself enough time to square away this company." He faced her, the sun casting a bright glow around him. That boyish charm returned with his half-smile. "We'll have to find a way to work together. I'm not calling my brother to interrupt his honeymoon about colors of letters and type of food to serve at some little holiday party they won't even attend."

Even in his adorable accent, he'd managed to diminish her job to some *little* holiday party.

"With the workload I'm facing, I don't see how I'll have time to plan a party."

"You won't have to do any of the planning. I just need you to make decisions." She tapped the screen on her computer, bringing up the to-do list for the holiday party, hoping he'd get on board. "I think if we start at the top." She typed in a new number one, biting her lip to keep from laughing. "We can work our way down, and you'll see that it's not as hard as it sounds." She picked up her computer and crossed the room.

He sighed. "What's number one?" He took the laptop from her, adjusting the screen to read. "Convince the stuffy, Cambridge-educated lawyer to have fun and host a holiday party."

She set her hands on her hips, waiting for a response. The longer he took, the more she began to wonder if she'd just shot herself in the foot. This wasn't the job to let her attitude get the best of her, but she needed his help.

He continued to skim down the rest of the list without comment. "Most of these questions I'll leave to you and Shelley to decide." He handed her back her laptop and crossed his office to the door. This was it. He was going to kick her out. Damn it. If she lost this account, there wasn't a chance in hell that she'd get that promotion. In fact, she'd probably get fired.

"Shelley, can you come in here for a moment, please?"

Shelley entered with a pad and pen in hand. "Yes?"

"Ms. Richardson is planning a holiday party for the company."

Shelley's eyes lit up, and a broad smile spread across her face. "My word."

The corner of his mouth twitched at her evident happiness. "You'd never guess, but party planning wasn't something I studied at Cambridge." He held Keegan's eyes a moment longer than comfortable. "Can you help her with the fine details?"

"I'd love to! Is it for the Atlanta or Miami employees?"

"Ms. Richardson?"

She ticked her chin up a notch. "Both, if it's possible."

She waited on Brady to make some type of derisive comment. He opened his mouth and then shut it. "I'll let you both decide that as well."

Keegan set her hands on her hips. "Then a joint party. I assume the two offices interact in the business. It will be fun to let them meet face-to-face."

Her stomach relaxed. Finally, they'd made a decision.

Shelley set her hand on her hip. "At which location, honey?" She winked, and Keegan smiled and relaxed. At least his secretary was excited about the party.

"Are you up for sunny Miami?" Keegan asked.

Shelley threw her arms in the air. "Honey, my bags are packed!"

Keegan shot Brady a sharp look. "I hope you have a swimsuit, Mr. Hayes. Looks like we're headed to Miami."

Look for *Forbidden Present* out May 2021!

First paperback edition April 2021

Cover Design by Triumph Book Covers
Editing by Kimberly Hunt, Revision Division

ISBN 978-1-7333968-7-5 (paperback)

www.palmerjoneswrites.com

SERIES BY PALMER JONES

A Southern Kind of Love Series
Hiding From the Sheriff
Falling For Her Client
Dreaming of Her Movie Star
Engaging Her Enemy
Kissing Her Rescuer
Finding Her Leading Man

O'Keeley's Irish Pub
Her Irish Boss
Her Irish Chef
Her Irish Flirt

Rosalind Brewery Series (Brewing Chemistry)
Ava
Reese
Frankie
The Christmas Truce

Family Ties Series
Entangled Past
Entangled Present
Entangled Future

Made in United States
Orlando, FL
05 June 2023

33833566R00173